FULL BLAST

FULL BLAST

Janet Evanovich
and Charlotte Hughes

ISIS
LARGE PRINT
Oxford

First published in Great Britain 2004
by Headline Book Publishing,
a division of Hodder Headline

Published in Large Print 2005 by ISIS Publishing Ltd,
7 Centremead, Osney Mead, Oxford OX2 0ES
by arrangement with Headline Book Publishing,
a division of Hodder Headline

British Library Cataloguing in Publication Data
Evanovich, Janet
    Full blast. – Large print ed.
    1. Holt, Max (Fictitious character) – Fiction
    2. Love stories 3. Large type books
    I. Title II. Hughes, Charlotte, 1954–
    813.5'4 [F]

ISBN 0–7531–7431–6 (hb)
ISBN 0–7531–7432–4 (pb)

Printed and bound in Great Britain by
T. J. International Ltd., Padstow, Cornwall

Many thanks to Jen Enderlin a.k.a. SuperJen for giving us a great book idea! Special thanks to Eric Hughes for coming up with the title for this book.

CHAPTER
ONE

Jamie Swift had been in the newspaper business long enough to realize it was a lot like being a waitress. You had to meet the needs of those you served — the rich, the poor, the in-between, even the crazies who complained no matter what you did. And like a waitress, you had to hope the tips were good. A big tip could make all the difference. A big tip in her case meant headlines, and she was in the business of finding headlines. But they didn't come easy in a small Southern town where life was, for the most part, uneventful, even predictable. She had to scramble for newsworthy events.

So here she was, once again, sitting at her desk, sifting through stories, looking for a new slant or an idea to make it more interesting to the reading public. She was so intent on what she was doing that she jumped when someone tapped on her door.

Sixty-year-old Vera Bankhead rushed into Jamie's office and closed the door behind her. "You are *not* going to believe this!"

Jamie glanced up. "What is it?" Jamie asked, straightening in her chair and trying to work the kinks out of her neck from sitting in one position for so long.

She had come in early, hoping to work undisturbed. "You got a good tip for me?" she asked the woman before her. "Give me a headline, and I'll kiss the ground you walk on."

"This is even better." Vera paused, as if to add a little drama to what she was about to say. The hairpins had popped out from her gray beehive hairdo, and her glasses were askew. She shoved them high on her nose and glanced about as if to make certain they were alone. She eyed the large plate-glass window overlooking the courthouse square where automatic sprinklers were doing damage control to a parched lawn brought on by a record-breaking July heat wave. Vera marched over and snapped the blinds closed.

Jamie arched one brow. "This must be big."

"It's bigger than when Lorraine Brown caught her husband doing the nasty with Beth Toomey on a sofa in the back office of the VFW Hall."

"Wow. Wasn't she jailed for going after them with a letter opener?"

"Yeah, and Tom refused to bail her out until she signed an agreement stating she wouldn't do him bodily harm afterward. She kicked his butt anyway the minute they released her."

"So tell me."

"You're not going to believe it," the woman repeated.

"Vera, out with it already!"

Vera held up a white paper sack. She reached into it and pulled out a brownie. "Taste it."

Jamie's mouth watered at the sight of the chocolate goodie. "I really shouldn't. I've already had three

2

doughnuts this morning. I can barely button the top of my jeans."

Vera gave her *that* look, the one that said she wasn't going to take no for an answer. And Vera could be fierce. Although she still worked as Jamie's secretary, fear and intimidation had prompted Jamie to promote her to assistant editor of the *Gazette*, as well. That and the fact Vera carried a .38 Smith and Wesson in her purse. Jamie was almost sure she wouldn't pull it on her; Vera was the closest thing she'd had to a mother, but it was best to humor her.

"OK, OK." Jamie reached for the brownie and tasted it. "Yum, that's good." She finished it off in three bites.

"Do you feel any different?" Vera asked, eyeing her closely.

"Yeah, I want another one. I can always buy larger jeans."

"This isn't just *any* brownie," Vera said in a conspiratorial whisper. "There are rumors floating around that Lyle Betts is putting aphrodisiacs in them."

Jamie arched one brow. Lyle Betts owned Sunshine Bakery, and was considered a pillar of the community. He coached Little League, and played Santa Claus for the children's unit at the hospital every year. "No way," she said.

Vera crossed her heart. "As God is my witness."

Jamie pondered it. Vera was a strict Southern Baptist; she only lied when absolutely necessary.

"Do you have any more?"

"Yeah, I bought extra. I figured we should do a little experimenting. We'll eat a couple more, and then compare notes."

"Oh, Lord," Jamie said, as Vera divvied them up. The last thing she needed was to start feeling horny. It had been three weeks since she'd laid eyes on sexy and mysterious Maximillian Holt, the man who blew into her life from time to time just long enough to turn her world upside down and inside out. The same man she had already voted most likely to climb beneath the sheets with first chance she got.

"I've already had three," Vera said, "and I don't feel a thing except for a little indigestion. Chocolate does that to me."

"I'm sure it's just a bunch of hype to sell brownies," Jamie said, hoping she was right. Lately she'd been having X-rated dreams where she and Max played starring roles. They did things she was certain were illegal in most states.

"And get this," Vera said. "Maxine Chambers quit her job at the library and just opened a lingerie shop right on Main Street. And guess what she named it? Sinful Delights."

Jamie couldn't hide her surprise. She couldn't imagine the prim librarian doing such a thing.

"And that's not all," Vera went on. "Folks say she's got a whole display of unmentionables hanging in her window where God and everybody can see them. She just undraped it today. Elbert Swank said his jaw fell open so hard when he saw them that he almost lost his dentures on the sidewalk out front. I would have given anything to see that."

"A new lingerie shop," Jamie mused. "Imagine that." She tried to keep her excitement at bay. Beaumont needed a good lingerie store, a place where cotton panties and practical bras weren't the order of the day.

"Of course I got my information secondhand so I'll have to get over there and check it out personally. You know how I am about getting my facts straight."

"Maybe she'll advertise with us," Jamie said. "We can always use the business."

"Oh, pooh. We're going to make money on that new personals section you started. How many people have advertised so far?"

"We must have about ten total; seven from men, three from women. Pretty good for a small-town newspaper, don't you think? And people are starting to write back!" Jamie had hoped the ads would bring in well-needed revenue and attract more readers. It was too early to tell, but she remained confident.

"I'm keeping my fingers crossed," Vera said. She stepped closer. "One ad in particular caught my attention," she almost whispered. "It was in yesterday's paper. The heading read 'Ready, Willing, and Able.' Sounds like a winner to me, seeing as how most men in my age bracket have a little trouble in the *able* department."

Jamie laughed out loud. "Vera Bankhead, I am *shocked*!"

Vera grinned. "Hey, even a woman my age has needs."

"Perhaps you should respond to the ad."

"What if he's ugly? You know I can't abide an ugly man. Maybe you should give me his name first."

Jamie shook her head. "You know the ads are strictly confidential."

"I'll bet I could figure out who he is. I know everybody in this town."

Which was why Jamie had insisted on handling the personals section, she reminded herself. She kept the ads locked in a file cabinet in her office. As much as she loved Vera, it was a well-known fact the woman was the biggest gossip in town. Jamie shrugged as though it made no difference. "I would see that your letter reached him."

"I'll have to think about it."

Jamie sighed wistfully. "Well, one thing is certain. Love is definitely in the air in the town of Beaumont, South Carolina. I think it's romantic." Jamie had only recently come to realize just what a romantic she was, and she knew Max Holt was responsible. She had begun to daydream about their relationship, had begun to wonder where it was going. She wanted him in her life permanently, and that scared the hell out of her.

"Sounds more like L-U-S-T to me," Vera replied. "It's the heat. Everybody in town is acting strange. If they start eating these brownies they're going to be out of control."

Jamie didn't want to talk about lust because, once again, it brought Max to mind. Max, who was too gorgeous for his own good and knew it. Max, who clearly lusted after her but kept his true feelings to himself. Not that she didn't have a bad case of lust, as well; it's what drew them together like iron shavings to a magnet, what made her skin literally ache for his touch.

It had been that way from the moment they'd first laid eyes on each other, when Max had come to Beaumont to aid his brother-in-law, now the mayor, in an attempt to clean up town corruption. Max had ridden in on his white horse, or in his case, a two-million-dollar car with enough technology to run a small country. Max's investigation had dragged Jamie right into the middle of it; she'd found herself dodging bullets from hit men, almost getting blown to smithereens by a car bomb, and landing in the path of a monster-sized alligator.

OK, so maybe she was exaggerating the size of the alligator, but all alligators looked big when you were treading water and happened to be in their path.

Most women with half a brain would have grabbed their purses and said, "See ya," but not Jamie. She had followed Max to Tennessee to find the person responsible for hiring the hit.

Simply put, Max was a philanthropist with brains and money, and as long as there was a cause or an injustice, he would be there, come hell or high water.

"My stomach feels funny," Vera said. "I think I ate too many brownies."

Jamie looked up. "Yeah?" She wouldn't tell Vera she was having a bad case of butterflies. The woman would attribute it to the brownies, but Jamie knew better. She was thinking about the last time she and Max were together in what could only be described as a compromising position. Sooner or later, things were bound to come to a head.

She and Max couldn't go on this way forever, but she was afraid to hope for more. She could fantasize all she wanted about a lasting relationship, but Max did not impress her as a man who could be tied down to any woman for very long.

"It's probably all in my mind," Vera said. "Lyle Betts most likely started the rumor just to get people into his bakery." She glanced about the office. "Where is Fleas, by the way?"

"Huh?"

"Are you even listening to me? Where is your dog? You know, that ugly hound you bring to work with you every day because he sulks if you leave him at home?"

"He's at the vet. And he's not ugly."

"I hope he's getting his anal glands expressed. I can't live with that flatulence problem much longer."

Jamie had *inherited* Fleas, a wrinkled, forlorn-faced bloodhound some weeks back. At the time she had desperately needed a vehicle, and, trying to save money, had bought a rust bucket of a pickup truck. The car salesman, who claimed the dog was attached to the truck, had knocked fifty bucks off the price of the truck as an incentive for her to take the dog. They were bonding rather well or at least as well as could be expected with a dog that had chronic gas.

"He's being neutered today," Jamie said. "Poor thing," she added. "I'll bet Dr. Adams has his nuts on a chopping block as we speak."

Vera shuddered. "I don't even want to think about it."

They were interrupted when someone tapped on the door. "Pardon me," a female voice said.

Vera and Jamie glanced toward the door. Jamie felt her jaw drop to her collarbone. Vera gaped, as well.

"I'm sorry to disturb you," the woman said, "but there was nobody out front."

Jamie continued to stare. The woman had coal-black hair that fell to her waist. Sparkly blue eye shadow colored her lids, and her lashes were long enough to paint the side of a barn. "May I help you?" Jamie managed.

The woman stepped into the room. Her skirt was short and tight; her low-cut blouse emphasized perfect oversized breasts. Jamie decided either God had been very generous in the boob department or the woman was stuffed to the gills with silicone.

"My name is Destiny Moultrie," she said in a husky voice. "I'm here about the job."

Vera tossed Jamie a suspicious look. "What job? You've decided to replace me, haven't you? You'd rather have some Elvira — Erin Brockovich look-alike with big knockers sitting out front."

"I don't know anything about this," Jamie said, holding out both hands. She looked at the woman. "What job?" she asked, echoing Vera's question.

"The advice columnist. You've been turning it over in your mind for weeks."

"I have?"

Vera looked at Jamie. "You have?"

Jamie shifted in her seat. "Um, well —"

"You never mentioned it to me," a very peeved Vera interrupted. "You've always come to me with your ideas."

The woman looked from Vera to Jamie. "I didn't mean to cause friction. Perhaps we should discuss this in private, Miss Swift."

Vera took offense. "*Miss Swift* doesn't keep secrets from me. I know more about what's going on around here than anyone else." She tossed Jamie a dark look. "At least I thought I did."

Jamie couldn't mask her confusion. "Vera, please, not now."

But Vera was not deterred. "First, you take the personals section away from me because you don't trust me, and now *this*. I should quit. I should hand in my resignation and go on one of those senior citizens' cruises that serve seven meals a day. I could meet a nice widower, and sow a few wild oats. I still have a few oats left, you know."

"Vera —" Jamie fought the urge to crawl beneath her desk. They were acting anything but professional. But she knew better than to argue. In Vera's mind, Jamie was still an unruly kid who'd never been properly disciplined by her father.

"Seven meals a day?" Destiny said. "That's a lot of food. I would bust right out of my clothes."

"You're *already* busting out of your clothes," Vera said. She turned to Jamie. "On second thought, I'm *not* quitting, because I've been here longer than anyone, and I'm not going to risk losing my benefits.

Furthermore, you *can't* fire me. It was your daddy, God rest his soul, who hired me, not you." She gave a huff and marched from the room, but not before slamming the door behind her.

"Uh-oh, I blew it," Destiny said.

Jamie turned to her visitor. She was intrigued. "Please sit down, Miss Moultrie," she said, using her professional voice. She smiled serenely, as though it were an everyday occurrence for her secretary to pitch a fit. OK, so it *was* an everyday occurrence, she reminded herself. Vera was probably out front right now polishing her .38.

"Please call me Destiny," the woman said. She took one of the chairs directly across from Jamie's desk. "I'm sorry for barging in like this, but I sensed you would be making a decision soon, and I wanted to be the first to apply."

Jamie merely looked at her.

"You *have* been thinking about starting an advice column, right?" Without warning, the woman smacked her forehead. "Oh, man, I hope I'm not in the wrong place."

"The wrong place?" Jamie realized she was repeating a lot of what was being said.

Destiny pulled out a small notebook and flipped through several pages. "Is your middle name Leigh?"

Jamie nodded. "Yes. It was my mother's first name." Now why had she gone and given out personal information to some stranger she'd probably never see again?

"Yeah, I know about your mother. She walked out when you were still in diapers."

Jamie arched both brows. "Excuse me, but I don't see the point of all this."

Destiny looked up. "Sorry. I shouldn't have mentioned the part about your mother. I know you still find it painful at times."

"What else do you know?"

"There's an old tire swing hanging in your backyard, am I right?"

Jamie snapped her fingers. "I've got it. You're a private investigator, aren't you? Who hired you, and for what reason?"

"No, I'm not. Just answer this one last question. Do you have a bar of Dove soap in your lingerie drawer?"

Jamie felt the color drain from her face. "Who are you? How do you know about the soap?"

"I just do."

Jamie leveled her gaze at the woman. Her astonishment had an edge of anger to it. "Tell me more about the soap."

"Are you sure?" When Jamie nodded, she went on. "The scent reminds you of your mother, even though you remember little else about her."

Jamie felt the goose bumps rise on her arms. She was quiet for a moment. "I'm going to ask you again. How do you know this?"

The woman sighed. "I'm psychic. Sort of."

Jamie did a gigantic eye-roll. "Sort of? What does that mean?"

"I have visions, and I'm right a lot of the time, unless I'm under a lot of stress, then I might make a mistake now and then. It's a simple case of performance anxiety; sort of like sex. But I get it right more often than not."

Jamie sighed. It was really turning out to be a weird morning. First Vera with her brownies, and now she was conversing with a woman who claimed to be psychic. She had time for neither because she had to concentrate on getting a newspaper out. "Miss Moultrie, um, Destiny —"

"I'm working on getting better," Destiny said. "I practice every night." She paused. "You don't believe in psychics, do you?"

"Not exactly."

"See, I knew that." The woman licked the tip of her finger and drew a short imaginary line in the air as though marking her success. Turquoise rings circled every finger, bracelets jangled on her wrists. "There are a lot of phonies out there. Some claim to be one hundred percent accurate. There's no such thing."

"I wasn't, um, looking for a psychic. Just an advice columnist." There. She'd gone and admitted it. "The idea was to sort of complement —"

"Your new personals section," Destiny said. "People would be more intrigued by a psychic. And I've got the perfect name for it. The Divine Love Goddess Advisor." She pulled out an envelope and handed it to Jamie. "Why don't you look over my résumé and give it some thought. I wouldn't be able to start for a day or two since I just moved here and have to unpack. But I travel light."

Jamie shifted uneasily in her chair. "Why Beaumont, South Carolina?" she asked. "This town isn't exactly a booming metropolis. And the *Gazette* is rather small."

"I was sent here for a reason," Destiny said. "I'd never even heard of this place, but it came to me in a vision. So I used a small pendulum, and Beaumont came up on the map. I had to use a magnifying glass to see it, but now I'm sure I'm in the right place. Well, pretty sure."

Jamie simply nodded. She figured it was best to humor the woman until she could get rid of her.

Destiny smiled. "I know it's a lot to take in, but you can rest easy, my column will bring in many new readers."

"You know this for a fact?"

"Yep. I also have a very good feeling you're going to hire me. This interview is just a formality."

Jamie had no intention of hiring her. The last thing she needed was some kook working for her. "I'll have to think about it. I'll keep your résumé on file in the meantime."

"I know you have doubts," Destiny went on as though she hadn't heard. "And I don't blame you. This newspaper is very important to you after what you've been through. You've struggled for so long to keep it going. I admire your tenacity, Jamie, but you have to stop comparing yourself to your grandfather."

Once again, Jamie felt the tiny hairs on her arm prickle. "What do you know about my grandfather?"

"He started this newspaper from nothing and did extremely well. He passed it on to your father when he died, but your father didn't fare so well. He never wanted to be a newspaperman to begin with."

"You're pretty good," Jamie said, "but this is a small town where everybody knows everybody's business. You'd only have to ask around to get your information." Even as she said it, she wondered how the woman had found out about the soap in her dresser drawer. She decided to humor her. "While you're at it, tell me this. There's this man in my life."

"Yeah, I know all about him. He sort of saved your behind when you had financial problems so he's a silent partner. You're afraid of falling in love with him, but I would advise you to follow your heart."

"How does *he* feel?" Jamie surprised herself by asking.

Destiny looked thoughtful. "He's hard to read." Suddenly, she sneezed.

"Bless you," Jamie said.

Destiny's eyes watered, and she sneezed again. "You'll have to forgive me. This always happens when I start picking up on stuff. Do you have a tissue?"

"Don't you know?"

"Look, I can't be expected to know *everything*."

Jamie reached into her side drawer and pulled out a small box of tissues and handed it to her, just as Destiny let out another sneeze.

"I have to go before it gets worse." The woman stood and wiped her eyes. "Oh, by the way, I'm not going to charge you for my services. I've been married five times so I get plenty of alimony. This is just a hobby."

"Five husbands, huh?"

Another sneeze. "Yeah, and I'm not even forty years old. A girl has to work fast to rack up that many husbands in such a short period."

Jamie sat back and studied her. "Didn't you know the marriages were going to fail?"

Sniff, sniff, sneeze. "I was in love with them at the time, so what could I do? How about you call me when you're ready for me to start? My new number is on my résumé." She made for the door, and then paused. "This man you're thinking about?"

Jamie remained silent.

"He's going to be back in your life very soon."

Jamie perked. "And?"

"Fireworks."

Jamie arched one brow. "Fireworks?"

Destiny smiled. "Fireworks."

CHAPTER
TWO

Vera eyed Destiny suspiciously as she stepped into the reception area. "It was very nice meeting you, Vera," Destiny said, dabbing her nose with a tissue. She sneezed several times as she made her way toward the front door. She opened it, and then turned. "By the way, I'm sorry you're having car trouble."

Vera hitched her chin high. "Excuse me? There's not a darn thing wrong with my car."

Destiny shrugged. "Whatever." She hurried out.

"What was all *that* about?" Vera demanded when Jamie stepped out of her office. "Am I fired?"

"Don't be ridiculous, you'll still be here when I'm dead and gone. I was thinking about starting an advice column to complement the personals section."

"Why wasn't I told?"

"Because I haven't made up my mind."

Vera frowned. "Then how —"

Jamie was beginning to feel weary. "Destiny Moultrie is psychic. Or so she says."

Vera pursed her lips. "Oh, good grief, you don't believe in that hocus-pocus, do you?"

"She was very convincing, but, no, I think it's all a crock." That didn't mean she didn't feel uneasy about some of what Destiny had told her.

"Hogwash, that's what it is," Vera said. "And that woman needs to get on allergy medication. One of these days she's going to sneeze too hard, and those T-I-T-S are going to pop a button, and somebody is going to get hurt."

Jamie waited until after lunch to check on Fleas. The vet's assistant assured her the surgery had gone well. "You can pick him up in the morning," she said. "We'll give you a list of things to look out for during his recovery. You're going to have to make sure his stitches don't pull free, and he's not going to be able to go for walks for about ten days."

"That shouldn't be a problem," Jamie said, "since all he does is eat and sleep."

Jamie hung up a moment later. Stitches? Recovery? She did a mental eye-roll as she imagined Fleas lying on her sofa with an IV of ice cream dripping into his veins. Once again, she reflected that she was not the perfect dog owner. But what could she do? The animal refused to eat the healthy dog food she bought for him. He preferred cheeseburgers, fries, butter pecan ice cream, and Krispy Kreme doughnuts. And Jamie, who practically lived on junk food, ate the same things.

She told herself that despite their bad eating habits, as best she could figure, they were close to getting in the essential food groups.

★ ★ ★

18

The rest of the day passed quickly for Jamie, approving layouts for the newspaper and getting it to print. She had begun working for her father at the newspaper — performing small jobs after school like emptying wastepaper baskets and keeping pencils sharpened — since first grade, earning three dollars per week. Looking back, she realized he'd preferred bringing her to the office instead of leaving her with a baby-sitter.

As she'd grown, so had her duties, and, until she'd gone off to college to study journalism, she'd worked in every department, earning little money but loving the work so much that she would have done it for free. She'd earned extra cash by selling subscriptions, which her father claimed she had a knack for, what with her big blue eyes, blond hair, and winning smile.

"You're like your grandpa," her father had told her not long before he'd died. "You've got ink running through your veins. You love this newspaper as much as he did. You'll do well by it."

Jamie smiled fondly at the thought, the good old days, when she and her father had worked side by side in order to make deadlines. And thinking of her father brought Destiny Moultrie to mind once more. The woman was about as strange as they came, but just thinking about all she'd known of Jamie's life gave her a bad case of heebie-jeebies. Jamie's father had *not* wanted to be a newspaperman, and the paper had suffered as a consequence. Jamie had begged and pleaded for permission to leave college in order to relieve him of some of the work, but he had absolutely refused to let her quit. His staff, all of them as devoted as Vera, had been invaluable in seeing that the paper made it to print on time.

Jamie couldn't help but wonder how Destiny had managed to get as much information as she had, but she knew there had to be a logical explanation. There were gossips in town who would be only too happy to share what they knew.

Except for one thing, she reminded herself, the soap in her drawer. That couldn't be explained.

Jamie and Vera headed out the front door shortly after five p.m. Jamie lingered beside Vera's car, in no hurry to go home to an empty house. She hadn't realized just how much she'd come to depend on Fleas's company.

"You headed any place in particular?" she asked Vera as the woman slid into the driver's seat of her old Buick.

"We usually have church on Wednesday night," Vera said, "but we're having Vacation Bible School so that's out. Maybe I'll bake a cake for my sick neighbor. What about you?"

"Oh, I've got a million things to do," Jamie lied. "You know me, busy, busy." Jamie tried to think of what she could do to pass the evening.

Vera closed her door and rolled down the window. "This car is hotter'n Hades. Next car I buy is going to have a decent air conditioner."

Jamie continued to stand there. "Well, then, you have a nice evening."

Vera nodded, stabbed her key into the ignition, and turned it. Nothing happened. "What in the world? It was running fine this morning." She tried again. The car didn't respond.

"Uh-oh," Jamie said. "Sounds like you're having car trouble. Sounds like the starter."

Jamie's eyes widened. The two women locked gazes. "Uh-oh," she said.

"Don't be ridiculous," Vera said, as if reading her mind. "It's just a coincidence."

An hour later, Jamie led Vera into her garage where a red 1964½ Mustang convertible sat. It was an exact replica of the one Jamie had received from her father as a graduation present years before, only hers was white. Even though she'd spent a lot of money maintaining it, she still drove it with pride and wouldn't have thought of replacing it. It was in that very garage that Jamie had helped her father rebuild old cars, and each time he sold one, he'd tucked the money into her college fund.

Vera stepped up to the car and ran her hand along the hood. "It looks like it just rolled off the showroom floor. Are you sure Max won't mind if I borrow it? I mean, he bought it for you. It was a gift."

Jamie shrugged. "He only bought it because it was his fault mine was riddled with bullet holes." Luckily, it had since been repaired.

Vera shook her head sadly. "Do you know how strange that sounds? How many people send their cars to a body shop with bullet holes? That is precisely why I think Max Holt is the wrong man for you. I appreciate what he did for this town, but trouble seems to follow him everywhere."

Jamie figured it was best not to get into a debate with Vera over Max. Not that Max couldn't charm Vera's Hush Puppies right off her feet, mind you, but nobody had ever been good enough for Jamie as far as Vera was concerned. It didn't matter that Max was filthy stinking rich and turned every female's head between the ages of eighteen and eighty; he was a moving target for con men, bad guys, and the mob.

What Jamie also wouldn't tell Vera was that Max was more dangerous to her heart than any other body part. The three weeks she'd gone without seeing him seemed like forever. She knew he was a busy man, his company, Holt Industries, had offices all over the world; but surely he could have found time to pick up a telephone.

"So, you wanna take it for a spin?" Jamie said, chasing Max from her thoughts.

Vera opened the door. "Oh, Lord, it's a stick shift. I haven't driven one of those in years."

"All you need is a little practice."

Twenty minutes later, they were cruising Main Street with the top down, Vera grinning like a sixteen-year-old who'd just gotten her driver's license. "Hey, I'm pretty good at this," she said, shifting the gear into first after pausing at a stop sign.

Jamie grinned, as well. "See, I told you you'd pick it up in no time."

Vera glanced at her. "I don't look silly, do I? I mean, me driving around in such a snazzy car at my age. I'm no spring chicken, you know."

Jamie looked at her. Vera's beehive had already lost its hairpins and fallen to her shoulders, but the excitement in her eyes made up for her mussed hair. "You look great. And, no, you do not look silly." If anything she looked younger.

The woman hitched her chin high. "I want to take it around the courthouse square again. Maybe I'll see somebody I know."

Jamie smiled at Vera's enthusiasm. She had to admit it was more fun riding around town with her than sitting home alone worrying about Fleas.

Vera circled the square. The downtown area had received a face-lift in the past couple of years. Each shop owner had painted his or her store in what was referred to as an historic color. They'd added awnings and massive flowerpots out front, hoping to draw business from the strip mall on the outskirts of town.

Jamie knew the town well. Despite changes to the outside, the Downtown Café still served the best coffee in town, and she knew the regulars who gathered first thing in the morning for the $2.99 breakfast special of eggs and bacon and the best homemade biscuits she'd ever tasted. There was Coot Hathaway's doughnut shop where you could buy glazed doughnuts straight from the oven and sticky buns that stuck to the roof of your mouth and chocolate mocha doughnuts that were her personal favorite. And nobody made better sandwiches than Donnie Maynard, who owned the local sandwich shop. He bought his bread fresh from Sunshine Bakery, and his meat-loaf sandwiches, served cold, always drew a crowd. He used a secret ingredient that he swore he would take to his grave, and no matter how hard folks tried they couldn't figure it out.

The courthouse square was as quaint as it had been in Jamie's younger days. People still fed pigeons or read the daily newspaper or gathered in small groups to catch up on the latest gossip. The Garden Club had replaced the old shrubbery with new — in late spring, the azaleas blazed with color in every imaginable hue. Fall brought with it colorful mums, and pansies were planted in winter. Even the bandstand had been given a fresh coat of white paint.

"Oh, look!" Vera said. "There's Robyn Decker and Betty Hamilton from my Sunday school class. Wait'll they get a look at me in this hot car." Vera braked and tapped the horn several times, and the women looked up. They gaped in surprise and hurried over. Both wore lightweight jogging outfits and sneakers.

"Vera, is that you?" Betty said. She was tall and slender and wore a mop of short gray curls that had obviously been sprayed into place because not one strand strayed.

"What in heaven's name are you doing in that car?" Robyn asked. Her hair was the same light gray, on the frizzy side, tucked back with hair combs. She was on the heavy side. A sheen of perspiration coated her forehead.

"I'm taking a test-drive," Vera said, winking at Jamie. "Ya'll want to cruise with us?"

The two women looked at one another. "Sure," Betty said. "It's too hot to try to get our exercise."

Jamie had to agree. Not only was it hot, the humidity hung over the town like a woolen blanket. She got out of the car, and pulled back the seat so the two women

24

could climb in. "Fasten your seat belts," she said, once they'd settled themselves and Jamie reclaimed the front seat.

"You sure you know how to drive this thing?" Robyn asked.

"Vera drives it like a pro," Jamie told her.

They shot off, and the women in the back seat giggled like teenagers. "Hey, maybe we can pick up some guys," Betty said.

Robyn Decker gasped. "Why, Betty Hamilton, I don't believe what just came out of your mouth. You know we can't fit any men into this back seat, what with the size of my rear end." More giggles.

"Holy marolly," Vera called out. "There's Maxine Chambers's new store." She whipped the Mustang into a parking slot directly in front.

All four women leaned forward as if trying to get a closer look from where they were sitting. Finally, Jamie opened her door.

"Where are you going?" Vera asked.

"I want to check it out."

Double gasps from the back seat. "What if somebody sees you?" Betty said.

Jamie shrugged. "Aw, come on, ladies. The ground is not going to open up and swallow us just for looking."

"I don't care if the ground does swallow me up," Vera said. "I figure it's worth it." She pulled the seat forward, and the two in back reluctantly climbed out.

All four women hurried to the front of the store and gazed at the window display.

"Oh, my," Betty said. "I can't believe a proper Southern woman like Maxine would fill her window with unmentionables. What are our young people going to think? It might be dangerous. It might raise the testerone level in some of the boys, and that could spell trouble."

"Testosterone," Jamie corrected. "And I seriously doubt it's something they've never seen before. You know how inquisitive boys can be."

Vera eyed the merchandise. "I don't think I would even know how to wear some of this stuff."

Jamie perused the items in the window, making a mental list of what she planned to buy. "Maybe Maxine provides a list of instructions." But she was as surprised as the others that prudish Maxine Chambers would actually open a sexy lingerie shop.

"What are those lacy things hanging over there?" Vera asked. "Between the garter belts and the see-through bras."

Jamie followed her gaze. "Those are thong bikini underwear."

Vera arched both brows. "They don't look as though they would do much good in covering your behind. Why, if a cold wind blew up your skirt —"

"Oh, Lord, ya'll are *not* going to believe who is heading our way," Robyn said.

Betty turned. "Oh, heavenly days, it's Agnes Aimsley and her grandson. The gig is up."

Jamie turned as Agnes, frail and white-haired, inched her way toward them. Her sneakers looked out of place with her prim dress. The man beside her, a twentysomething preppie type, had her arm tucked through his protectively. His brown hair was cropped short, and he wore oversized tortoiseshell glasses that had gone out of style long ago.

Vera looked grim. "Agnes teaches our Sunday school class," she told Jamie. "You may have heard she had a heart attack last year. She's such a devout Christian that she'll have another one if she sees what's in Maxine's window."

"We're talking de-vout," Betty emphasized. "If she dies, Jesus is going to have to move over and let her sit next to God. I hear her grandson's one of those religious fanatics. I hear he can be a real cuckoo clock at times."

"Hello, ladies," Agnes called out pleasantly. "I see you're taking advantage of the nice weather the good Lord has provided."

"Um, hello, Agnes," Vera said.

Jamie tried to suppress a smile as Vera, Betty, and Robyn backed against the store window, no doubt attempting to block it from Agnes's view.

"Have ya'll met my grandson, Brent Walker? He's visiting for the summer while on break from Emory University where he is studying to be one of God's messengers."

They all shook hands. "Very nice to meet you, ladies," Brent said politely. He glanced up at the sign hanging over the window. Agnes looked up as well.

"'Sinful Delights,'" she read aloud, and suddenly smiled. "I didn't know we had a new chocolate shop in town. I hope they sell Godiva, that's my favorite. Scoot over, I want to see."

She and Vera did a little jig as Vera tried to stop her from looking past her.

"Believe me, Agnes, you're better off not knowing," Betty said.

Jamie cleared her throat and tried to remain straight-faced. The grandson looked confused.

"Perhaps we should move on," Brent said, as if taking his cue from the looks on the women's faces.

Agnes wasn't deterred. "Would you ladies please step aside so I can see what's in the window?"

It was like the parting of the Red Sea, Jamie decided, watching Vera, Betty, and Robyn clear the way so Agnes could step closer. "Oh, my," she said. Her eyes glazed over in shock.

Brent's face turned a deep red. "What is the meaning of this?" he demanded. "Who would open such a place?"

Vera started to answer, but he cut her off and pulled a small tablet from his back pocket.

"I demand to know the name of the owner."

"Maxine Chambers," Betty supplied. "Actually, we're shocked, as well."

He scribbled the name on his pad. "This place looks like something straight out of Sodom and Gomorrah. I'm going to have a talk with this Chambers woman. I feel it's my Christian duty."

"Would somebody please explain what *those* are," Agnes said, pointing to a pair of underwear.

"They're edible undies," Jamie said, only to have Brent glare at her. Jamie shrugged. "Well, she asked."

"Edible undies?" Agnes said. "I don't understand." Suddenly, as if a lightbulb had gone off in her head, she gasped and covered her breast with both hands as if to keep her heart from leaping out. "Oh, my."

"Let's go, Gram," Brent said, taking her by the arm. And not a moment too soon. Agnes swayed and fell into a dead faint.

Brent caught her in his arms. "Somebody call 911!"

"Well, thank God it wasn't a heart attack," Vera said when she dropped Jamie off at her house two hours later, after sitting in the ER waiting on word of Agnes's condition.

"It was probably a good idea that her doctor decided to keep her overnight for observation anyway," Jamie said. "I'll tell you, that grandson of hers is a nut."

"Yeah, he's a real fruitcake," Vera said, putting the gear into neutral. "Oh, by the way, you're not feeling a little weird, are you?"

"What do you mean?"

"You know, from eating those brownies?"

"You mean horny?"

Vera rolled her eyes. "Yeah, that."

Jamie decided she wouldn't tell Vera she got horny every time she thought of tall, dark, and drop-dead gorgeous Max Holt. "Yeah, I'm feeling a little frisky," Jamie confessed, although she suspected it was just her imagination. "I'm thinking maybe a cold shower is in order."

Vera sighed. "I'm thinking the same thing. Must be my wild oats acting up."

Jamie arrived at work the next morning, just as Destiny Moultrie climbed from a cream-colored Mercedes. The woman hurried over.

"I know I promised to give you a day or two to think about the column," she began, "but I'm anxious to get started."

Destiny was dressed in silk khaki-colored slacks and a matching jacket that hung open to expose a tight purple bustier that barely contained her breasts. Cleavage seemed to be Destiny's middle name.

"I'm really busy," Jamie said.

"I was hoping we could talk it over this morning. And I'd like to discuss another matter with you. It's pretty important."

Jamie did a mental sigh. That meant all the doughnuts would be eaten by the time she got to the small kitchen in back, but she figured she at least owed Destiny the truth. She had no intention of hiring a psychic for her column, even if there was to be a column, which she hadn't decided on one way or the other.

"I can only afford a few minutes," she said.

"I knew you'd say that." Destiny followed her to the front double-glass doors.

Vera looked up the minute they stepped inside. Her gaze immediately fell on Destiny. "How did you know I was going to have car trouble?"

Destiny shrugged. "I just had a feeling. I didn't want you to find yourself stranded."

"You didn't tamper beneath my hood, did you?"

"Vera!" Jamie said. "That was not a nice thing to say."

"It happens all the time," Destiny said. "People don't want to believe in things they can't see."

Vera gave a grunt. "So what's it going to cost me to get my car repaired?"

Destiny shrugged. "I have no idea."

Vera looked at Jamie. "See, I told you there was nothing to this psychic stuff."

"What I meant to say," Destiny began slowly, "is I have no idea how much a new engine costs."

"A new engine!" Vera cried.

"Man, that's going to cost you," Jamie said, then caught herself. What was she thinking?

"New engine, my foot," Vera said. "There's not a darn thing wrong with my engine."

"Maybe we should step into my office," Jamie said, motioning Destiny inside.

The woman followed. Jamie paused at the door and glanced back at Vera. "Has Mike come in yet?" Mike Henderson was Jamie's fresh-out-of-college editor. She was trying to raise him to be a real newspaperman since he was organizationally challenged and spent much of his time chasing women.

"He's covering the city council meeting, and then he has an appointment to interview the new high school football coach."

Jamie nodded and closed the door. She turned and almost bumped into Destiny.

"I have something to tell you," the woman said.

Jamie took the chair behind her desk and motioned for Destiny to sit. "What is it?"

"Last night I had a vision. You were in it. There was a man with you."

Jamie perked up and thought of Max. "Oh, yeah? Were we naked?" She slapped her hand against her forehead. Now why had she gone and said something like that? The last thing she needed to do was encourage the woman.

"It wasn't that kind of vision," Destiny said. "This man was in uniform, and he was asking you a lot of questions."

Jamie remained quiet.

Destiny didn't seem deterred by her silence. "The situation was, um, dire, because I had this heavy feeling in my chest afterward."

Jamie figured any woman with Destiny's breasts would have a heavy feeling in her chest. She sighed. "OK, Destiny, I'll play along. Who was asking these questions and what were they?"

"I don't know." At Jamie's look, Destiny went on. "Hey, I'm doing my best here, OK? I can't give you every little detail." All at once she glanced to the chair beside her. "Shut up, OK? I don't need your help."

Jamie's eyes widened as she followed Destiny's gaze to the empty chair. "Uh, Destiny, who are you talking to?" she asked.

32

The woman didn't hesitate. "His name is Ronnie. He's from the spirit world. He doesn't have enough sense to know he's dead. Follows me around."

Jamie gripped the arms on her chair as chills raced up her spine. Time to bolt, she told herself.

"He's just an old redneck, don't worry, he's harmless." She glanced back at the empty chair. "Yes, you heard me right, Ronnie, you *are* a redneck. Anybody who gets sloppy drunk and falls out of the back of a pickup truck doing sixty miles per hour is a bona fide redneck in my book." She looked at Jamie. "That's how he died. He's kinda between worlds."

"Oh, well, that certainly explains it." Jamie glanced at the door. It would take her less than three seconds to reach if she ran like hell.

"Hey, I know it sounds crazy," Destiny said, "but that's the way it is. I have dead people show up all the time. They don't usually stay long. So, when do you want me to start?"

Jamie blinked. "Huh?"

"The job? I got a lot of my stuff unpacked last night so I'm ready to roll."

Jamie decided the woman had enough problems so she tried to let her down easy. "I'm thinking maybe I should hold off on the column," she said. What Jamie was actually thinking was that Destiny needed to be hauled off in a straitjacket.

"I suggest you announce the new column in your newspaper as soon as possible."

"Well, like I said —"

Destiny sighed in exasperation. "Dammit, Ronnie, would you *please* stop yakking and let me finish this conversation?" She shifted in her chair and regarded Jamie. "Look, I don't have all day. Let's do this. Run the announcement. If you don't get a substantial amount of responses, I promise I won't bother you again."

Once again, Jamie glanced at the chair beside Destiny. "Does he follow you everywhere?" she asked, thinking it would be best to have all the facts before she reported the woman to the authorities.

"Who, Ronnie?" Destiny sighed. "Hell, I can't even take a shower without the pervert getting in there with me. But don't worry; as soon as his pea brain realizes he needs to move on, he'll be out of my life." She rolled her eyes. "Dead people," she said on a sigh. "They can be such a pain in the ass." All at once, she sneezed. "Uh-oh, gotta run before I go into a sneezing frenzy." She stood and made for the door. "I'll call you later."

Jamie stopped her. "Um, Destiny?"

She turned. "Yeah?"

Jamie almost felt sorry for her. "How about I call you when I've made my decision? In the meantime, don't tell Vera about your friend, OK?"

"Vera, I need to run an errand," Jamie said, shortly after Destiny left. "I won't be long."

"No problem, I'll hold down the fort."

Jamie picked up her pocketbook and left the building, hurrying down the street toward Maxine

Chambers's shop. She couldn't wait to see what was inside. She opened the door and stepped in, and was greeted by the smell of lavender.

Maxine was standing behind the counter. She had changed her mousy brown hair to a flattering red and wore makeup, something she had never bothered with when she'd worked at the library.

"Well, Jamie Swift, it's wonderful to see you again, only this time we don't have to whisper like we did at the library."

"I just came by to offer my congratulations on your new store," Jamie said.

Maxine smiled. "Well, you're the first. Everyone else is shocked that I would do such a thing, and some preacher wannabe is calling constantly, accusing me of corrupting the town. And get this; he wants to meet with me so he can pray for my soul. I told him to take a hike."

Jamie knew Brent Walker had been the one to call. "I'm sure it's going to take time for some folks to adjust. I'd just ignore him." She glanced around. "Now then, why don't you show me around? I've been dying to come in."

"What did you have in mind?"

"I'm not sure. Something a little sexy." She thought of the edible underwear. "Without going overboard," she added.

"Come on and let me show you my new European lace collection. They're elegant but simple. Sexy *and* classy," she added.

Jamie followed her to an aisle where Maxine held up the most beautiful bras and panties she'd ever seen. "Oh, my," she said.

"Aren't they lovely?" Maxine said proudly. "And look at this baby doll sleepwear in satin. Think how nice that would feel against your skin."

Jamie ran her hand against the material. "I've never felt anything so nice."

"I agree," Maxine said. "This is top-of-the-line. Oh, and I've got these beautiful teddies and body suits. Aren't they wonderful? And you've got just the figure for them."

"Why, thank you, Maxine." Jamie paused and studied the woman. "I don't mean to be nosy, Maxine, but what made you decide to open a lingerie store?"

The woman smiled. "I guess I'm the last person in the world people would expect to find running a store like this, but it's always been a secret fantasy of mine. So one morning I woke up and reminded myself I wasn't getting any younger, and that's when I started getting serious about it. Unfortunately, I haven't had a lot of customers since I opened."

"Then you'll have to let me write an article about your store," Jamie said, "along with a nice advertisement. It'll be my celebration gift to you."

"Why, thank you, Jamie. That's very kind of you. You know, I've always liked you. You were so careful with your library books. You never dog-eared the pages like some folks, and you always brought them back on time." She sniffed. "Not all people respect books like you do. Why, I could tell you stories —"

"Show me what else you've got," Jamie said, wanting to change the subject. Maxine probably did have a lot of stories, but she didn't have time to listen to them.

Maxine gave her a complete tour of the store. In the end, Jamie selected a number of items from the European collection.

"Good choice," Maxine said, "and since you're one of my first customers, I'm going to give you a ten percent discount." She rang up the merchandise, then wrapped the bras, panties, sleepwear, and body suits in tissue paper and put them in a beautiful lavender-colored bag.

Jamie handed her a check. "Why don't we meet for lunch early next week so we can talk about your store?" she said. "In the meantime, I'll send my editor over to get a picture of you for the ad."

Maxine looked pleased. "Well, now, I think that would be quite nice. You just call me when it's convenient."

"I'll check my calendar and get back to you." She left the store a few minutes later with her purchases and walked by the bakery, thinking how good a brownie would taste right about now. She didn't really believe they contained an aphrodisiac, but if on the off chance they did she'd better steer clear of them. Her libido was giving her enough trouble these days.

And that made her think of Max. She wondered when she would see him again. At the same time, she questioned why she had allowed herself to become so involved. She knew very little about the man except that he was a gazillionaire who owned a whole slew of companies and had dated his share of celebrities. She knew he'd once been married, but that it hadn't worked out, and it was probably one of the reasons he wasn't in a hurry to marry again.

What she didn't know was how she felt about their situation. After an engagement gone badly, Jamie had pretty much decided marriage wasn't on the cards for her, at least not in the near future. But now she was beginning to have second thoughts, and it was all because of Max. Knowing herself as she did, she was aware that she wasn't cut out for the short-term flings Max was accustomed to. She wanted more.

Damn. She had tried so hard not to fall for him. She had fought her growing attraction to him every step of the way, only to realize that she was beginning to entertain thoughts of a possible future with him.

As she saw it, she had two choices. She could try to get the man out of her system and wonder for the rest of her life if anything would have become of them or she could continue to wait.

Neither option sounded particularly appealing.

CHAPTER
THREE

Happy Paws Veterinary Clinic was decorated with vinyl chairs and floors, obviously to make it easier to clean up after nervous cats and dogs. Which explained the strong disinfectant smell, Jamie thought upon entering the reception area shortly after lunch. Some furry friend had either suffered a sudden loss of bladder control or heaved up a helping of meat chunks. From somewhere in back, a cacophony of barking persisted.

As Jamie waited for the receptionist to get off the telephone, she studied the large bulletin board that served as a lost-and-found center. Another bulletin board listed a variety of puppies and kittens to sell or give away.

She thought of adding Fleas's name to the list. Owning a pet was more trouble than she'd thought. Only, she couldn't think of a person who'd want to take on a dog with emotional problems and missing hair.

When the receptionist hung up the phone, she smiled at Jamie. "Oh, you're Fleas's mommy, aren't you?" the woman said in a voice that sounded too small and squeaky for someone who appeared to be at least one hundred pounds overweight.

"That's me," Jamie said.

"Hold on one sec, hon, and I'll get him."

Fleas did not look happy to see Jamie, but then the sagging brown skin and folds along the hound's face and jowls gave him a perpetual look of sadness and discontent. This time it seemed to be mixed with outright annoyance.

Oh, great, she thought. He's pouting.

"Okeydokey," the receptionist said. "His heartworm test was negative, so you can start the preventative medicine. You can give him his first dose today, then he has to take one every month. You'll need to mark your calendar."

"He won't eat it," Jamie said dully. "Unless I can hide it in his ice cream."

The woman laughed as though it were the funniest thing she'd ever heard. "Oh, dogs love them," she insisted. "It comes in a meatlike treat."

"Can I put it between a hamburger bun with cheese on top?"

More laughter. Which was rather annoying for Jamie since she was serious.

"And then there's the flea preventative. You'll want to apply it once a month. It'll be easier to remember if you do it at the same time you give him his monthly heartworm medicine. I gave you a six-month supply of each. That's what people usually request." She hesitated and looked about the room as if to make sure nobody was listening. "Have you ever owned a pet, hon?" she whispered.

Was it that obvious? Jamie wondered. "This is my first, um, experience."

"There's a booklet inside his goody bag. It'll give you all sorts of information. And you can call us if you run into problems."

Jamie pulled out her checkbook and pen. "How much do I owe?"

"Well, now, let's see." The woman pulled up the information on the computer. "He had a full exam, we clipped his toenails, took blood for the heartworm test, performed the surgery —" She looked up. "We expressed his anal glands. I have to tell you, it wasn't pretty. Our technician had to go home for the rest of the day." She burst into giggles. "Just kidding."

Fleas sank to the floor and covered both eyes with his paws.

Jamie tightened her grip on the pen as she prepared to write the check. This was going to be bad.

"Oh, and there was a charge for anesthesia, of course, and his nerve pills."

"Nerve pills?"

"You mentioned he had a bad case of separation anxiety. Don't worry, Dr. Adams started him on a teensy-weensy dose, but it should take the edge off. Try giving it to Fleas with peanut butter. It's easier that way."

Jamie looked at Fleas. The dog had serious emotional problems, including shell shock from his coon-hunting days.

The woman behind the counter looked up from her computer. "Okeydokey, it comes to four hundred and eight dollars."

Jamie's eyes almost popped out of her head. She looked at Fleas. "You realize I paid less than that for the truck."

Fleas got up and shook hard. His long ears flapped annoyingly. Finally, he sat back on his haunches and began to lick himself.

Jamie cringed.

Police Chief Lamar Tevis was waiting for Jamie when she arrived back at the office, Fleas on her heels. The serious look on the man's face told her something was wrong. He held his cap in his hands, and his sandy-colored hair was still flat from wearing it. Vera was on the telephone. She shrugged at Jamie as though she had no idea why the chief of police wanted to see her.

"Hello, Lamar," Jamie said. "May I help you?"

He glanced at the bloodhound beside her. "Wow, that's about the ugliest dog I've ever seen. Is he a stray?"

"He belongs to me," Jamie said.

"Sorry, I didn't know he was yours. How come he's missing hair on his back?"

"A raccoon attacked him."

"I didn't know you liked to hunt coons. Why, me and my buddies —"

"It happened before I, um, came into ownership." Jamie saw that Lamar was still staring at her dog as though he were ugly. She hitched her head high. "Actually, he's pure bloodhound. Comes from championship bloodline," she added. It was a lie she told often.

"No kidding. What's his name?"

This was the part Jamie hated most. "Fleas."

"Uh-oh." Lamar stepped back.

"He doesn't actually *have* fleas, somebody just named him that. So what brings you to this neck of the woods, Lamar?"

Lamar glanced at Vera, then back to Jamie. "Perhaps we should talk privately. No offense, Vera."

Vera hung up the telephone. "Like I won't find out," she said. "So you can just kiss my royal behind, Lamar."

"Spoken like a true Southern Baptist," Lamar said with a chuckle.

"Any word from Mike?" Jamie asked, wishing her editor would check in more often. He was probably sweet-talking one of the counter girls at Dairy Queen.

"He called while you were out. Said he was working a hot story and would be in shortly. He wouldn't give me the details, he was acting real secretive and all. You know how dramatic he gets."

Jamie nodded. "Pray for a decent headline." She led Lamar inside her office and closed the door. He waited for Jamie to sit before he took the chair in front of her desk. Fleas plopped down beside Jamie's feet and gave a huge sigh.

"I guess you haven't heard the news," Lamar said. "Luanne Ritter was found murdered in her home late this morning. Suffered a fatal blow to her head," he added.

"Oh, my God!" Jamie said. Luanne Ritter owned Ritter's Loan Company.

"Yup. That's where your editor has been all morning. At the murder scene," he added. "I didn't want to say anything in front of Vera. Not until I gave you the news."

"Do you have a suspect?"

"It's too early to tell. Her neighbor, Elaine something-or-other —" He paused and reached for notes. "Elaine Brewer is her name. Anyway, she went over to Luanne's house to borrow some coffee, knocked several times, but there was no answer. She found the door unlocked and almost tripped over Luanne's body on the kitchen floor. Coroner said Luanne had been dead at least ten or twelve hours. Sounds a little suspicious to me," he added.

"Oh, yeah?"

Lamar leaned closer. "Get this. The neighbor drinks decaf. Luanne drinks only regular coffee. I'd think after being neighbors for ten years this Brewer woman would have known. We've taken her in for questioning."

Jamie just looked at him. Lamar was a good honest man, but he wasn't the smartest investigator she'd ever met. "This is unbelievable," Jamie said.

Lamar glanced up quickly. He looked defensive. "You don't think I'm making this up, do you? The murder, I mean? My men will vouch for me. Your editor, too."

Jamie blinked. "What I meant was it's hard to believe someone just murdered Luanne in cold blood."

"I have the body to prove it. I can take you over to the morgue if you want to see for yourself."

Jamie did a mental eye-roll. "Let's start over, Lamar. What can I do for you?"

Lamar reached into his shirt pocket and pulled out a small section of newspaper. He unfolded it and handed it to Jamie. "This was on Luanne's night table. Nobody knows about it except the responding officer and me. I'd like to keep it that way for now." He pretended to zip his lips. "Get my drift?"

Jamie found herself looking at a copy of her personals section that had been cut out of the newspaper. She glanced at Lamar. "You're not thinking my personals section had something to do with Luanne's murder?"

"There may be nothing to it, but I thought you should know." He leaned back in his chair and crossed one leg over the other. Fleas sat up and began to scratch. Lamar watched, an uneasy expression on his face. "Luanne wasn't very popular in this town," he went on, "what with her line of work. Way I heard, she could lean pretty hard on someone if they were late on their loan payment."

Jamie shook her head as she continued staring at the ads. Her hands trembled. "It has to be business related, Lamar. I think this —" She paused and held up the section of newspaper. "This is just a coincidence."

"Could be. I've sealed her place of business, and we're planning a full investigation. Like I said, I don't want this ad stuff getting out. I just wanted to make you aware." He took it from her, refolded it, and stuffed it into his pocket. "Also, I need your help."

Jamie knew where he was headed. "You know I can't give you the names of those who've submitted an ad without a court order."

"No judge is going to give me an order to look into every name on your list," he said. "All I'm asking is that you keep an eye out for anything that looks suspicious. In case we have some kook on our hands."

"Yes, of course."

"I do have one other question. Did Luanne run an ad?"

"No."

Lamar shifted in his seat. "She had a message on her answering machine from a man regarding an ad. Said he'd call her back. Unfortunately, Luanne didn't have caller ID, and the tape must've been old because the voices weren't that clear."

"She must've answered his ad."

"She had another call from a fellow who claimed he was a man of God, said he wanted to meet with her immediately. He didn't leave his telephone number, told her he'd call back. Once again, it was hard to make out the message."

"Wonder why he didn't leave his name," Jamie pondered aloud.

"We also found religious literature stuffed inside her mailbox so he obviously knew where she lived."

"Was there any indication of forced entry?"

"No. Luanne opened the door for the person who killed her, so whoever it was must've not presented a threat. She might have opened the door for a preacher. This is all speculation, of course."

Jamie nodded. She thought of Agnes Aimsley's grandson, Brent Walker, then pushed it aside. Brent might be a bit on the kooky side, he might even leave religious material in Luanne's mailbox, but he wasn't a murderer. But she kept quiet, knowing how quickly Lamar could get sidetracked.

"By the way," Lamar said. "Where's Max Holt?"

Jamie would have loved nothing more than to say, "Jeez, last time I saw Max he had my skirt shoved to my waist and his hands on my thighs." Instead, she shrugged. "Who knows? He's a busy man."

"He's your partner."

"Max is my *silent* partner, Lamar. I run the newspaper."

"Max is good at this sort of thing. Investigative work," he added.

Jamie was not surprised by the remark. Lamar had witnessed firsthand just how good Max was when he'd almost single-handedly discovered who was involved in the town's corruption, which had bled taxpayers of their dollars for years. "You thinking of hiring him on as a deputy?" she asked, grinning, if for no other reason than to lighten the mood.

Lamar grinned back. "I tried, but he turned down the job. I reckon he has bigger fish to fry."

Despite her attempt at flippancy, Jamie could feel her stomach knotting. "Lamar, tell me you don't really think Luanne's murder is connected to my personals section, because if you think it is, I'll stop running the ads immediately."

"Then we risk losing the killer *if* it's connected. Are you going to help me?"

"I'll do what I can legally."

"That's all I'm asking," Lamar said. He left a few minutes later.

Jamie reached for the telephone. It was time to call Max.

Max Holt was in the boardroom of Holt Industries when he received Jamie's call. He immediately excused himself and hurried into his private office. "What's up, Swifty?"

Jamie had not forgotten the sexy pitch of his voice, or the teasing lilt he often used with her. Just hearing his voice again did all sorts of soft and fuzzy things to her insides. And that reminded her of how little she knew about the man. He moved in mysterious circles, dined with royalty, and made business deals that ended up on the pages of the *New York Times*.

"Max, do you have any idea what I had to go through to reach you?" Jamie said. "I had to bypass a receptionist, a secretary, and your personal assistant, all of whom insisted on knowing my business with you."

"What did you tell them?"

"I said I had a small oil-rich country for sale and that you might be interested in buying it."

He chuckled. "Well, I'm glad you were able to reach me. What's up?"

Jamie wondered how he could sound so casual when every nerve ending in her body was tingling. She wondered if he'd though about her these past weeks. "I have a problem on my hands," she said. She told him about the personals section she had started, Luanne Ritter's murder, and the fact Police Chief Lamar Tevis suspected the two might be connected. She figured, as her partner, Max should know. OK, so maybe there was more to it than that. It was a good excuse to call him.

"And here I thought you were calling to say you missed me," Max said. "You and I have some unfinished business, you know."

Jamie felt a thrill of delight race up her backbone at the thought. They had come so close the last time. She shook her head, trying to push the image from her mind. "Max, this is serious," she said, wondering how he could just pick up where they'd left off after three weeks of no word.

"Does Lamar Tevis have proof the two are connected?"

"No. But what if they are?"

"Don't assume the worst before we have time to look into the facts," he said. "Listen, I'm driving down tomorrow for Frankie's birthday party. I can't believe my brother-in-law is reaching the big five-oh."

Jamie had received her invitation the week before. Jamie had met Frankie and his wife, Deedee, when they'd moved to Beaumont some ten years prior, after Frankie had retired from wrestling as Frankie the Assassin. They'd become fast friends, but it was hard to believe Max and Deedee were brother and sister. "Of course I'm going," she said.

"My schedule will be tight," Max said, "but I can swing by your house and pick you up on the way."

Jamie took her time in answering. It was no surprise that Max would just assume she would attend the party with him. And on a Friday night of all nights when most reasonably attractive single women had dates. She almost preferred cutting her tongue out with her dull letter opener than telling Max she was dateless.

Be cool, she told herself.

"I, um, didn't know you were coming, Max, so I sort of made other plans," she said, then wanted to smack her own mouth. Her and her dumb pride, she thought. But Max had a way of bringing out the worst in her when it came to male — female stuff.

"Oh, yeah?" He sounded more amused than annoyed. "Well, if we put our heads together I'm sure we can think of a way to ditch him. I have to get back to a meeting and wrap things up here so I can leave, but do me a favor. Wear that blue dress you wore the first night I met you."

Jamie heard a dial tone. She hung up. She felt something nudge her foot and glanced down at Fleas who was watching her. "OK, so I made up that part about having a date," she said. "Sometimes things just fall out of my mouth before I have time to think about them. Especially when it comes to *that* man," she added.

The dog thumped his tail against the floor.

50

"It's complicated with Max and me," she went on. "I never know where I stand with him." She couldn't tell Fleas the truth, that she couldn't get Max out of her mind, that she was just itching for the chance to be alone and naked with him. It wouldn't be fair to discuss sex in front of the poor animal since he'd just been neutered. Not that she could imagine Fleas interested in chasing a female dog, since it would take effort on his part. And Fleas was allergic to effort.

Jamie gave a huge sigh. Suddenly, her thoughts took a drastic turn, and she snapped her head up. Holy cow! Destiny Moultrie had warned her she would be talking to a man in a uniform, and it would be bad. She had been right on the money. Jamie picked up the telephone and dialed the woman's number. Destiny answered on the first ring.

"We need to talk," Jamie said.

"I demand to know what's going on," Vera said, standing in the doorway of Jamie's office. "And I'm not going to take no for an answer."

Jamie noted the determined look on Vera's face. "You're not armed, are you?" she said.

Vera pressed her lips into a grim line and ignored Jamie's question. "You've never kept secrets from me. Why was Lamar Tevis here? What'd you do now? Are you in trouble with the police?"

Jamie gave a sigh. Why did the woman always assume she'd done something wrong? "Luanne Ritter was murdered."

Vera's brows shot up in surprise. "No kidding? Well, I'm sure she had it coming."

"Vera!"

"Nobody liked her anyway. Folks only borrowed money from her when they were desperate. And Luanne liked to talk. If someone's credit rating was low, she blabbed it all over town. Why, I heard that one of Luanne's employees roughed up a couple of customers who fell behind on their payments. And to think, Luanne's husband, God rest his soul, was such a nice man. If he knew how Luanne treated her customers he'd have reached right out of his grave and snatched her bald-headed."

"Well, now, that's something to think about," Jamie said, not knowing how to respond.

"I'm telling you, that woman was no better than a loan shark. So why did Lamar come to you?"

Jamie didn't meet her gaze. She didn't like lying to Vera. "Um, Mike was on the crime scene, and Lamar doesn't want vital information printed in the paper."

Vera suddenly looked indignant. "Why didn't Mike call me? I'm the assistant editor. I should have been there to take photos."

"I suppose he felt he had to move fast since it was a murder investigation." Jamie was proud that Mike had made it to the scene. He was a good editor, but his poor time-management skills and sexual exploits had interfered with his work in the past. He now made a concerted effort to get to work on time.

Vera didn't look placated. She sniffed, a definite sign of annoyance. "Well, I have to leave for a hair appointment," she said. "Helen is going to cover the phones. Besides, I want to be the first to tell everybody at the beauty shop about Luanne."

Five minutes later, Mike rushed into Jamie's office. As usual, his clothes looked as though he'd slept in them. His light brown hair was mussed, as though he'd finger-combed it on his way out of the house. "Have you heard the news?" he asked.

"Yes. Lamar was here earlier."

"I'm going to get right on the story. We're going to have a kick-butt headline. Oh, and you're not going to believe this one. They were hauling Luanne out of her house on a stretcher, and the body bag slipped. Luanne hit the ground."

"Oh, jeez. Please don't mention it in your article."

"Lamar almost had a stroke."

"So did Vera when she found out you didn't call her to take pictures."

"Uh-oh. Maybe I should leave town for a couple of days," he said. "By the way, are you going to Frankie Fontana's birthday party tomorrow night? It's the talk of the town, what with him being the new mayor and just turning fifty and all."

"Yeah, I'm going."

"You should take me with you. I could get pictures for the society column."

Jamie hadn't thought of that. Frankie's wife, Deedee, would go all-out for the party, and the photos would fill up space. With the exception of Luanne Ritter's murder, there just wasn't enough going on in Beaumont these days. "You'd have to rent a tux."

"I've already got one. Come on, Jamie, I need a night out. My life is as boring as yours."

"My life is not boring."

"Whatever. So, what do you say?"

Jamie pondered it. At least it meant she wouldn't have to show up alone. Not that she'd ever let that stop her before, but this was different since she'd already told Max she had a date. She had to save face. "OK, you can go as my escort."

"Your escort? Oh, I get it. You couldn't find a date."

Jamie gave him a look.

"Hey, I understand. It's not like I've never had to scramble to find someone to go with me at the last minute. It's harder for women to go alone, though. They tend to look desperate."

Jamie drummed her fingers on her desk. "Mike, don't you have an article to write?"

"Hello?" a voice called out.

Jamie looked up to find Destiny standing in the doorway. Mike looked, as well. "Well, hello to you," he said, straightening his tie and squaring his shoulders as if to make himself appear taller. "May I help you?" His eyes were fixed on her breasts.

"I'm here to see Jamie."

He went on as if he hadn't heard. "I'm her editor, Mike Henderson." He rubbed a hand over his head, smoothing out his rumpled hair. "You've probably seen my byline."

"Destiny Moultrie," she said in her husky voice. "And, no, I haven't had the pleasure of reading your articles. I've just moved to Beaumont."

"You just moved here?" he repeated. "Well, then you probably haven't had a chance to dine at our best restaurants or see the sights. I could —"

"I don't eat out much," Destiny said. "I'm a vegetarian."

Mike smiled broadly. "A vegetarian? Well, now, isn't that a coincidence. It just so happens I'm a vegetarian, too."

Jamie tried to suppress a smile. Mike lived on fast food and probably wouldn't recognize a zucchini from a cucumber. "Um, Mike, about that article —"

"Yeah, yeah." He reached into his pocket. "Here's my business card, Miss Moultrie."

"Call me Destiny," she said, taking the card.

"If you should find yourself in need of a tour guide, I'm the man for the job. Oh, and use my pager. That's quicker."

"Thank you, Mike."

He was still smiling as he backed from the room and closed the door.

"Nice man," Destiny said to Jamie.

"Yes, Mike can be very, um, charming," Jamie said. She motioned for Destiny to take a seat. "Thank you for coming right over," she said. "I have something I want to discuss with you."

"Have you decided about the job?"

"I'm still thinking about it." She paused. "Something terrible has happened." Jamie debated whether or not to tell her about Luanne and decided to hold off.

Destiny leaned forward. "Oh, my, what is it?"

"I was hoping you could tell me."

Destiny shook her head. "I haven't had any more visions if that's what you're asking."

"Nothing about the man in uniform who was supposed to question me?"

"No, nothing. Why?"

Jamie leveled her gaze on the woman. "I was questioned by the chief of police this morning about a murder that took place last night."

Destiny simply looked at her. "I'm not surprised. Who was the victim?"

Jamie told her what she knew.

Destiny listened carefully. "I'm not getting anything on it, but that doesn't mean it won't come to me later." She suddenly glanced behind her. "Ronnie, I asked you to wait in the car."

Jamie looked up at the vacant spot behind her. "Your dead spirit came with you?"

"Sorry. Just ignore him."

Jamie nodded as though it were an everyday occurrence to have a dead spirit in her office. "Destiny, I don't know anything about psychic ability; in fact, I don't really believe in such things."

"I know that, but I hope you won't let it stand in the way of giving me a job. I am perfect for it. I have feel for what people really need help with. I *can* help them, Jamie. I've done this sort of thing before with a lot of success."

Jamie considered it. If an advice column pulled in more readers it could only mean more revenue for the newspaper. "Tell you what. I'll announce the new column in an article and see if we get any responses. If we get a significant number, the job is yours. As long as you realize I have editorial control on what goes out," she added.

"Are you going to announce to your readers that I'm psychic?"

"The jury is still out on that one." Jamie wasn't sure how the citizens of Beaumont would accept it.

"Don't forget, I want to be referred to as the Divine Love Goddess Advisor. I think it's catchy, don't you?"

Jamie didn't have a clue. Probably folks would laugh her right out of town. "You realize I'm going out on a limb here."

"I won't let you down," Destiny promised.

Vera walked through the door two hours later. Jamie sat back in her chair and stared, her mouth agape. "Wow!" The gray was gone, and her hair cut in a flattering style.

Vera preened. "Susie colored it, added a light frosting, and then cut it. She says this haircut is the rave in Hollywood. Susan Sarandon and Sharon Stone are wearing this style. Mitzi, the cosmetologist, did my makeup. Of course, I ended up buying fifty dollars' worth of foundation, powder, and eye shadow from her, but she showed me how to use it to enhance my best features."

"You look great," Jamie said and meant it. "In fact, you look ten years younger."

"That's what everyone said. It sort of made up for the fact they already knew about Luanne Ritter. News travels fast in this town." She paused. "Um, Jamie, would you mind if I kept the Mustang for a few more days? It's going to cost a fortune to fix my old car."

"What's wrong with it?"

"Don't ask."

"It's the engine, right?"

"Yeah, but that doesn't mean your psychic friend is on the up-and-up."

"You're saying it's just another coincidence?" Jamie asked.

"I'm saying my car is old, and the engine was bound to give out sooner or later."

Jamie just looked at her.

"Frankly, the car is not worth what it would cost to replace the engine so I need to look around, see if I can find something affordable."

"You're welcome to keep the Mustang as long as you need it," Jamie replied.

"You're a doll. By the way, I hear your friend Deedee is throwing a big birthday party for Frankie tomorrow night. You plan on going?"

"I wouldn't miss it."

"Who are you going with?" Vera asked.

Big pause. "Mike."

"*Our* Mike? What's wrong, couldn't you find a real date?" She didn't wait for Jamie to respond. "Well, I don't blame you for not wanting to go alone. Not with people still talking about your broken engagement and all."

Jamie felt her ego plunge to her toes. "That wasn't my fault." Which was true. She'd broken up with Phillip Standish because his mother had been the ringleader of

58

the town's corruption scandal. "Besides, I didn't love him." That was true, too. She'd simply wanted to belong to a real family for once. Security and predictability had been important to her at the time. Seemed those days were gone forever. Her life was about as predictable as a tornado. And that tornado had a name: Max Holt.

"Oh, nobody is blaming you," Vera said. "It's just, well, I don't want folks feeling sorry for you. I wish you could have found a better date than Mike. I mean, he's so young. He can't be more than twenty-four or five."

"I'm hoping he'll look older in his tux," Jamie said.

"I'm hoping he'll remember to wash behind his ears."

Leave it to Vera to make things worse, Jamie thought. "It's not a *real* date, OK? He's just acting as my escort. Besides, he wanted to go so he could snap some pictures for the society column." Jamie regretted the words before they left her mouth. Snapping pictures was supposed to be Vera's job.

"I've already heard about the birthday cake your friend Deedee chose for Frankie," Vera said, as if she were more interested in the latest gossip than she was in snapping pictures. "Lyle Betts baked it if that tells you anything."

Jamie leaned back in her seat. "Oh, yeah?"

"The way I heard it, Lyle has an 'Adults Only' book to order from. The cake is supposed to be of a naked woman."

Jamie chuckled. It sounded like something Deedee would do; she could be outlandish at times. Which was why some of the more genteel families had had trouble accepting the couple when they'd first moved to Beaumont. Deedee had arrived wearing rhinestone outfits, and Frankie had shocked the town when he'd invited his old wrestling buddies for a visit. Jamie had taken them under her wing and invited them to all the social events, and the two had become a hit. It was a known fact they could liven up even the dullest party with their presence. And when Frankie had run for mayor, promising to clean up town corruption, he'd won hands down.

"And get this," Vera said. "People are lining up at Lyle's bakery to buy brownies. Wouldn't surprise me if half the women in this town ended up pregnant before long," she added with a knowing look.

Jamie promised herself she'd steer clear of the brownies.

The following night, Jamie slipped on her blue silk dress, and checked herself in the mirror. Her makeup and hair were perfect. She had taken a long bubble bath, slathered herself with lotion from head to toe, and then given herself a manicure and a pedicure. She tried to convince herself it had nothing to do with Max.

She'd even tried to convince herself that her trip to Maxine Chambers's lingerie shop had nothing to do with Max, but beneath her clothes she wore a body suit that was designed to make a man's tongue fall to the floor. The fact that she'd spent close to two hundred dollars in the shop had almost caused her to swallow her own tongue.

60

The doorbell rang at precisely six forty-five. Jamie opened the door and found Mike on the other side. He wore a baby-blue tux that was outdated, and at least one size too small. Ruffles peeked out from his sleeves. "Oh, jeez," she said.

"I know it's a little snug," he told her. "My parents bought it for my high school prom. I guess I've filled out."

"You look fine," Jamie told him, not wanting to hurt his feelings. She knew he tried to help his parents financially from time to time, and odds were he couldn't afford to rent a tux. Probably nobody would notice his white socks anyway. Besides, it wasn't a date. Mike was going as part of his job.

"Hey, you look gorgeous," he said, taking a long look. "You should dress up more often, and you wouldn't have so much trouble finding a date. Hey, speaking of gorgeous, what's your friend Destiny doing tonight? I'm here to tell you, that woman is hot. You should fix us up."

"Don't you think she's a little, um, mature for you?" Jamie asked.

"Age is not an issue with me. I'm taking you out, aren't I?"

Jamie shot him a dark look. "May we leave now?"

Jamie did not see Max among the crowd of people when she and Mike came through the door at Frankie and Deedee's, and her heart sank. What if he'd been unable to get away? Or maybe he'd had a better offer in the way of female companionship. Max Holt would naturally have his share of offers. Jamie pushed the thought aside. Max would not renege on a promise to be at his brother-in-law's fiftieth birthday party. She craned her head, trying to see above the tall heads in the room.

Max spotted Jamie the minute she stepped through the front door. He smiled at the sight of her so-called date, who immediately headed toward the dining room where the buffet was set up. His smile broadened when he noticed she was looking for him, but he was hidden from view at his place beside one of the round, floor-to-ceiling columns inside the house. He simply stood there for a moment watching her. Finally, he moved toward her until he was standing directly behind her.

"Looking for someone?"

Jamie felt the hairs stand on the back of her neck at the sound of his voice. Every nerve in her body sprang to life as she turned and found herself looking into Max Holt's handsome face. For a moment all they could do was stand and stare at each other. It was as though all the people in the room had evaporated.

"Hello, Max," she said, trying to sound cool. But cool wasn't easy, what with her heart beating like a conga drum in her chest. Damn, he looked good in his black tux, which, unlike Mike's, was simple and elegant and probably tailor made. Of course, the man looked good no matter what he wore.

Max was all male — sinewy muscle, gorgeous olive complexion, hard jaw. He was as polished as they came,

62

with an underlying air of danger that oddly made her feel safe in his presence.

His smile was slow and lazy as a winding river. "You amaze me, Swifty. I thought you couldn't get any prettier. I was wrong."

Jamie offered him a benign smile, meant to make him feel as though she were immune to his charm. "Thank you, Max. Coming from a world-renowned womanizer I consider that quite a compliment."

He grinned. "So, who's the boy?"

"Excuse me?"

"Your date?"

"You know Mike Henderson. I hardly think he qualifies as a boy. He's, um, not exactly a real date, he just escorted me. He's here to take pictures for the society column."

"If he were any younger I'd have to report you to the authorities."

"Same old Max."

"Tell you what, Swifty. I'm going to be a gentleman about this, seeing as how you probably think I took you for granted. I assumed you wanted to see me as badly as I wanted to see you. But let's get something straight." His tone dropped, and there was a slight huskiness to it. "You leave the party with me."

CHAPTER
FOUR

Jamie's stomach quivered at the thought of going anywhere with Max. "I don't know if that's wise."

He stroked one finger down her arm. Her skin prickled.

"There you go again," he said. "You're thinking too much." He gave her a private smile. "You're wearing the blue dress. I can't wait to see what's under it."

Jamie gulped. Yikes, the man was seducing her right there on the spot. And damned if there was anything she could do about it because her tongue had suddenly become plastered to the roof of her mouth.

And now, here she was, wondering what *he* was wearing, if anything, beneath that dignified-looking tux.

"I need a drink," she said, if for no other reason than to change the subject. Max knew what he did to her, and he was probably enjoying every minute of it.

Max motioned, and a waiter appeared instantly, carrying a tray of white wine in tall, long-stemmed glasses. "Would you like a glass of chardonnay?" the man asked.

Jamie concentrated on keeping her hand steady as she reached for one of the goblets. She could feel the perspiration beading her upper lip, and she hadn't put any tissues in the small bag she'd chosen to bring.

"Are you hot?" Max asked.

Jamie tried to play it down, suspecting Max was enjoying her discomfort. "There are too many people crammed into this place. I think your sister invited half the town."

"Deedee does have a way of going overboard," Max said, looking about the room.

Mike returned balancing a plate stacked high with food, camera dangling from his neck. "Hi, Max. Hey, nice tux. I'll bet you didn't rent it in Beaumont." He looked at Jamie. "Why is your face all sweaty?" He didn't give her a chance to answer. "I haven't eaten all day. I hope I don't make a pig of myself." He bit into a finger sandwich. "Wow, check out the brunette who just walked through the door. The one in the red dress," he added. "I should go over and introduce myself. Maybe she'll let me take her picture." He winked at Jamie. "Don't tell Destiny. I'm saving myself for her." He hurried away.

Jamie shook her head as she caught the amused look on Max's face. He pulled a handkerchief from his pocket. "May I?" When Jamie merely shrugged, he very carefully mopped her forehead and upper lip. "There now, good as new."

Jamie drained her glass. "I should find Frankie and wish him a happy birthday."

"Great, we can go together."

Deedee Fontana and her assistant Beenie appeared out of nowhere. "Oh, Jamie, I'm so glad you could come!" she cried, hugging her tightly. "You too, little brother." She and Max hugged, as well.

"You look beautiful," Jamie said, noting Deedee's ankle-length, Kelly-green cocktail dress. It set off her green eyes and red hair. Jamie was certain Beenie had handpicked the outfit for her; he'd long ago tossed her slinky rhinestone garb, before husband Frankie had been elected as town mayor. Beenie was dressed in Ralph Lauren, his dark hair combed straight back, emphasizing a perfect oval face.

"Frankie will be thrilled to see you," Deedee said in her Betty Boop voice that gave the former beauty queen a childlike quality most people found endearing.

"We wouldn't have missed it for the world," Jamie said, and then wished she had used a singular pronoun. She didn't want anyone, least of all Max, to think she was his date for the evening. "You look gorgeous as always," she told the woman quickly, hoping no one had caught the slip. Deedee seemed to sparkle. Well into her forties, she passed for thirty, thanks to a plastic surgeon in Hilton Head that she kept on call.

"Where *is* Frankie?" Max asked.

Deedee giggled. Coming from anyone else, it would have sounded silly, but Deedee's little-girl quality and naïveté made people, especially her husband, want to take care of her. "He and several of his old wrestling buddies are at the bar. Snakeman, Big John, Choker, and Dirty Deed Dan flew in to celebrate with us."

Jamie recognized some of the names as Frankie's old wrestling buddies. Snakeman had toured with a twenty-foot boa during his wrestling days. "Is there a

66

snake in residence?" Jamie asked, hoping that wasn't the case.

Another giggle from Deedee. "No, the snake died a while back, and Snakeman decided not to replace him because it made traveling difficult. The snake was just part of the show."

Jamie tried to hide her sigh of relief. The last thing she wanted was something wrapping itself around one of her ankles.

Deedee offered them a conspiratorial grin. "Wait till you see the cake I ordered."

Beenie rolled his eyes and tapped his fingers against his lips. "It's designed to look like a naked woman. It starts at the shoulders and ends at her navel, and get this, she's wearing a nipple ring. Tacky, tacky, tacky."

Deedee pretended to pout, something else she pulled off very well. "You didn't think the one that looked like a man's buns was tacky."

Beenie struck a pose. "Now that was a work of art." He shrugged. "Besides, I like men's buns." He went on. "Anyway, as I told Deedee, this is *not* the time or place for such decadence. We have visiting dignitaries, and they will probably be offended. I would have chosen something elegant but simple. Less is always more."

The waiter came by. Jamie grabbed another glass of wine. Max grinned.

"Oh, Beenie, stop acting like an old maid and loosen up a bit," Deedee said. "It's not going to kill you to have a little fun now and then."

Jamie couldn't help but smile as Deedee and Beenie continued to fuss. Deedee had hired Beenie away from an exclusive spa in Hilton Head. They were inseparable, but they tended to argue like brother and sister.

"And guess what else we ordered from the bakery?" Deedee said in a conspiratorial whisper. "Aphrodisiac-laced brownies. Everybody in town is shocked that Lyle Betts is making them, but he claims he can't bake them fast enough. Isn't that a scream?"

Jamie wasn't about to tell her she had already tried them. "Oh, here's the birthday boy now," she said as Frankie joined them. Standing well over six and a half feet, with a barrel of a chest, Frankie Fontana struck an imposing figure. Jamie had not known Frankie in his wrestling days, but as a teenager, Max had seen him in the ring a number of times and assured her he had been quite formidable. Now, having been retired more than ten years, Frankie wore a good-natured smile and easygoing attitude that made him appear as harmless as a kitten.

"Glad you could come," Frankie said, pumping Max's arm enthusiastically and giving him a hearty slap on the back. He hugged Jamie lightly as though realizing his own strength.

"Happy birthday," Jamie said and Max seconded it.

Frankie grinned from ear to ear, looking much like an overgrown kid despite his graying temples. "I guess Deedee told you about the cake. Snakeman is going to remove the nipple ring with his teeth, and then we're going to have arm-wrestling matches in the kitchen. Better place your bets while there's still time."

Beenie looked aghast. "Do you realize the lieutenant governor is here?" he hissed.

"Yeah, he's the one taking up the bets," Frankie said.

Deedee patted her husband's hand. "Well, I'll put my money on you any time, sweetie," she said. He kissed her lightly on the lips although it was obvious he would have preferred something more passionate. Twenty years of marriage had not dampened their desire for each other.

Frankie looked at Jamie. "I'm especially glad to see you. Deedee has a dilemma."

"Frankie's right," Deedee said. "I need to find a cause."

"A cause for what?" Jamie asked.

Deedee giggled. "You know; a cause. Now that Frankie's the new mayor, I think I should make some sort of contribution to this town."

"That's a wonderful idea," Jamie told her friend. "You could volunteer at the hospital."

"Eeyeuuw!" Deedee shuddered.

"Deedee doesn't like being around sick people," Frankie explained. "We wouldn't want her to catch any germs."

"There's a telephone number in the phone book for people wanting to volunteer their time," Jamie offered. "You could call them and see what they need. I'm sure you'll find something that interests you."

Deedee suddenly brightened. "I could work for a hotline service. You know, help people out who have personal problems. I'm a good listener."

Jamie and Max exchanged looks. Jamie couldn't imagine Deedee trying to solve anyone's problems. God bless her, but Deedee's answer to everything was a new piece of fine jewelry or a shopping trip to New York.

"I don't know about the rest of you, but I'm hungry," Frankie announced. "Let's grab some grub."

A few minutes later, Max and Jamie carried their plates and glasses of wine to one of the love seats adorned in faux leopard. Deedee had decorated the room in a jungle theme, complete with animal-skin sofas, banana plants, and wooden giraffes. Max sat close enough so that their thighs touched. It didn't go unnoticed by Jamie.

"Max, we really need to talk," she said, trying to ignore the tingling that started at her hip bone and spread right down to her painted toenails. Her stomach took a nosedive as she imagined his hair-roughened thighs touching hers without benefit of clothes. Lord, what the man did to her!

"You smell nice," he said.

"Thank you." She didn't want to think about how good he smelled. She tried to remember what she had been saying before he'd touched her and her mind had taken leave. "I'm, uh, really concerned about Luanne Ritter's murder and that the personals section may be connected to it. I told Lamar I'd pull the ads, but he disagreed. He's afraid if the murder had something to do with the ads, we might lose the killer. I think it's too risky."

"Give me a few more details," he said.

70

Jamie told him about her conversation with Lamar, trying not to leave anything out.

"We're going to have to work fast, Swifty," he said.

"We'll have to work at night, after the office is closed. Nobody is supposed to know. Not even Vera."

"What about the production staff?"

"They never come up front. Besides, even if they did, they'd have no idea what we were working on."

"You have records of the people who've written in?"

Jamie nodded. "I keep them locked in my office for confidentiality's sake. Vera pitched the fit of all fits when I told her she wasn't privy to the information, but you know how she loves to gossip." Jamie paused. "By the way, I lent her the red Mustang. Her old car gave out on her."

He grinned. "Does she drive it with the top down?"

God, if only he wouldn't smile like that, Jamie thought. She could handle almost anything but those bone-melting smiles. "Yes. She even got a new hair-cut so the wind wouldn't mess up her hair so badly."

"I can't wait to see that." He glanced around the room. "Tell you what. We'll wait until the birthday cake is served, then slip out and drive to the office." He suddenly smiled. "Unless you need to get your date home in time for his curfew."

Jamie shot him one of her looks.

Frankie's cake was rolled out on a serving cart an hour later, and the guests gathered around and sang "Happy Birthday," even as some gasped at the sight of the naked figure of a woman with size-D breasts. Frankie

71

blew out his candles and hugged Deedee as everyone clapped. Snakeman made a production of removing the nipple ring with his teeth and received rousing applause.

"Speech!" someone shouted from across the room.

Frankie laughed. "I'd have thought you guys had heard enough of my speeches during the mayoral campaign," he said. "OK, but I'll make it short. First of all, I'd like to thank you all for being here to share my birthday. Deedee and I are very lucky to have so many friends. And because we consider all of you friends, I would like to make an important announcement."

Max and Jamie looked at each other and shrugged.

Frankie paused and smiled tenderly at Deedee. She beamed. "After all these years, my wife and I are expecting a baby."

Everyone clapped. Jamie looked at Max. "Well, there goes that perfect figure she's worked so hard to keep," she said, knowing Deedee went bananas if she gained a pound.

Max merely grinned. "Sounds like she and Frankie have been eating brownies."

Max and Jamie left the party shortly afterward, but not before they'd offered Frankie and Deedee their congratulations.

"I'm going to be an uncle," Max said, his tone incredulous, as they pulled away from the Fontana house, which was really an estate. An estate on which

72

sat a pink house that Frankie claimed was salmon-colored and caused a lot of snickering from his wrestling buddies who referred to it as the Pink Palace.

Jamie still couldn't believe the news. "Deedee is going to have to give up her rigid dieting. She's eating for two now."

"Hello, Jamie," a voice called from the dashboard. "What's this about Max being an uncle?"

Jamie smiled. "Hey, I've missed you, Muffin," she said to the voice-recognition computer that ran Max's business from a dashboard that was more complicated than most jets; thanks to a team of first-rate computer whizzes. Max had hired them away from top government contractors, and with his help, they'd created the car's instrumentation using state-of-the-art equipment.

Spread out among luxury automotive goodies like a tachometer, an altimeter, and a global positioning satellite system were a highly enhanced PDA, a keyboard, a digital speech-recognition module, a photo-quality printer, fax, satellite phone, HDTV display screen, and a full video-conferencing suite, all operated by a high-powered computer that was smaller than an ashtray, "She" had a Marilyn Monroe voice, but because she was constantly fed information from a team of experts, she was the only one capable of matching Max's genius.

Not only that, Max had created technology in her that was able to make judgment calls, not based on data but on simple human emotion. His competitors, including the federal government, claimed it couldn't be done. Now they wanted to buy that technology.

"Deedee's pregnant," Jamie said at last.

"Uh-oh."

"My thoughts exactly," Max said. "We can expect drastic changes in the Fontana household."

"Wait a minute," Muffin said, "I thought she was going through menopause."

Jamie smiled, although she was still stunned by the news. "You ever heard of a change-of-life baby? It happens."

"How's she taking the news?"

"She looked thrilled," Jamie said, "and I think she'll make a wonderful mother. Deedee is very softhearted. And Frankie is going to enjoy spoiling the little tyke."

"I'm going to start looking into all the best baby books," Muffin said. "I'll get every piece of data I can, then Deedee and I will talk."

"I can't wait to see her in maternity clothes," Jamie said. "I'm sure Beenie will insist on the best designer money can buy."

Max gave her one of his slow easy smiles. "You sound a little exuberant there, Swifty. Sounds like you wouldn't mind having a little bambino of your own. You might need to give it some thought, what with that ticking biological clock thing that women worry so much about."

"My clock is ticking just fine, Max," she said, "and no, I don't think I'm ready for motherhood. I can't even raise a dog properly, but at least he won't be sitting in some therapist's office thirty years from now complaining what a crummy job I did."

"Ah, Jamie, you'd be a great mom," he said.

"Really?" The sincerity in his voice touched her.

"Excuse me," Muffin said. "I think we're missing something here. A father, maybe?"

Max and Jamie locked gazes. "How *is* Fleas, by the way?" Max asked.

Jamie thought he'd done a clumsy job of changing the subject. "I just had him neutered."

"See, that makes you a responsible pet owner," Max said.

"Uh, Muffin," Jamie began, "back to love and marriage and baby carriages, how's your love life?" Muffin had been having an on-again off-again on-line romance with a laptop computer at MIT. Max had also programmed Muffin with a personality. She had attitude.

"We're sort of taking a break from each other," Muffin said. "I think I intimidate him. I think he's chatting with someone else."

"He'll be back," Max said. "A smart man never walks away from a good thing."

Jamie felt his eyes on her, but she didn't dare look his way. As she had told Fleas, their relationship was complicated. "I suppose you told Muffin what's going on in Beaumont," she said, realizing she had been the one to change the subject this time. Each time things got too personal between them, one or both of them backed off. Besides, if Max started sweet-talking her they'd never make it to the newspaper office.

"Yeah, what do you think?" Muffin asked.

"I think I'm going to feel guilty for the rest of my life if my personals section is involved in that poor woman's murder."

"You can't take everything Lamar Tevis says as fact," Muffin said. "We're not dealing with Columbo. Do you have backup info on the people writing the ads?"

Jamie felt herself nod even though she knew Muffin couldn't see her. "Yeah, I have to keep the letters on filè in case someone gets a response, and we've had quite a few replies already."

"Anybody else have access to the letters?" Muffin asked.

"Not even Vera."

"Oh, man, I'll bet that pissed her off. So, here's what we do," Muffin began. "You give me the names and any other pertinent info, and I check them out. If I find anyone who looks suspicious, we'll take a closer look."

Twenty minutes later, Max pulled into the parking lot of the *Beaumont Gazette*. A cream-colored Mercedes was parked in one of the slots. "Boy, you must've given somebody on your staff a really good raise," he said.

"Oh, no, that's Destiny Moultrie," Jamie said with a sigh as the woman climbed from her car. Destiny had not picked a good time to show up. "She's going to be our new Divine Love Goddess Advisor."

Max frowned. "Come again?"

"I'll explain later."

Destiny raced around to the passenger door as Jamie climbed out. The woman was wearing her bathrobe and

76

bedroom slippers. "Oh, thank God I found you," she cried. "I drove by your house, but you weren't home. I figured I'd check here just in case."

Jamie could see the woman was upset about something. "Um, Destiny, this is my partner, Max Holt."

Jamie didn't miss the knowing look in Destiny's eyes as she looked his way. "It's about time you showed up," she said. Max arched both brows in question, but Destiny turned to Jamie and grasped her hands tightly. Jamie was surprised to find them icy cold.

"I had a vision." Destiny glanced to her side. "Ronnie, get lost, this is important."

Jamie winced inwardly. Just what Max needed to hear, she thought.

"The name is Max Holt, not Ronnie," Max told her.

"Destiny isn't talking to you," Jamie quickly said. "Ronnie is from the spirit world."

"Actually, he's between worlds," Destiny said. "He doesn't know he's dead, so he follows me everywhere."

Max simply nodded as though it made complete sense. "OK."

"I've been eating garlic pickles all day," Destiny told Jamie.

Which explained her breath, Jamie thought.

"I know it sounds crazy, but when I eat garlic pickles I dream a lot." She looked from Jamie to Max. "Sometimes I have waking dreams or visions where I see things."

"Destiny claims she's psychic," Jamie told Max. She wasn't sure what kind of reaction she expected, but she was surprised when Max merely smiled politely.

"Nice to meet you, Destiny."

"Same here." Once again, she turned to Jamie. "Anyway, I awoke about an hour ago, and —" She paused and shuddered. "I saw this woman. Her skull was crushed."

"You're right, Destiny," Jamie said. "A woman *was* found dead this morning. Remember, we discussed it."

"No, Jamie. You don't understand. I'm talking about another woman. A second victim," she added. "It hasn't happened yet."

CHAPTER
FIVE

Jamie felt a sense of fear, a feeling of dread wash over her. Then she reminded herself she didn't believe in psychics. Yes, but Destiny had told her things, things that couldn't be explained. She suddenly realized Destiny was shivering, despite the warm night. "How do you know these women are not one and the same?" Jamie challenged.

Destiny sneezed. "I just do. The second woman will put up a fight. There will be scratches on the killer's arms."

"Did you see the victim's face or the face of the killer in your vision?" Max asked, surprising Jamie.

"Believe me, I tried."

"This sounds a little far-fetched," Jamie said, no longer knowing what to think about the woman's predictions.

"It's true," Destiny said.

Max looked thoughtful but remained silent.

Jamie wanted to send Destiny on her way, but the woman appeared too upset to drive. "Destiny, we need to get you inside," she said. "You don't look so good."

Max followed them. Jamie noticed he didn't seem a bit skeptical when Destiny announced that Ronnie was right behind her. Jamie turned and eyed Destiny suspiciously. "If you're so certain this murder is going to take place, why can't you see the killer?"

Destiny paused and looked at her. "I'm blocked, OK? Everything is murky. I don't know where or when the murder is going to take place, but one thing is for sure —" She suddenly sneezed. "It's only a matter of time."

It wasn't until Jamie had gotten Destiny inside and sat her down in the small kitchen with a fresh cup of coffee that she stopped shivering. "All I keep seeing is this poor woman," she said. "Fighting for her life," she added, followed by another sneeze.

Jamie grabbed several tissues and handed them to her.

Max leaned in the doorway listening. Jamie gave him a cup of coffee and he quietly thanked her, all the while watching Destiny closely, as though trying to make up his mind about something. Jamie wondered if he was trying to decide whether Destiny was the real thing, and she couldn't help feeling surprised. Did Max actually believe what she was saying? Of all the people in the world, Max Holt struck her as the last person on earth who would believe in psychics.

Jamie joined Destiny at the table. She had her eyes closed. "What are you doing?" Jamie asked.

"Looking for a face," Destiny said. "All I'm getting is a view of her, the victim, from her shoulders down. Struggling and fighting for her life."

"Is she wearing something unusual?" Max asked. "Maybe something with a monogram on it?"

Jamie glanced up quickly. Was Max merely trying to humor her?

"I'm not getting anything." A fat tear rolled from Destiny's left eye and slid down her cheek. "There's no use trying to force it. It either comes to me or it doesn't."

"What about the garlic pickles?" Jamie asked.

Destiny shrugged. "That's something my grandmother used to do. It sometimes works, but not always."

Jamie tried to think, tried to open herself up to what she was hearing. What she knew about psychic phenomena was next to nothing. But she was certain Destiny believed somebody was about to die.

Max put down his coffee cup. "Jamie, may I have a word with you?"

Jamie looked at Destiny.

"I'm OK. Besides, I need a minute to myself."

Max and Jamie didn't speak until they'd reached her office and closed the door. "Max, I know all this sounds and looks strange, but —"

"Not really."

Jamie couldn't hide her astonishment. "Are you saying you believe in this sort of thing?"

"I don't disbelieve. I think there are some things in this world that can't be explained. And I believe the woman saw something. She's obviously hysterical."

"She spooks me, Max. I mean, she shows up in my parking lot in her bathrobe with stories of visions and murder and some guy named Ronnie from the spirit world. You don't think that's strange?"

"Have any of her predictions come true?"

Jamie told him about Destiny's vision concerning Lamar. "I want to believe her, but she has a ghost following her around, for Pete's sake. I don't know whether to take her seriously or call a doctor."

Max put his hand on Jamie's shoulder. "Listen, I'm not saying she's the real thing, but I think she bears listening to. That's why I'm going to put Muffin on the case. I think we should use every possible means to catch the killer before he strikes again. If what Destiny says is true," he added.

"I'm scared, Max," Jamie said. "I honestly can't bear the thought of my column being responsible for Luanne Ritter's death. I don't care if everybody in this town *did* hate her; she was still a human being. And the thought of somebody else getting killed is more than I can handle."

Max took her in his arms. "Then we'd better get to work."

Jamie unlocked the file drawer in her office and pulled it out. She found what she was looking for right away. She joined Max and Destiny.

"Max and I thought maybe you could look through some of these ads and see if you get a feel for them."

Destiny looked doubtful. "I've never been real good at psychometrics, but I'll give it a try."

Max slid forward in his chair. "Jamie, before you get started, I'd like for you to make a copy of the ads so I can fax them to Muffin."

"Sure, Max. It won't take but a couple of minutes. Please help yourself to more coffee if you like. Also, there are soft drinks in the refrigerator and maybe a couple of stale doughnuts." Jamie hurried into the reception area where the copy machine and fax were situated along one wall near Vera's desk. She felt like she had stepped into a bad science fiction movie.

When she returned, she found Max and Destiny talking softly. He seemed genuinely interested in what she was saying. "Here are the copies." Jamie handed them to Max, and showed him to the fax machine. "Call me if you need me."

He nodded and went to work.

Finally, Jamie joined Destiny on the sofa. "OK, here's what we've got."

"There's only one problem, Jamie," Destiny said. "Even though I've never been really good at this sort of thing, it works better if the object is handled by the original person only."

Jamie gave her a blank look. "Come again?"

"In this case, the actual author of the ad." She reached for one of the sheets of paper. "The way psychometrics works is that you feel the energy from the person who touched the object."

Jamie tried to hide her skepticism. "You're saying since I was the last one who touched these ads they will hold my energy?"

Destiny nodded. "At least some of it. What we can do is look at the ads and see if anything stands out. Maybe something will come to me. It might help later in a vision, who knows?"

Max returned and reclaimed his seat. "OK, I faxed the info to Muffin, and she's already at work on it."

"I'm afraid we're not having much luck," Destiny said. Jamie nodded in agreement. "We're just looking through the ads, seeing if anything sounds unusual or, um, ominous. For example, the heading on this ad reads 'Looking for discreet relationship. Must be open to new experiences.'"

"You're right, that's scary," Max said.

Jamie realized he was teasing her. "We don't know what it means," she said. "'Open to new experiences' could mean he's into kinky stuff."

Destiny pondered it and finally shrugged. "Or maybe he just likes sailing or horseback riding," she said. "That could be one way of looking at new experiences."

"But why would he insist on discretion?" Jamie asked. "Doesn't that sound a little paranoid?"

Max shrugged. "It could mean he doesn't want people to know he found a date through a personals ad. That doesn't mean we don't check him out, though."

"How many ads do you have there?" Destiny asked.

"Only seven, since I just copied the ones from the men. I have all their addresses and phone numbers. The way it works is, they pay for the ad, which includes a couple of dollars extra for postage, and when I get a reply I forward it to them. It's a new feature, of course, and I'm hoping it'll catch on. As least I was until I heard about Luanne Ritter's murder."

"Did you happen to notice any return addresses from those who responded to the ads?" Max asked.

"There weren't any," Jamie told him. "They obviously wanted to keep it confidential. Small town and all," she added.

"Take a look at this ad," Max said after a minute.

Jamie shuffled through the pages. "Yeah, I remember that one."

Destiny leaned forward and read, " 'Till Death Do Us Part.' "

"Did you not think that sounded strange when you read it?" Max asked.

Jamie shook her head. "No. It could simply mean this person is looking for a lifetime partner, which is what a couple of the ads say. Now that someone has been killed it sounds pretty menacing, and we definitely need to check it out."

"Don't you have anyone who sounds like a guy I'd want to meet?" Destiny asked, surprising them both. "Hey, I'm new in town; I wouldn't mind meeting a nice guy. He'd have to be open-minded, of course."

Jamie almost welcomed the change of subject. "My editor Mike Henderson has a crush on you"

"Oh, yeah?"

"He's a little young."

"Young is nice. Two of my husbands were old and died on me. It's such a hassle planning a funeral."

Max cleared his throat. "I believe we have work to do, ladies," he said.

Jamie nodded. "OK, this ad reads, 'Don't Pass Me By,' and another one, 'Walking on Sunshine.'" She suddenly chuckled. "Oh, listen to this. 'Offer Good for a Limited Time.'"

Even Max chuckled at that one.

"They all seem to be searching for the same thing," Jamie said. "A woman looking for a good time who might be interested in a long-term relationship." A sheet of paper fell to the floor. "Oh, I almost missed one. Listen to this. It reads, 'Deeper Than the Night.'"

"That sounds nice," Destiny said.

"Yeah, listen to his ad. He says, 'No matter what path you choose, keep it simple, but put your heart into it.'"

Destiny sighed. "Wow, that's deep." She glanced to an empty space in the room. "Oh, stop acting jealous, Ronnie. Remember, you're dead? It's not like I can go bowling or coon hunting with you." She rolled her eyes at Jamie. "That's Ronnie's idea of a good time, if you can believe it. At least the last guy that attached himself to me had a little class. He was an English professor."

Jamie just stared at her.

"How old is this guy who claimed to be deeper than the night?" Destiny asked.

"Thirty-five and never been married."

"Which means he doesn't have children," Destiny said. "Believe me, I've had my share of stepchildren. I should take the ad home and put it beneath my pillow tonight. Maybe something will come to me. You should give me his name and address. I could drive by his house; see if I get any vibes."

"These are confidential."

"You didn't mind letting me hold them a few minutes ago," Destiny objected.

"That was different. I was seeking your, um, professional opinion. If you want to meet this guy you'll have to go through the proper channels like everybody else. Only, I'd hold off until we look into the murder."

Max checked his wristwatch. "It's after midnight. We need to go home and get a good night's sleep. By morning, Muffin will have a lot of the information I requested, and we can start from there."

They left the building a few minutes later, once Jamie had locked up. Destiny pulled away in her Mercedes as Max helped Jamie into the passenger's side of his car. He joined her in the front seat a moment later.

"Max, we need to talk about Destiny," Jamie said. "I know she sounds convincing, but surely you don't believe in the supernatural."

"I simply try to keep an open mind," he said. "I've seen and heard of instances where psychics have taken investigators right to the crime scene. In fact, I was personally involved in one of those instances."

Jamie looked at him. "You were involved with a psychic?"

"The son of a close friend of mine was kidnapped for ransom five years ago. A woman just appeared at his front door with all the information the police needed to find the boy. They still call on her from time to time."

Jamie felt the goose pimples rise on her arms. "But what about this Ronnie, this dead spirit that Destiny claims follows her everywhere?"

Max grinned. "Yeah, that's pretty strange, but from what I've read, and this is only what I've read, some people get lost between worlds when they die suddenly or violently because they're confused and don't know they should go to the light."

"The light?" Jamie shook her head. "Max, do you know how that sounds?"

He laughed. "Yeah, I know, but there have been cases reported. Some priests believe in it. Why do you suppose exorcisms are performed? It's believed that a dead spirit can attach itself to a live human. I read all this stuff when I was a kid. I was really fascinated with that sort of thing."

"You're really scaring me now," Jamie said shuddering. "I don't think I want to talk about it anymore."

"I know it all sounds far-fetched like you said, but I believe the woman in your office tonight saw something that frightened her. I don't think she was faking it."

"I've lived in a small town too long," Jamie said. "I believe in what I can see. Could we change the subject?"

"Yeah." Max looked at the dashboard. "Muffin, are you there?" he asked.

"Yes, and I've been listening to every word. I'm with Jamie. This whole thing gives me the creeps."

"Then let's talk facts. You got anything yet?"

"Do you know what time it is?"

"I know it's late, but —"

"So, go to your hotel and get a good night's sleep. I should have something for you in the morning."

Jamie was glad they were headed in a different direction. That's exactly what she wanted to hear: facts. "You're not staying at Frankie and Deedee's?" she asked.

Max shook his head. "I need a place to work while I'm in town, and I wouldn't be able to think straight with Frankie and his wrestling buddies around. Besides, I'm not into arm wrestling."

"Where are you staying?"

Max shrugged. "Where am I staying, Muffin?"

"You have reservations at the Carteret Street Bed and Breakfast."

"It's really nice," Jamie said. "Probably not as nice as you're accustomed to," she added, suspecting Max had stayed in some of the best hotels in the world. "But you should be comfortable there."

"You have a suite on the first floor," Muffin said. "It has a sitting room, courtyard, and private entrance on the east side. Guaranteed late arrival; you'll find a key waiting for you beneath the doormat."

Max looked at Jamie. "You should stay with me tonight."

"Uh-oh, here it comes," Muffin said. "I'm outta here."

"I can't stay with you," Jamie replied. "I know the owners. I went to school with their daughter. I wouldn't feel right."

"I have my own private entrance, remember?"

It sounded so tempting. And Jamie hated to waste the body suit she'd spent forty bucks on. And in all honesty, she wasn't sure she wanted to stay by herself after hearing about dead spirits and exorcisms. But she had a dog to care for.

"You're going to have to show me how to get to the place anyway," he said. "I'll get lost."

Jamie looked at him. "Oh, puh-lease. You could find your way to Mars in this car, Max."

"Yeah, but —"

"Why don't you ask Muffin for directions to the Carteret Street Bed and Breakfast?"

"Because she doesn't have beautiful blue eyes like you." He stopped at a red light. "C'mon, Swifty, what d'you say?"

She sighed. "Oh, Max —"

"You're doing it again, Jamie. You're thinking too much. You're doing the 'what-if' thing."

She knew he was right. It was time she stopped doing so much thinking and just enjoyed being with Max because, well, in all honesty, she wanted him as much as he wanted her. And it wasn't like she had to stay all night. She could go home later and let Fleas out. Later, after she got over her case of the heebie-jeebies.

"Turn left at the light."

CHAPTER
SIX

Carteret Street Bed and Breakfast was a massive, two-story Colonial with verandas on both floors. Oversized rocking chairs and baskets of ferns gave it a welcoming look. Once Max had parked his car and grabbed a bag from the trunk, Jamie pointed him toward a narrow, flower-laden path where old-fashioned street lamps lit the way. They found themselves standing at the door to his room. Sure enough, a key had been placed beneath the doormat. He unlocked the door, opened it, and motioned for Jamie to go through first.

Fresh daisies sat on a highly polished cherry coffee table. The rust- and cream-colored furniture was comfortable looking while maintaining a look of simple elegance. The ornate crown molding and woodwork were a deep mahogany, and repeated in the oversized fireplace. A tasteful rug covered heart-pine floors. Max opened a set of French doors and found a sink, small refrigerator, and microwave.

"Nice," he said. "Where's the bedroom?"

Jamie's stomach dipped to her toes. "Through that door."

He took her hand in his and led her in that direction. An old four-poster rice bed and matching highboy, both in cherry, greeted them. The comforter was pure linen, as were the curtains. Jamie had visited the bed-and-breakfast several years ago when it had been redecorated, and she had praised it in an article. She was glad Mrs. Hobbs had given Max the nicest suite.

The Hobbs were an older couple — short and stout as a teacup, as Vera liked to say, but Mrs. Hobbs was worse than Vera when it came to gossip. Vera did most of her gossiping on the church lawn after Sunday services; Myrna Hobbs preferred holding court at the local Piggly Wiggly grocery store, where she could often be found picking up food items for her guests. Vera claimed Myrna exaggerated, that a soul couldn't believe a word that came out of the woman's mouth. Vera believed in sticking to the facts.

Max reached for Jamie.

"I, um, thought maybe you'd like to see the garden first," she said quickly. "It's really very nice. Mrs. Hobbs hired a man who designed a garden at one of the old plantations in Charleston."

Max suddenly smiled. "You're nervous, aren't you, Swifty? You're remembering last time. I have to tell you, you're all I've thought about the past few weeks."

She smiled. "Really? Gee, I wish I'd known." Jamie hated to bring up the fact he hadn't contacted her in the three weeks since that time, but she figured it needed saying. It had to be the wine talking. She'd had three glasses at Frankie and Deedee's, which was well over her quota.

"I was out of the country most of that time. I'm not real good at sending postcards." When she didn't say anything, he went on. "I guess I could do better." He sighed and raked his hands through his hair. "Do you still want to look at that garden?"

Jamie opened the French doors leading from the bedroom. Taking Max's hand in hers, she led him down a brick walkway and across a small footbridge that covered a pond. Once again, old-fashioned street lamps lighted the way. Jamie was glad Mrs. Hobbs had left them burning for Max's arrival.

"The pond actually has goldfish in it," Jamie said. "Huge ones."

Max studied his surroundings with only a hint of interest. "So, can you tell me the names of these plants?"

"Sure." Jamie glanced around. "That tree is a hemlock. And the plants growing beneath it are hosta plants. Or plantain lilies as they're sometimes called," she added. "They're shade plants." She pointed. "And that's caladium, and growing next to it is ostrich fern." She caught sight of Max's grin. "What?"

"How do you know this?"

"Just because I never have time to mow my lawn or weed my flower beds doesn't mean I don't know about plants. I planted a whole bunch of daylilies around the pickup truck in the back yard to try to make it look more attractive."

"Did it work?"

"No. But you know how attached Fleas is to that truck."

"Does he sleep in it?"

"Are you kidding? He has this giant pillow that I bought for him so he can sleep on the floor in my bedroom, but when I wake up each morning I find him sprawled across the foot of my bed."

"That's going to present a real problem for us."

Jamie's stomach fluttered. "I think he's become somewhat spoiled since you last saw him," she said, changing the subject.

Max stroked her arm. "I'd like to go inside and spoil you."

More fluttering. "OK, but you didn't get to see the entire garden."

This time, Max captured her hand and led her through the French doors into the bedroom. A breeze blew in from the doorway, bringing with it the scent of magnolia. Moonlight dappled the room. Max pulled Jamie into his arms and kissed her.

Jamie leaned against him, delighting in the solid planes of his body and his scent. He offered more than a mere distraction from spending part of the evening talking about bogeymen, and she had been waiting for this moment all evening. No, she had been waiting much longer than that. Common sense had told her it was sheer folly, but her heart refused to listen. She returned Max's kisses with a hunger that surprised even her.

Max cupped her hips in his hands, pressing her flat against him so there was no doubt that he was as eager for her as she was for him. He slid his fingers through her hair, anchoring her head between his palms as he

94

kissed her more deeply. Jamie clung to the jacket of his tux.

She slipped her arms around his neck and tilted her head back, parting her lips beneath his so his tongue could explore the inside of her mouth. Max's hands moved to her breasts, warming them through the clothes she wore.

"I want you, Jamie," he whispered. "I have since the first time I saw you."

Damned if she didn't want him too. She just wasn't sure she could get him out of that tux quickly enough. "I need to use the powder room first," she said.

He gazed down at her, a promise in his eyes.

Jamie slipped from his arms and stepped inside the bathroom, purse in hand. An old claw-foot bathtub dominated the room. The mahogany woodwork had been softened with beige linen wallpaper and ivory towels. Still a bit rattled, Jamie checked behind the shower curtain, and then told herself she was being silly. From the next room, she heard soft music and realized Max had turned on a radio. She swayed to the sound as she reached for the zipper of her dress, slid it down and shrugged out of it. She gazed at her flushed face in the mirror, noted the worry lines on either side of her mouth.

She wished she weren't so edgy.

She reached into her purse for the minibottle of Kahlúa that she had stuffed into her pocketbook before leaving the house that evening. Deedee had given it to her, as well as a raw-silk jacket, when she and Beenie had returned from a shopping trip in New York. Jamie had suspected things might turn romantic with Max before the evening was over, and she'd hoped the Kahlúa would settle her nerves. She opened the small bottle and took a sip. What if she was making a mistake? What if she fell head over heels in love with Max, knowing how reluctant he was to make a long-term commitment? What if? Oh, the hell with it, she thought. She drained the small bottle.

Bravery had never tasted so good. She could feel her shoulder muscles relaxing, and the knots loosening in her stomach.

It was about time she took a few chances in life.

Max undid the knot of his bow tie and walked into the sitting room. He opened the small refrigerator and reached inside for a container of bottled water. He turned and started for the bedroom when a light tap at the door stopped him. He unlocked it and opened it, finding a squat, gray-haired woman on the other side. She held a tray of food.

"I hope I'm not disturbing you, Mr. Holt," she said quickly, "but I heard you come in and thought you might enjoy a light snack from the kitchen."

"You must be Mrs. Hobbs," Max said, backing away so the woman could enter.

"Yes, but you can call me Myrna." She set the tray on the coffee table. "I trust you've found everything you needed."

"Everything is fine."

"I hope you like croissants. I also brought several cheeses and grapes. Fruit and cheese always go together so well, don't you think?"

"You wouldn't happen to have a bottle of champagne handy, would you?" Max asked.

Mrs. Hobbs sniffed. "I don't keep alcoholic beverages on the premises, Mr. Holt. I guess it comes from my strict Baptist upbringing, but I've always been a teetotaler. My husband accuses me of being far too prim and proper, but I'm afraid it's a little late in life for me to change."

"I understand, Myrna, and I respect your beliefs. Thank you for bringing me the snack." The woman didn't seem to take the hint.

"Tell me, Mr. Holt," Myrna said, her eyes bright with curiosity. "What's it like being a big-time celebrity with all that money?"

Max laughed and shook his head. It didn't look like Myrna was in a hurry to leave.

Jamie had freshened her makeup and sprayed perfume in places she was certain would shock Vera's church friends. She fluffed her hair, hoping it gave her a sexy, untamed look.

She turned for the door, felt her head swim. She was loose as a goose. Maybe she shouldn't have drunk the whole ounce of Kahlúa, especially since she'd had more than her share of wine at Frankie and Deedee's party. Not only that, she'd barely touched her food.

Oh, well, it was too late to worry about it now. Besides, she was single and over twenty-one, and if she wanted to act a little wild and crazy every now and then, so be it. Max accused her of thinking too much, of being too predictable.

Let him get a look at the new Jamie Swift.

The music was coming from the alarm-clock radio on the bedside table; Johnny Mathis singing "Chances Are." The bed was empty. Jamie wondered why Max wasn't already naked and in it. Maybe he'd sensed just how nervous she was and wanted to take his time. She turned for the short hall leading to the sitting room, almost tripping over her own two feet.

OK, so she was a little tipsy.

"'Chances are,'" she sang off-key as she started down the hall, failing miserably at her attempt to walk straight. Finally, she called out. "OK, here I am, ready and willing." She stepped inside the sitting room, did a little dance routine, and then froze when she found Max standing at the door with Myrna Hobbs.

The woman looked Jamie's way, and her mouth formed a gigantic O.

"Jamie, I'm sorry you're so embarrassed," Max said, once he'd packed her inside his car and pulled away from Carteret Street Bed and Breakfast.

"I'll get over it."

Max shook his head. "I can't believe Myrna Hobbs kicked me out of my room."

Jamie wasn't surprised. "Oh, that's nothing. Myrna will beat it to the Piggly Wiggly the minute they open tomorrow. By noon, everyone in town will know what happened." She did a massive eye-roll. "Did you hear

98

what that woman called me, Max? She called me a drunken floozy."

"Yeah, well, I think I got it across to her that I didn't appreciate it."

Jamie had to admit it was true. Max had called Myrna Hobbs on the carpet for that one, which was why the woman had asked him to leave the premises. "Thank you for defending me."

He grinned. "I'll have to admit, you *did* sort of look like a drunken floozy, but I liked it. You looked cute."

Jamie groaned.

"Hey, I think it's great you've loosened up, Swifty." He gave a low whistle. "And that thing you're wearing under your dress," he added. "Where can I buy you ten more just like it?"

So he'd liked the body suit. At least one good thing had come of the evening.

A voice sounded from the dashboard. "Excuse me? What are we up to *now*?"

Jamie put her finger to her lips in an obvious attempt to stop Max from telling Muffin what had just occurred. He smiled and turned down the volume switch. "Wait a minute. You're worried about what my computer will think of you?"

"Muffin is not just *any* computer," she whispered.

Max turned up the switch.

"Hello?" Muffin called out. "Is anyone home?"

"I'm here," Max said.

"Why'd you hit the volume switch?"

"None of your business," he said, grinning.

Silence. Finally, "Don't piss me off, Max. You need me. I make you look good."

"Yeah, yeah, yeah. I need the name of another hotel. Something with a work station so I can go on-line. You know the routine."

"What was wrong with the last one?" Muffin asked.

"Too stuffy. See what you can find."

Jamie was only vaguely aware of the conversation between the two. She didn't feel well, her stomach was churning and her head hurt, no doubt from the alcohol she'd consumed. She was glad when Max turned into her driveway. She waited until the safety bar rose before reaching for the doorknob. "Well, I'd invite you in, but I have to go throw up."

"Rule number one: never mix your alcohol."

"Jeez, I could have used that information earlier."

Fleas nudged Jamie awake the next morning at five a.m. She rubbed her eyes and looked at him. "Gee, thanks for rescuing me from the possibility of sleeping late on a Saturday." Since becoming housemates with the bloodhound, she rarely slept until the alarm clock sounded during the workweek, and she never slept late on weekends.

"This must be what it's like to have kids," she grumbled, knowing Fleas probably had to go to the bathroom. After that he would want something to eat. She sighed.

The doorbell rang. Max, no doubt. The man was like a vampire. He could live on four hours' sleep. She stumbled from the bed and into the living room. Her head hurt, and her eyes felt gritty. She checked the peephole, and sure enough, Max stood on the other side.

She opened the door. How could he look that good in the morning? "What?"

"How's your head?"

She noted the amused look. "I think a couple of aspirin might help. Is that why you stopped by?"

"I know you don't like getting up before seven," he said. "That's why I brought coffee and doughnuts. To sort of soften the blow."

"Chocolate doughnuts?"

"Chocolate mocha cream."

Damn the man for knowing her every weakness. She opened the door. He stepped inside and followed her into the kitchen, staring at her wrinkled sleep shirt. "I was kind of hoping you'd still be wearing that black thing this morning," he said, setting down her coffee and the folder he carried under one arm.

Jamie reached for the aspirin bottle beside her sink. She popped two in her mouth and followed it with a sip of water. "I burned it," she said.

"God, please, no."

"OK, I'm *thinking* about burning it."

"Don't do it, Jamie. Burn that shirt instead."

She took a sip of her coffee. Naturally, Max knew just how she liked it. He grinned at Fleas and the two reacquainted themselves, Max giving the animal a hearty rub on the head. "Have you taught him any tricks yet?" he asked Jamie.

She looked into the bag of doughnuts and pulled one out. Fleas licked his chops. "Yeah, he's learned to wait until I leave the house before getting on my sofa so he doesn't get yelled at."

"Good dog." Max offered the dog a sympathetic look. "Sorry to hear she had your gonads cut off, guy. You're looking a little depressed."

"Speaking of his unmentionables, he needs to go out." Jamie unlocked the back door, opened it, and Fleas ambled outside as though he had all the time in the world. "Don't pee on my rosebush," she said, as he hiked his leg on a small bush of tiny yellow tea roses.

Max chuckled. "Yeah, you've trained him real well."

Jamie carried her coffee and doughnut to the kitchen table and sat down. "Not that I'm not thrilled to see you, Max, but is there a specific reason you felt you had to visit the minute the sun came up?"

He grabbed his folder and joined her. "Yeah, Muffin has all kinds of information for us. I figured you'd be interested."

"I'm all ears," she mumbled.

"Remember the ad that read 'Till Death Do Us Part'?"

"Yeah, that was spooky," Jamie said.

"He's a minister who performs a lot of marriage ceremonies. He obviously doesn't believe in divorce."

Jamie glanced up quickly. "A minister? Lamar said someone called Luanne saying he was a man of God. Max, we could be on to something."

"That's why I told Muffin to dig deeper."

"Anything else?"

"All the men are either single or divorced. We've got an auto mechanic, a dentist, a chef and —" He paused and chuckled. "Remember the ad that read 'Offer Good for a Limited Time'?"

"Yeah."

"He's a car salesman."

Jamie laughed. She had finished her doughnut and was debating having a second, but she wouldn't rush. She didn't want Max to think she lacked discipline. She sipped her coffee, counted to ten.

"Just get the doughnut and be done with it," he said, as though reading her mind. "I bought extra."

Jamie got up, grabbed the bag and carried it to the table. "I don't normally eat more than one, but —"

"Save it, Swifty. This is me you're talking to. I've seen you go through a dozen doughnuts in two days flat."

She frowned at Max but took a bite from the second doughnut nevertheless. "I was under a lot of stress at the time. So the guys you mentioned seemed to check out OK?"

"Yeah. Their ages vary, but most of them just want to meet someone who likes to go to a movie or dine out, that sort of thing."

"Um, what about the guy Destiny and I thought was so cool. You know, the ad that read 'Deeper Than the Night'?"

"I was waiting for you to ask about him. What do you know about Samuel Alister Hunter, or Sam Hunter as he's called?"

Jamie arched both brows. "I didn't recognize the name until just now, but then I'm not used to seeing his full name. And I can't tell you much about him except that he was a hunk in high school. Unfortunately, I was in middle school at the time so I didn't stand a chance. He went off to college, and eventually went to work on Wall Street. I haven't seen him since. I had no idea he'd returned to Beaumont."

"He just moved back. He's semiretired after making his money in the stock market, but he's looking to buy land which he plans to develop."

"No kidding? I wonder if he's still a hunk."

"Control yourself, Swifty. You're hot for me, remember?"

"I should probably try to set up a date with him," she said. "Just in case he's the murderer," she added.

"You're a brave and admirable woman," Max said, "to put yourself in harm's way in order to protect others."

"That's me, Max, brave and admirable. Willing to risk life and limb for the safety of others."

Max leaned back in his chair and regarded her with a half-smile. "You didn't sound so brave last night when we were discussing the supernatural."

"I hope we're not going to get on that subject again," Jamie said.

Fleas scratched at the back door. Jamie let him in, gave him a doughnut and poured him a bowl of milk.

"That's the most ridiculous thing I've ever seen in my life," Max said. "He should be eating meat."

"He has a cheeseburger every day for lunch." Jamie switched on her coffee maker, hoping the coffee would ease her throbbing head. She leaned against the cabinet.

"Back to the subject of Sam Hunter," Max said. "We don't really know much about the guy, and he returned to Beaumont three days before running his ad."

"Why would a guy with his looks be interested in someone like Luanne Ritter?" Jamie pondered aloud.

"Maybe he didn't know her."

"That's hard to believe, everybody knew Luanne."

"What did she look like?"

"She was so-so," Jamie said, trying to think of a nice way to describe the woman.

"I've got all the addresses, information, everything. We need to check these people out. You're going to have to arrange a date with them. Quickly," he added.

"I can't date all these men that fast," Jamie said.

"You're only going to contact the ones who allowed their phone numbers to be printed," Max said. "Unless you want to tell them that you were processing their ads at the newspaper office and liked what you saw. Maybe we can enlist Destiny. She can contact half of them. Besides, she already knows what's going on."

"That's a great idea," Jamie said, sarcasm slipping into her voice. "Ronnie can chaperone."

"Yeah, well, we'll have to talk to her about bringing Ronnie. We don't want to spook these guys. But I think between the two of you, we'll be able to get the job done quicker. I'll be close by, of course."

"We're not going to be able to find out who the murderer is in one date," Jamie said.

"You're right. We're going to have to watch them. If I have to call in some of my people, I will."

"We don't have a minute to waste, Max. We need to get to work on this immediately."

He stood, crossed the distance between them, and pulled Jamie against him. "It's still early. We could toss out that shirt."

Jamie's stomach fluttered in response. He had a point there. It wasn't even eight o'clock. Murderers usually waited until after dark to strike. She was about to respond when the doorbell rang several times.

"So much for that idea," Max said, releasing her with a sigh.

Jamie hurried into the living room and peered through the peephole. "Oh, damn. It's Vera," she called out to Max. "She's probably already heard the news. Myrna works fast."

CHAPTER
SEVEN

Jamie reached for the doorknob and opened it. "Good morning, Vera. Max and I were just having coffee and doughnuts. Won't you join us?"

The woman stepped through the front door. "I just ran into Myrna Hobbs at the Piggly Wiggly. Were you really drunk and doing the hootchy-kootchy in one of her suites last night?"

"Aw, Jamie was just having a little fun," Max said, coming up behind her. "Mrs. Hobbs overreacted."

"Yeah, I was just having a little fun," Jamie echoed.

"At least you're being honest with me," Vera told her, "which is a good thing. I couldn't bear the thought of your being a slut *and* a liar."

Jamie rolled her eyes. "I'm not a slut. There aren't enough eligible men in this town for me to be a slut, even if I wanted to."

Vera looked at Jamie. "Well, for your information, I slapped Myrna's face and told her she'd better never make another derogatory comment about you as long as she lived."

"Good for you," Max said.

"You actually slapped her?" Jamie asked. "In the Piggly Wiggly?"

"Yeah, the security guard threw me out of the store, threatened to have me arrested if I didn't leave. I can't afford to go to the slammer because I have to teach Sunday school for Agnes Aimsley tomorrow. She's still in shock after seeing all those unmentionables hanging in the window of Sinful Delights." Vera had to pause to suck in a deep breath.

"Myrna Hobbs will think twice before she decides to pull me over in frozen foods and start talking trash about you. I told her it was OK if I called you a slut, but she'd better keep her fat mouth shut."

"Thank you for defending me," Jamie said. "I think."

Vera shrugged as if it were no big deal. "Look, I know you're all grown-up, but if you insist on sleeping around you're going to have to be discreet. I hope you're on the pill and practicing safe sex. I probably should have had this talk with you long before now. I probably shouldn't have fed you all those brownies."

Max regarded Jamie. "You never mentioned you were promiscuous."

Jamie pressed the ball of her hand against her forehead. "Vera, could we talk about this later? I have a small headache."

"She's hungover," Max said. "She mixed wine with Kahlúa."

"Yeah, Myrna mentioned you had an alcohol problem," Vera said. "You might want to get help with that."

Fleas came up beside Jamie and nuzzled her leg as though he sensed she was in need of his support. Jamie sighed. "Would you guys give me a break? I have less

108

sex than this dog, and he's been neutered. And I'm *not* an alcoholic."

"She's in denial," Max said, obviously enjoying the whole thing.

Vera turned to him. "Now that we've got that settled, I want you to come outside and look at this Ferrari I'm test-driving. I thought maybe you'd take a ride with me, see what you think."

Max shrugged. "Sure."

"You're test-driving a Ferrari?" Jamie said incredulously. "Why?"

"Because I'm thinking of buying it. I can buy a Ferrari if I want to."

Jamie had just realized Vera was wearing Capri pants. Vera, who never wore anything other than dresses. "Do you have any idea how much they cost?"

"Yeah, but it's ten years old, and the guy is going to cut me a deal. I'm thinking I need something a little sporty. I'm thinking I need to reinvent myself. I've signed up for a class on line dancing. I might meet someone. All the men at church are on their last leg." Vera started out the door, then paused and glanced over her shoulder at Jamie. "You might want to change into something else. That shirt you're wearing isn't very flattering."

By the time Max returned, Jamie had showered and changed into shorts and a cotton T-shirt. She wore only a hint of makeup, and had pulled her wet hair into a ponytail. Luckily, her headache had dulled.

Max paused when he saw her. "Damned if you don't have the best set of legs I've ever seen on a woman. No wonder you have such a reputation with men."

Jamie gave him one of her looks. "Tell me Vera isn't really going to buy a Ferrari," she said.

"I think I convinced her not to. The mileage was too high, and it's kind of beat-up. I told her I could probably find her a good deal on a car if she'd give me a few days, but I think she's having a good time looking. Now, why don't we get to work?"

"OK, I'll call Destiny and see if she can help," Jamie said, although she wasn't thrilled at the prospect.

Destiny arrived an hour later. "Here are the ground rules," Max said, addressing both women. "You meet the guy in public, and you carry a cell phone that I will provide for each of you, complete with a GPA."

"What the heck is a GPA?" Destiny asked.

Jamie answered. "It's a device that lets Max know where we are at all times."

"You two have done this sort of thing before, haven't you?" Destiny asked.

Jamie nodded. "Yeah, and we always get the bad guy in the end." She paused. "Um, Destiny, Max and I didn't want to bring this up, but it might be distracting if you start talking to Ronnie on your, um, dates."

Destiny turned to the empty chair beside her. "Did you hear that, Ronnie? We're trying to find a killer. You're going to have to keep your mouth shut." She paused. Finally, she turned to Max and Jamie. "He promises to cooperate if I'll hang out with him at the bowling alley afterward. That's Ronnie's idea of a good time." She rolled her eyes.

"OK," Max said. "Muffin, my assistant, was able to get much of the information we need. The guy with the 'Till Death Do Us Part' ad is a minister. We just found out he does a lot of marriage counseling, even has a little wedding chapel and provides everything a couple needs for the auspicious occasion, right down to the flowers and catering. He's very anti-divorce and insists on counseling couples for an extended period of time before he'll agree to marry them. He accepts fairly large donations for the sessions, and the use of his chapel. I think Jamie and I should check him out just in case. We could pose as an engaged couple."

"That'll never work," Jamie said. "He'll see right through us."

"Not if you act like a real fiancée," Max said. "You're going to have to be nice to me, hold my hand, and simper at me a lot. That's what engaged couples do. It isn't until after the marriage that they learn to dislike each other."

Jamie just looked at him, Leave it to Max to make marriage sound like a prison term.

"Aw, come on, Swifty, it'll be fun," Max said, as though he hadn't realized he'd made a blunder. He reached for a cell phone in his pocket and punched a button. "Muffin, why don't you see if the Reverend Heyward can schedule us after lunch," he said. "In the meantime, Jamie and I are going to check out one Larry Johnson, author of 'Offer Good for a Limited Time.'"

"I'm on it," Muffin said. "What else?"

"Just hold tight." Max turned to Destiny. "I want you to call the dentist. He takes Saturday-morning appointments. Can you fake a toothache?"

She shrugged. "I've faked orgasms, that's gotta count for something. Besides, my wisdom teeth have been bothering me for months. I can kill two birds with one stone."

Larry Johnson owned and operated Beaumont Used Cars and reminded Jamie of a weasel with his beady, close-set black eyes. He held a hand-flex exerciser in one fist and pumped it furiously as he questioned Max about his Porsche look-alike. "That didn't come off an assembly line," Johnson said.

"You're right," Max said. "I had it custom designed."

Johnson changed the flex device to his other hand before taking them on a tour of the lot.

"My therapist advised me to use this," Larry told Jamie when he caught her staring. "I work out every morning at the local gym. It's supposed to help with stress."

"Does it?"

"No." He chuckled. "The only thing that works is a double shot of scotch straight up."

Jamie and Max pretended to find his words amusing. "I can certainly relate to that," Jamie said, thinking it was a good way to break the ice. They needed to get a fix on the guy, and in order to do that they needed good rapport. "I prefer Kahlúa," she added with a grin.

Larry smiled at her but didn't let up on his flexing. "That's a girlie drink."

She batted her lashes, something Deedee would have done with ease but which she found taxing. "So, I'm a girl."

Larry paused and gave her a long hard look. "Yeah." He cleared his throat. "So, do you folks see anything you like?" It was obvious Larry had seen what he liked.

"I want to take a second look at the white Chevy Corvette convertible," Max said.

Larry nodded. "Good choice. Just so happens that's my old car, and I took damn good care of it. Low mileage, too," he added. He hitched his shoulders high. "Just bought me a brand-new one. Unfortunately, it's about the only nice thing I own since my divorce. Child support payments, you know? But I'm real proud of it. Got a security system on it that'll wake the dead."

They walked over to the used Corvette, and Max climbed in. "You mind if I take it for a test-drive?"

"No problem, pardner." Larry dropped the keys into Max's hand. "It runs like a charm."

"I'll stay here and wait for you," Jamie said, giving Max one of her looks. She glanced Larry's way. "I might just find something on the lot I like."

The comment seemed to fly right over Larry's head, Jamie noticed, but then he probably thought she and Max were a couple. Jamie figured she could change that easily enough. She looked at Larry. "You got any coffee inside?"

"Sure."

Max took off in the Corvette, and Jamie followed Larry inside a small building. The dark paneled walls were adorned with pictures of race cars. Jamie noted a nondescript woman sitting before a computer. "This is my secretary, Mabel," Larry said. The two women nodded, and Mabel handed Larry several messages. "Come into my office and I'll pour you a cup of java," he told Jamie.

"Actually, Larry, I don't care for coffee," Jamie said once he'd closed the door behind them.

"Well, then, we'll just chat until your, um" — he glanced at Jamie's ring finger, which was bare — "until your significant other returns."

Jamie sat on a fake-leather couch. "Max and I are just friends. You know, good buddies."

"Oh, well, that's nice." Flex, flex. "You can never have too many friends in this crazy world," he said. "Me? I'm a loner."

"Sometimes it's good to have someone to talk to after you've ended a relationship. I speak from experience."

"Sorry to hear that, Jamie. Is it OK if I call you Jamie?"

She nodded. "I know what you're feeling right now because I've gone through it. The pain and emptiness." She sighed heavily. There were times she thought she would have made a damn good actress. "The loneliness," she added.

He was flexing triple time. "I can't imagine a woman with your looks being lonely. Maybe you should get out more."

Jamie gave a grunt of disgust. "Most of the men in this town are either married or downright ugly. It's not every day a woman meets a guy who owns his own business and is attractive to boot."

He nodded. Finally, he jerked his head up as though a lightbulb had just gone off inside. "Oh, were you talking about me?"

Jamie wagged her finger and made a tsking sound with her tongue. "You're playing games, Larry. I don't like games."

He sat up straighter in his chair. The man's eyes registered interest. "Maybe you and I can get together for a drink sometime. Soon," he added, after a few seconds.

"How about this evening?" Jamie asked.

He looked surprised. "Well, sure. I usually leave here around six. I could meet you in the lounge at the Holiday Inn around six-fifteen. They have happy hour until seven-thirty. Free food, half price on drinks." He gave a self-deprecating smile. "That's usually where I eat my dinner. Not that I can't afford to take a lady someplace nice once in a while and buy her a real meal," he added quickly. "Why, we could —"

"The Holiday Inn will be fine, Larry. Six-fifteen," she added.

The Corvette reappeared, and Max climbed from it. Jamie watched him walk toward the building. She wondered if Max had any idea just how good-looking he was, how no men came close in comparison.

Jamie and Larry rejoined Max. "What'd you think of the car?" Larry asked.

"I like the looks of it," Max said. "Let us talk with our friend. If she's interested, we'll bring her over."

"I look forward to hearing from you," Larry said. He winked at Jamie. He seemed so excited at the thought of meeting her later that he didn't even bother with a sales pitch.

Max and Jamie climbed into Max's car and pulled from the car lot. "I'm meeting Mr. Johnson for a drink at six-fifteen," Jamie said. "The lounge at the Holiday Inn."

"Boy, you work fast," Max said. "I didn't even have time to get the VIN number off the car so Muffin could check it out. No wonder you've got such a reputation in this town."

Jamie rolled her eyes.

Muffin came on. "Make sure you don't get into Larry Johnson's car," she warned Jamie. "He's got a couple of DUIs on his record."

"Hmm," Max said. "And I'd stay away from the Kahlúa tonight, Swifty, or you'll be doing the hootchy-kootchy on the tables at the Holiday Inn."

Jamie looked at him. "Go ahead and have your fun. I, on the other hand, have a job to do." She paused. "Speaking of which, have you heard from Destiny?"

"Yeah, she's waiting to see the dentist."

Dr. Kevin Smalls, a thirtysomething man, was almost completely bald, and his belly tugged at the buttons on his shirt. The examining room was decorated in a pale blue-green; obviously to make patients feel less anxious, but it wasn't working on Destiny as she drummed her long nails against the arm of her chair.

"Just relax," the dental assistant said and smiled. "We haven't lost a patient yet."

Finally, Dr. Smalls pulled the small mouth mirror from Destiny's mouth. "OK, I'm done here. I'll meet you in my office." He got up and left the room.

Destiny was shown to his office a moment later. Smalls shook his head sadly. "It's no wonder your wisdom teeth have been bothering you, Miss Moultrie," he said. "You know, most people have them extracted at a much earlier age."

"Really?" Destiny asked, not looking too pleased. She glanced around the office, her eyes resting on a bag of golf clubs.

"They're crowding the back of your mouth. I suggest we set you up with an oral surgeon as soon as possible."

"Do you play golf, doctor?" she asked.

He glanced at the bag of clubs. "When I have time. My wife and I share custody of our children so my weekends are pretty much taken up with them."

"So, what do you do for fun?" she asked.

"Well, I hadn't really thought much about it."

"Maybe it's time you started taking care of your own needs. You could start by inviting me to lunch."

Max and Jamie grabbed an early lunch at Maynard's Sandwich Shop where Donnie Maynard convinced Max his meat-loaf sandwich was the best thing in the world next to indoor plumbing.

"I'll give it a try," Max said.

"Make that two," Jamie told Donnie and wondered if Max had ever eaten a meat-loaf sandwich.

Max paid for the order, and they carried their drinks to a table. The walls inside the shop were of old brick, the tables and chairs battered and scarred, yet sturdy. Max took a sip of his iced tea. As if noting the curious look on Jamie's face, he arched one brow. "What?"

"When's the last time you had meat loaf?"

"Are you kidding, my cousin's wife, Billie, used to cook it all the time."

"The people who practically raised you?" she asked, remembering he'd mentioned them before.

"Right. I was sixteen years old when I moved in with them. Nick taught me everything I know about the newspaper business and horses; Billie taught me to focus my energy."

"You lost me on the last part."

"I was pretty much a juvenile delinquent from the age of five."

"Too smart for your own good, I'll bet."

"Nick was instrumental in breaking my bad habits by having me muck the stalls each time I got into trouble. You ever mucked a horse stall?"

"Nope. Don't want to, either."

"Builds character."

Their sandwiches arrived. Jamie thanked Donnie and waited until he walked away before saying anything. She knew that Max's parents had pretty much given up on their son; that the only attention he'd gotten was from the servants and during his summer vacations with cousin Nick. "Do you ever see your parents?"

"I swing by now and then if I'm in the vicinity. They're older and have more time for me than they used to." He took a bite of his sandwich and nodded his approval. "Hey, this is good," he said.

Jamie bit into her sandwich, as well. As usual, Donnie had outdone himself on the meat loaf. "He has a secret recipe. Neither love nor money will get him to part with it." But her thoughts were elsewhere. She pondered what Max had just said about his parents having time for him now. There had been no bitterness in his voice. He'd obviously come to terms with their relationship. "What about Nick and Billie?" she asked. "Do you see them often?"

"I usually spend holidays with them. They have two kids; Christie and Joel." He chuckled. "Well, they're not really kids anymore, Christie is probably about thirty, and Joel is a couple of years younger. They both work for the newspaper. We're all pretty close." He smiled.

"Why are you smiling?" Jamie asked.

"I'm thinking about Billie. She goes all out decorating the house for Christmas, and every year she swears it's going to be her last. Somehow, she ends up doing even more the next year." He paused. "You would like her. She's simple and down-to-earth. So is Nick."

"I'll bet they're proud of you."

Max looked surprised. "Thank you. I believe that's the nicest thing you've ever said to me."

"Well, look at all you've accomplished, Max."

He shrugged. "Nick taught me to go after what I wanted. The only time he disagreed with me was when

I told him I was getting married. He and Billie didn't feel I was ready. It didn't take me long to realize they were right."

"Is that why you're dead set against marriage now?"

"Let's just say I learned my lesson. I'm in no hurry to repeat that mistake."

"Don't you think you're being a little harsh?" Jamie asked. "I mean, look at Frankie and Deedee. After twenty years they're still madly in love."

"I'd say they're the exception, as are Nick and Billie."

They concentrated on their lunch after that, although Jamie realized she didn't have much of an appetite. She wondered how long it would be before Max became bored with her and moved on, and the thought was not a pleasant one. But she couldn't think about that right now because she had to work with him to solve Luanne Ritter's murder.

In the meantime, she needed to protect her heart.

Once they'd finished lunch, they thanked Donnie and headed out the door. Muffin was waiting for them.

"Good thing I don't take lunch breaks or we wouldn't get anything done," she said.

"What's up?" Max asked.

"The Reverend Heyward claimed he was much too busy to see you, but I was able to get you in at two o'clock, once I hinted that a hefty donation would change hands."

"Great," Max said. "That'll give us time to check out a couple of addresses." Max reached for a folder beside his seat. He handed it to Jamie. "How about looking at

120

the ad entitled 'Open to New Experiences' and giving me the address," he said. "You know, the guy looking for a discreet relationship?"

Jamie flipped through the file of names and print-outs that Muffin had supplied. "Here we go. John Price, age fifty-five, new to Beaumont, recently opened his own accounting firm. He lives on the edge of town. I know the area. Just stay on this road until you hit the main highway."

Max followed her directions, and they ended up in a rural area. They found the house, a two-story frame with NO TRESPASSING signs on the property, and a Doberman pinscher on a long leash that was attached to the porch rail.

"Well, now, Mr. Price obviously doesn't want company," Max said. "What else have we got on him?"

Jamie glanced back at the file. "Like I said, he's new in town, lived here about three months," she said. "Been divorced about a year from his second wife. He has a daughter by his first wife; she's in college. No police record. He left a high-paying position in Atlanta to come here. He's renting the house."

Max picked up a pair of binoculars and trained them on the man's residence. "Interesting. He's installed a fairly expensive security system on a piece of rental property, and he's got a man-eating creature guarding the front door. Wonder what he's got guarding the back?"

"I'm not going to go look," Jamie said. "I don't want to arrive at my date with half my face ripped off.

Besides, he's accustomed to living in a large city where the crime rate is high."

Max looked at her. "Or maybe he's hiding something. Muffin, do what you have to do, but I want to know if Mr. Price is at work today. I want to have a look inside."

Jamie gaped. "You're not going in there?" When Max didn't respond, she went on. "See, this is why I should never have called you. I should have let Lamar Tevis handle it. You remember Lamar Tevis, our chief of police? He's the man who's going to throw you behind bars for breaking and entering."

"Just for the record, Max," Muffin said, "I want you to know I'm taking Jamie's side on this." She paused for a few minutes, and then came back on the speaker. "Mr. Price is with a client," she said.

Max grinned. "Perfect, Now, here's what we're going to do."

CHAPTER
EIGHT

Jamie watched Max slip around the side of the house and disappear. The dog out front barked ferociously. "I hate this," she said to Muffin. "Max has absolutely no respect for the law. He's either hacking through firewalls or breaking and entering, and I can't believe I always find myself in the middle of it. One day we're going to get caught, and they're going to lock us up and throw away the key."

Three minutes later, Muffin came on. "He's in." Then, a quick, "Uh-oh."

Jamie's heart leaped to her throat. "What is it?"

"There's another Doberman inside. A mean one."

"Holy Toledo!" Jamie cried. All at once, the dog out front began barking out of control.

"Hang on, Max," Muffin said. "I'll cover you."

"What's going on?" Jamie demanded.

"I just blasted both animals with an ultrasonic frequency that should draw their attention for a few minutes. Max and I have done this sort of thing before. Max," Muffin said. "Are you OK?"

Jamie's nails bit into the palms of her hands. "Put him on the speaker," she said. "I want to know that he's OK."

Max came on. "I managed to lock the dog in the bathroom. I'm going to search the place."

"Oh, boy," Jamie said. "Muffin, how do you plan to get him out?"

"Same way I got him in."

Jamie counted the minutes. "How long has he been in there?"

"Less than five minutes," Muffin said. "There's nothing we can do but wait."

"I wish I hadn't quit smoking," Jamie said. "I could use a cigarette about now."

"Don't worry," Muffin told her. "Max is good at this sort of thing."

Jamie watched the clock on the dashboard. The next ten minutes seemed to drag on forever. Once Max was finished searching the house, he alerted Muffin, and she hit the dogs with the high-frequency sound once again. Max emerged from the house looking calm. He started the car and pulled away. "The place is clean," he said. "I didn't find anything out of the ordinary, but that doesn't mean we're not dealing with a killer."

Jamie leaned her head against the seat and closed her eyes, waiting for her heartbeat to return to normal.

Once Max had driven a distance, he looked at her. "Are you OK?"

"I am now."

"So you were worried about me, huh?"

She just looked at him.

Max grinned. "Muffin, Jamie was worried about me. That says a lot about our relationship."

"What relationship?" Muffin asked.

124

"Thank you, Muffin," Jamie said, "for not feeding his enormous ego. He knows darn well why I was worried. I don't look good in stripes, and if I go to prison what's going to happen to Fleas? Nobody wants a dog with emotional problems and missing hair."

"You guys need to stop arguing," Muffin said. "You have an appointment with the Reverend Heyward in half an hour. You're supposed to be in love."

The Reverend Joe Heyward was a big man, standing well over six feet, with a broad chest that made Jamie think of Frankie. He looked to be in his early sixties. "So you two are thinking of getting married," he said, once Jamie and Max had joined him in his office. The paneled walls were adorned with pictures of happy brides and grooms.

"Yes, sir," Max said. "We're in love."

"Madly," Jamie said.

"Sometimes, love is not enough," the reverend replied. "There are trials and tribulations in this world that can tear a couple apart unless they are determined to work on their relationship every single day, every single hour, every single minute. You must be one hundred and fifty percent dedicated."

"Wow, that sounds like a lot of work," Max said.

"It certainly is," the reverend replied. "Otherwise, you'll end up in divorce court like half the couples in this country, and —" He paused and leaned forward. "I do not believe in divorce." He clasped his hands as if in prayer. "What God hath joined together let no man put asunder. Till death do you part," he added.

"We agree, don't we, honey?" Max said to Jamie.

"Huh? Oh, right."

The reverend went on as though he hadn't heard. "I was married to my wife for thirty years before the Lord took her. Do you think it was always easy? No, it was not. Oh, she looked real nice when I first met her, all dolled up at the church social. Prettiest thing I'd ever seen. But people change over the years, and you have to accept change."

The man pointed to Jamie. "She's a beauty right now, but what are you going to do when she gets fat and starts nagging with every breath? 'Cause you can count on that happening, son. Women love to nag. They can nag in their sleep. You fantasize about putting a pillow over their face and shutting them up for good." He paused and cleared his throat as if realizing he'd made a blunder. "Not that I would ever consider such an act, mind you."

Jamie almost shivered at his last sentence. The man sounded off his rocker. Luanne had obviously been desperate for male attention. Was he the one who'd called her the night of her murder? What if he'd decided to stop by and meet Luanne personally? Would she have opened the door if he'd mentioned he was a minister? So many unanswered questions.

"This marriage business sounds tougher than I thought it would be," Max said. He looked at Jamie. "And you *do* eat a lot of doughnuts. You keep that up, and you're going to be the size of a freight train."

"That's how big my wife was," Heyward said.

Jamie gaped at Max. "I don't eat *that* many doughnuts. And I don't nag."

"Oh, yes you do," Max told her. He looked at the Reverend Heyward. "And she can be disagreeable at times. It's not always easy."

"I'm not disagreeable," Jamie said. "You're just stubborn and arrogant."

Heyward shook his head sadly. "I can see that we have our work cut out for us." He reached for his appointment book. "Let me see when I can fit you in."

"Would you mind if we get back to you?" Max said. "I need to check my calendar." He handed the man a hefty cash donation.

Heyward's eyes widened at the sight of the money. "I suggest we begin as soon as possible, maybe meet a couple of times a week. Call me as soon as it's convenient. And don't be discouraged; a good solid marriage makes for a lot of happiness. As a matter of fact, I hope to marry again one day soon. I'm definitely in the market for a good wife."

Max was grinning when he and Jamie climbed into the front seat of his car a few minutes later. "What do you think?"

"I think the man is wacko. I don't think many women are going to jump at the chance to become the next Mrs. Heyward. And that business about putting a pillow over someone's face to shut them up." She shuddered. "I don't like it."

"I wouldn't mind knowing how his wife died," Max said.

"Muffin, are you there?" Jamie asked.

"Yeah, what's up?"

"How did the Reverend Joe Heyward's wife die?"

"She choked on a chicken bone," Muffin replied.

Jamie rolled her eyes. "No, seriously."

"I'm telling you, the woman choked on a chicken bone."

Jamie sat there for a moment. She felt Max's smile before she glanced over and saw it. "How can you possibly think that's funny?"

"Well, he said she was as large as a freight train. I'll bet she could put back a whole truckload of fried chicken."

"Max, that's not one bit funny." Nevertheless, Jamie could feel the corners of her mouth twitching. Max reached over and tickled her.

"Lighten up, Swifty. We're not letting Heyward off the hook that easily."

"I don't like being tickled."

"I plan to find all your ticklish spots before long," he said.

Jamie tried not to let her mind run amuck. "So what's next?"

Max didn't hesitate. "I think we need to pay Lamar Tevis a visit and see if he's got the tape of the phone messages Luanne received the night of her murder. Muffin, call the police department and see if the chief is in."

Lamar greeted Max with a handshake. "Good to see you again, Max," he said. He nodded at Jamie and invited them to sit. He reclaimed his chair. "Now, then, may I ask *why* you want to hear the tape?"

Jamie answered. "A minister ran an ad with me, Lamar, and you said a man called Luanne claiming to be a man of God. She might have contacted him and left her telephone number."

"Well, like I told you, the tape must've been old and worn because the voices aren't very clear. But I'll be glad to play it." He popped a small cassette into his answering machine and pushed a button. There were several brief messages, along with a lot of crackling on the tape. They were followed by the voice of the man who claimed to be a man of God and needed to meet with Luanne immediately.

Jamie felt the hairs rise on her arms. She looked at Max.

"It's not Heyward," he said.

"No, but I think I recognize the voice. It sounds like Brent Walker."

Lamar stopped the tape. "Who is Brent Walker?"

"Agnes Aimsley's grandson. He's visiting her from the seminary."

"Are you sure?" Lamar asked.

"Could you play the tape again?" Jamie asked.

Lamar did as she requested. He cut off the machine once the tape ran out. "What do you think?" he said.

"I've only met this Walker guy once, and you're right, the voices aren't very clear, but I'm almost positive it's him. I can't imagine why he'd be calling Luanne, though. He didn't run an ad."

Lamar leaned back in his chair. "I reckon I'll have to pay him a visit and find out."

"I'm curious," Max said. "Was Luanne robbed?"

Lamar looked at Jamie. "We haven't released this information, so this is off the record."

"Of course."

"I think it was made to look like a robbery," he said. "Her jewelry box was cleaned out, but she was wearing several expensive rings. A burglar would have noticed."

The lounge at the Holiday Inn was doing a good business when Jamie arrived. Obviously, the free hors d'oeuvres were a big plus; people were lined up at the two tables that had been set up with chafing dishes. Larry Johnson was sitting at the bar. He looked surprised to see Jamie, as if he'd expected her not to show.

He stood as she crossed the room. "You dressed up," he said. "I'm flattered."

"Of course I did," Jamie said. "I wanted to look my best."

"You succeeded very well. Would you rather get a table?"

"A table would be nice," Jamie said, thinking he would be more open to conversation if they had privacy. She needed him to feel comfortable with her.

Larry grabbed his drink and led Jamie to a table that was situated in a dark corner. A cocktail waitress appeared a moment later. Jamie ordered a club soda and lime; Larry a double scotch.

"I thought you liked Kahlúa," Larry said, once the waitress left them.

Jamie noted he looked disappointed that she hadn't ordered a drink. After what Muffin had said about his drinking history, she suspected Larry preferred hanging with boozers, and, despite all the ribbing Jamie had received after how she'd acted at Myrna Hobbs's place, she seldom touched alcohol. But once again, she needed Larry to feel comfortable around her or he wouldn't say what was on his mind.

"Actually, I love the stuff," she said, "but I'm still recovering from a hangover I got at a friend's birthday party."

He grinned. "I hope you don't mind if I have another."

"No, please, I insist."

"I'm afraid I'm not in the greatest mood tonight," he confessed. "I received a call from my ex-wife, and we got into it over the telephone so I closed the dealership at five and got the hell out of there."

Jamie hoped it meant he'd had time to belt back several scotches, "I take it the split was not amicable."

He gave a grunt. "Hardly. She got everything, including the house, and I'm paying child support out the ass. My apartment is crap, and I barely have any furniture. All I have to show for years of hard work is a decent car."

"I'm sorry." Jamie didn't know the man well, but she suspected he'd gotten exactly what he deserved. "I'm sure you feel a lot of animosity toward your ex right now, but perhaps it'll pass in time."

"Don't count on it. She put the screws to me. But I'm here to tell you, she's going to get hers."

Jamie caught the menace in his voice. "What do you mean?"

His answer was guarded. "As they say, what goes around comes around, know what I mean?" He suddenly looked apologetic, "I'm sorry. I have no right to unload on you. I invited you here for a good time."

"I *am* having a good time," Jamie said. "I don't get out much."

He looked doubtful. "A woman with your looks? I find that hard to believe."

"Remember, I mentioned I was involved with someone for a while? He didn't like to go out much."

"I go out every night." Larry shrugged. "Here, mostly, but it's better than sitting at home. The ex got the only decent TV set, too. I was mad as hell over that one. A guy shouldn't have to give up his TV."

They were interrupted when the cocktail waitress appeared with their drinks.

Larry shoved several bills at her, told her to keep the change, and she walked away. He stirred his drink. "My ex claims I have an anger problem, among other things. The judge ordered me to get counseling on anger management if I wanted to see my children. I think that sucks." He raised his glass, but it slipped from his hand, and his entire drink spilled on him, soaking the front of his shirt. "Oh, shit, now look what I've done."

Jamie tried to help him mop the spill with a napkin, but it was useless.

"I've got to get out of this shirt," Larry said. "It's sticking to me." He looked at her. "I only live a couple of miles from here. Why don't we run by my place, let me clean up, then we can grab a bite to eat someplace. I'll take you to a real restaurant so you can show off that nice dress."

Jamie hesitated. Max had specifically told her and Destiny not to leave a public area with the men.

"Hey, this isn't a pickup, OK? I just want to get out of this wet shirt."

Jamie knew Max would be mad as hell if she left the premises with Larry, but what could she do? If she refused to go she might lose her one chance of finding out whether he had ever met Luanne Ritter, much less visited her the night of her murder. He certainly had an anger problem, and his alcohol abuse made him a walking time bomb.

Besides, she owed Max for having scared the life out of her when he'd broken into John Price's house. "I'll follow you in my car," she said.

They left the lounge. Jamie climbed into her car and followed Larry from the parking lot, wondering if Max could see her from his vantage point at the other end of the lot. She grabbed her cell phone and punched in Max's number. He answered on the first ring.

"OK, Max, I know you're not going to like this, but I'm following Larry Johnson to his place so he can change shirts." She explained about the spilled drink.

"Bad idea," he said. "I specifically told you —"

"I know what you told me, but I think I'm on to something here. This guy looks suspicious."

"All the more reason to turn your car around and head in the opposite direction. I don't want you alone with him."

"Listen, Max, I can't see him intentionally killing Luanne Ritter, but he has serious problems. I think he feels he can talk to me."

"Oh, so you think you're going to get a full confession out of him?"

"Not exactly, but —"

"Turn your car around, Jamie," he ordered. "It's not worth the risk. I'll follow you to Frankie and Deedee's."

"No way, Max. Not when I'm this close. Trust me on this one, OK? And call Frankie and Deedee and tell them we can't make it for dinner. I'll be dining with Larry."

She hung up the phone in order to avoid arguing with him. The cell phone rang. She knew it was Max. She ignored it, knowing he would never agree to let her enter Larry's apartment. But she was determined to find out what she could. Besides, something told her she had nothing to fear with Larry Johnson. As long as she played along, she reminded herself.

Finally, the cell phone stopped ringing.

Five minutes later, Jamie followed Larry into the parking lot of a generic-looking apartment complex. She parked beside his car and climbed out. He hit a button on his key chain, and his Corvette beeped. "I don't trust the teenagers around here," he said. "If I ever catch them messing with my car I'm going to take a crowbar to them. Matter of fact, I keep one behind the seat of my car and another one beside the front door in my apartment."

Jamie suppressed a shiver. Luanne Ritter had died from a blow to the head. She tried to make light of it. "A crowbar would certainly scare me away," she said with a laugh. At the same time, she wondered what Larry's wife had found appealing about him. "Yes, sir, a crowbar would definitely get my attention," she added, causing him to grin.

She followed Larry to a door and paused beside him while he unlocked it. He opened it, stepped inside and flipped on a light switch, then motioned for Jamie to enter. "It's not much, but it's home."

Jamie followed him into a sparsely furnished living room. Larry had obviously found a good deal on fake leather furniture because the couch and chair matched those in his office. The apartment smelled of stale food and booze. Sure enough, there was a crowbar leaning against the wall beside the front door. "It's not so bad," she lied. "A few pictures on the wall, and the place would be really homey."

"I'm not much of a decorator."

No kidding, she thought.

"Hey, and I'm sorry about the mess, but I wasn't expecting company." He grabbed a pile of clothes from the sofa. "Have a seat."

Jamie sat down. He went about turning on more lights, then headed into the kitchen and made himself another scotch. "My shirt is plastered to me," he said. "Would you mind if I grabbed a quick shower and changed? Then I'll take you to dinner."

"No problem," she said.

He hurried into the next room. Several minutes later, Jamie heard the sound of running water. She stood and tiptoed into the bedroom and immediately started searching through Larry's dresser drawers. She was looking for jewelry. If Larry had indeed killed Luanne and tried to make it look like a robbery, he could very well have hidden his stash until he could dispose of it. A man with his financial problems would probably try to sell it when he felt it was safe.

If he'd been the one, she reminded herself. *If* the murder was actually tied to her personals ads. There were a lot of ifs, but Jamie knew she wouldn't have any answers unless she checked.

Nothing unusual in the drawers. Jamie glanced at the closet. She sometimes kept money tucked inside an old coat pocket. She heard a noise and turned.

Larry was standing in the doorway, a towel draped around his midsection.

She froze. Damn, damn, damn.

"Why are you in my bedroom?" he asked.

Jamie stared back at him for a full minute as she tried to find her tongue. She had been so engrossed in her search that she hadn't heard the sound of the shower being turned off or the bathroom door opening. Finally, she smiled. "Why do you think?"

"I should have known Jamie would pull something like this," Max said, having followed her car to Larry's apartment complex and watched her enter through one of the doors.

136

"What are you going to do?" Muffin asked.

Max stared at the door to the apartment. He noted Larry's Corvette out front. "She thinks she's so smart. Let her figure it out." He sat there for about twenty seconds. "Dammit," he muttered. He opened his car door and climbed out.

Larry smiled at Jamie and stepped closer.

"Why am I surprised?" he said. "I knew we had chemistry the minute I laid eyes on you."

Jamie wanted to tell him she felt about as much attraction for him as she did an eel. "Yes," she said in a husky tone meant to sound sexy. "I felt it, too."

"We don't have to go out," Larry said. "Besides, I'm hungry for you."

"Yes: I mean, no," Jamie said hurriedly. "On second thought, I think we should still go out. Someplace romantic," she added. "We shouldn't rush things."

"I could order pizza. Is that romantic enough?"

"Um, I was sort of hoping for soft music and candlelight. Maybe we could go dancing."

"Baby, we don't need all that." He suddenly pulled her against him. "Why put off the inevitable? You want it as bad as I do." He dropped his towel to the floor and pressed himself against her.

Jamie's skin crawled. The last thing she wanted to see was a naked Larry Johnson. He pulled her face close, studied her with those beady eyes. Oh, hell, he was going to kiss her, she thought.

He lowered his head, and their lips touched. Jamie felt herself stiffen.

"Relax," he whispered against her lips. "I'll go slow."

Jamie closed her eyes. It would be easier to let him kiss her if she didn't have to look at him. She braced herself. Think; think. His kiss deepened, and she started bargaining with God.

Please don't let him stick his tongue in my mouth. I'll even start going to church with Vera if I have to.

Larry pressed his tongue against her lips, trying to prod them open. "Come on, baby," he crooned.

Jamie's heart sank to her toes. She flattened her hand against his bare chest, hoping to push him away gently, when, all at once a loud siren split the night. They both jumped.

"Sonofabitch!" Larry yelled. "Someone is messing with my car,"

Jamie's head spun. "What?"

"That's my alarm system. Some asshole is trying to break into my car." He searched the room frantically and grabbed a pair of pants. He danced about, trying to get his legs into his slacks. He didn't bother zipping them as he raced from the room.

"Oh, thank you, God," Jamie whispered as she heard the front door of the apartment being flung open. She hurried into the living room, grabbed her purse, and ran out. She stood there for a moment, disoriented. Finally, she bolted toward her car.

And bumped into Larry and his crowbar.

"My car's OK," he said, and then gave her a funny look. "Where are you going?"

"I just remembered I have to go home and feed my dog."

"Feed your dog?" he said in disbelief. "Can't that wait?"

"He's hypoglycemic. If he doesn't eat every four hours his blood sugar level drops and —"

"Lady, what the hell are you talking about?" Larry scowled and began flexing his fists. "You get a man hard enough to break concrete blocks, and then you come up with this bullshit story about having to go home and feed your dog? What's with that?"

Jamie suspected he was on the verge of erupting. "Larry, things were getting out of hand. It's my fault. I haven't, well, you know, it's been *sooo* long since I've been with a man, and I'm really attracted to you, but I need more time. I don't want to do something I might regret later, you know? Especially since —" She paused, hoping she sounded convincing. "We might want to keep on seeing each other."

His facial muscles relaxed. "You're worried I won't respect you in the morning, is that it?"

"Something like that. You know how it is."

He seemed to ponder it. Finally, he nodded. "OK, then, I can wait. I'll call you."

"No. I'll call you. Just give me a couple of days."

He flexed a fist. "Well, OK."

Jamie covered the short distance to her car, climbed in, and punched the lock.

Max was waiting near the entrance to the apartment complex. He drove forward slowly as Jamie approached in her Mustang. She followed him for several miles before he pulled into the parking lot of the Piggly Wiggly supermarket. He slammed out of his car.

The look on his face told her she was in deep doo-doo. She rolled down her window. "Max, I —"

He jerked her car door open. "Get out."

Jamie gave a huge sigh but did as he said. "OK, go ahead and yell at me so we can get it over with."

"Just what the hell were you thinking?"

"I was trying to get information." She wasn't about to tell him she'd ended up in Larry's bedroom.

"You're off the job."

CHAPTER
NINE

Jamie blinked furiously. "Excuse me?"

"I'm calling in my own people. It's too dangerous, and I can't trust you to follow directions."

"You *can't* pull me off the job," she almost shouted. "I'm the one who called you. Besides, who are you to talk about taking chances when you broke into John Price's house today? At least I didn't break any laws."

"I knew what I was doing or I would never have gone in," Max said. "You acted irrationally by entering Johnson's apartment when we don't know if he's the killer or not. Jesus, Jamie, the man could have overpowered you. You're not thinking straight because you're emotionally involved in this."

"You're not taking me off the *job*, as you call it, but you're right — I *am* emotionally involved. My personals section could be connected to Luanne Ritter's murder. *That's* why I took the chance I did. If Larry Johnson killed Luanne, I want to know."

"At the risk of causing harm to yourself?" he asked.

"If I had felt threatened by him I would never have gone in. Besides, I got out before anything happened, didn't I?"

"I got you out by tripping the alarm system in his car."

She wasn't about to tell him how grateful she was for that or let him see how shaken she was over her ordeal. "It's a moot point now," she said, raising her voice. "I'm safe."

"You need to settle down."

"I *can't* settle down. Nobody in this town seems to care that a human being died. They keep thinking of the Luanne Ritter who ran a loan company and wasn't liked. Well, she may not have been the most popular person in town, but she didn't deserve to die. I don't know how I'll live with myself if my newspaper is involved."

"Well, you just might have to face that fact, so get over it."

"Gee, thanks."

"I'm being realistic. If you want to spend the rest of your life beating yourself up over something you had no control over, then do it."

"I shouldn't have called you. I should have let Lamar handle it."

"Then why *did* you call me?"

She hesitated, and her voice broke when she answered. "Because I was afraid Lamar couldn't handle the job. I knew you could. Satisfied?"

Without warning, Max pulled her against him. For a moment, he simply held her, waiting for Jamie to calm down. He sighed heavily. Finally, he pulled back so that he was looking into her eyes. "Look, I'm sorry I got

142

angry with you, babe, but I was worried as hell. Promise me you won't try anything like that again."

"I have to know the truth, Max."

"And we're doing everything we can." He released her. "Did you see anything in his place that looked suspicious?"

She told him about the crowbars. "He carries one in his car. If we could get our hands on it —"

"No way," Max said. "If he looks like our man I'll have Lamar Tevis check him out and send the crowbar to the crime lab. Also, I'm going to have Muffin check his and Luanne's telephone records."

"Luanne's picture was recently in the newspaper. We could take it to the Holiday Inn and show it around. See if anybody remembers her being there with Larry."

"He might find out, and we'll blow our cover. We just need to have him watched closely for the next couple of days until we can rule out the others. I suppose I could put Destiny on it."

"That's fine." Jamie had no desire to lay eyes on the man again.

Max checked his wristwatch. "We still have time to make dinner at Frankie and Deedee's."

Jamie was glad he hadn't canceled. She needed the diversion after what she'd been through. "I'll follow you."

Vera Bankhead stared at herself in the mirror as she tried on the new dress. On the bed behind her were two new pantsuits she'd purchased, as well.

Vera reached inside the little pocket of her purse and pulled out the ad she had cut out of the newspaper that day. "'Open to New Experiences,'" she read aloud. She often talked to herself, a result of living alone most of her life. "'Interested in discreet relationship with woman in fifties,'" she continued. "OK, I'm a tad older, but I look pretty good, and I can be as discreet as the next person. Lord knows I wouldn't want my preacher finding out that I was responding to a personals ad."

She hurried into her living room for her box of stationery.

Max and Jamie arrived at Frankie and Deedee's house around eight p.m. to find Deedee in tears.

"It's because of the lobsters," Frankie said miserably. "We had a tank installed in the kitchen. You may have noticed it when you were here for the party. Anyway, I had a bunch of lobsters flown in from Maine, and we were going to have them for dinner tonight, but Deedee —"

Deedee interrupted. "The chef was going to drop them live into a pot of boiling water, Max." Her bottom lip trembled.

"Honey, how do you think they cook lobster?" Frankie asked.

"Well, there *are* more humane ways to prepare them," Max said, "but I'm sure your chef knows that."

"I don't want to hear about it!" Deedee cried, palms pressed to her ears. "I want them sent back. Or find homes for them."

144

Max and Jamie exchanged looks. Jamie tried to imagine where one would find a good home for a lobster. It wasn't like they could drop them off at the local animal shelter and hope someone would adopt them.

Beenie had his arms crossed and was tapping his foot impatiently. "Well, I, for one, had my heart set on a nice lobster dinner, but Deedee said there will be no murders committed in this house so we'll all probably end up eating bologna and cheese sandwiches."

"I'd rather have a big old rare steak anyway," Snakeman said. "Come on, Big John. You and me can run to the store and pick up a load of 'em."

"I guess that will be OK," Deedee said. "Since the cows are already dead."

Jamie walked over to her friend. Deedee looked delicate in a cream-colored georgette dress that fell to her ankles. "Honey, I don't care what we eat as long as it doesn't distress you. You're just feeling a little sensitive now that you're pregnant, and you have every right."

Deedee sniffed. "I told them I wouldn't mind eating the lobsters once they grew old and died. I'm trying to cooperate."

"Does anyone know the life span of a lobster?" Beenie asked sarcastically.

No one had heard the chef come into the room. "This is nonsense, waiting for a lobster to die before we can cook him," the man said. "A lobster must be alive when you cook him or he's no good. I can put them in the freezer to numb them before I drop them into boiling water."

Deedee burst into tears.

"Scrap the lobster," Frankie said. "Snakeman is going to buy steaks."

"This is a crazy house," the chef muttered under his breath and pushed through the swinging door leading to the kitchen.

"Would you like to go upstairs and lie down for a while before dinner?" Jamie asked Deedee.

Beenie softened at the sad look in Deedee's eyes. "Of course she would. Come on, honey, you need to rest a bit, and then I'll repair your makeup."

"The rest of the guys are in the game room playing pool and darts," Frankie said to Max. "Why don't we join them?"

Beenie very gently placed a lavender-scented satin eye mask over Deedee's eyes as she half reclined on a settee, holding her Maltese, Choo-Choo, against her breasts. "I know everyone thinks I'm being foolish," she said, "but the thought of killing those poor lobsters is more than I can bear." She sniffed. "I was beginning to think of them as pets."

Beenie caught Jamie's eye and shook his head sadly. "Our Deedee has been feeling out of sorts all day," he said. "Tired and weepy," he added. "She was real upset over that woman's murder."

"That poor woman," Deedee said, removing her eye mask. "It's all I can think about."

"We're all very saddened by it," Jamie told her, "but I'm sure the police are doing everything they can to find the killer." She offered Deedee the closest thing she had to a smile and changed the subject. "You'll be relieved to know that Muffin is already doing research on pregnancy and child care. She's ordered a few books for you. By the time this baby comes into the world we'll all be experts."

Beenie did a quick repair job on Deedee's eyes. "I just hope I don't gain a lot of weight," Deedee replied. "You know how I am about my weight."

"Oh, pooh," Beenie said. "For once in your life stop worrying about your waistline. Besides, that new fashion designer I selected assured me you'd be the best-looking pregnant woman in town. In the country, even," he added. "You know what I think? I think a lot of celebrities out there will have their own designers trying to copy your style."

Deedee seemed to perk up at the thought.

"And of course the baby's nursery will look like something off a magazine cover," Beenie said. "I'm talking to interior designers who have been commissioned by the biggest names in show business."

"It sounds so exciting," Jamie said. "I can't wait."

Deedee touched her still flat tummy. "Eeyeuuw, I'm going to look like I'm carrying a giant melon," she said suddenly. "I won't be able to let Frankie see me in the buff."

"I've heard that a lot of men find pregnant women very sexy," Jamie said.

"But some women never totally regain their figures after having a baby," Deedee pointed out.

"That's not going to happen," Beenie said. "Your plastic surgeon can perform liposuction as soon as you deliver the baby. We'll have him on standby."

Jamie suppressed a shudder. It sounded rather drastic.

"And what do I know about being a mother?" Deedee said. "I've never raised anything but a Maltese." She sat up. "I have to speak to Muffin."

"*Now?*" Jamie asked.

"Yes. She always has the answers to all my questions, and I have a lot of questions."

"You want me to come with you?" Jamie asked.

"Yes. You can take notes." She glanced at Beenie. "You want to come?"

"No, I'm going to join the guys. I get hot being around all that testosterone."

"So you're saying you've been experiencing morning sickness for some weeks now?" Muffin said a short while later.

Deedee sniffed. "Yes. It isn't very pleasant."

"Your doctor has probably told you to keep soda crackers on your night table, right?" Muffin replied.

"I have trouble keeping them down."

"The nausea should go away after the first couple of months," Muffin told her. "There are medications to help you through it if you like."

"I just hate taking anything while I'm pregnant," Deedee said. "What bothers me even worse is the

148

fatigue. I get up in the morning and several hours later I'm ready for a nap."

"It happens to a lot of women," Muffin told her. "The first three months or trimester, as it's called, is the worst. Odds are, once you get into your fourth and fifth month you'll start feeling better. Of course, you're going to be the size of a refrigerator."

"Eeyeuuw!" Deedee cried.

Muffin chuckled. "Just kidding."

"Hey, pregnant women are cool," Jamie said. "Once you start getting big everyone opens doors for you and waits on you like a princess."

Deedee seemed to ponder it. "But people already do that."

Muffin spoke up. "Hey, I'll bet Frankie will start buying you more jewelry."

Jamie looked up from her notes. "Muffin, what a materialistic thing to say."

Deedee looked at her. "Maybe if I play my cards right I'll get that new ten-karat solitaire from Tiffany's I've been wanting." She looked thoughtful. "This pregnancy thing might just end up being the best thing that's ever happened to me, and when it's all over, I'll have a precious little baby boy or girl. It's a win-win situation."

"Do you plan on breast-feeding?" Muffin asked.

"Eeyeuuw, I hadn't thought of that." Deedee was quiet for a moment. Finally, she looked at Jamie. "What do you think?"

"Don't ask me, I can't even raise a bloodhound properly. Maybe you're trying to make too many decisions at once. You've barely had time to get used to the thought of being pregnant, much less buying maternity clothes, decorating a nursery, and deciding whether you should breast-feed. You need to relax."

"How come Frankie isn't worried about these things?" Deedee asked. "I feel like I'm going through most of it alone."

Jamie grinned. "He's too happy to be worried. The woman he loves more than anything in the world is going to have his baby. He's passing out cigars."

"Are you happy for me, Jamie?" Deedee asked.

"Of course I am. Why wouldn't I be?"

"It's silly, but I just wanted to make sure I had your support. And because I'm a little nervous. I want to be the best mother I can be. I never thought I'd feel like this about a baby. It's a miracle that I got pregnant after all these years, and I don't want to botch it."

Jamie reached across the seat and hugged her.

"Deedee, you are going to be a wonderful mother. And Frankie will be a great father. I think this is one lucky baby."

"How far along are you?" Muffin asked.

"Six weeks."

"Well, that'll give us plenty of time to learn everything we can about babies," Muffin said.

Deedee smiled almost dreamily at Jamie. "You know, I never thought I would be facing motherhood, but this would be more fun if you were going through it with me. I mean, you're my best friend. We'd have a blast if we were both pregnant at the same time. We could shop together."

150

Jamie almost swallowed her own tongue. "Um, maybe I should just concentrate on raising Fleas right now."

It was shortly after eleven p.m. when Max and Jamie arrived back at her house. Fleas was spread-eagled on the sofa. He didn't move as they came into the house.

"That's some watchdog you've got there," Max said.

Jamie walked up to the animal, hands on hips. "Excuse me, but are you supposed to be on the sofa?" she asked.

The dog didn't budge.

"OK, play your games, but Max and I are going to have ice cream."

One of Fleas's eyes popped open. He raised his head.

"I figured that would get your attention," Jamie said, going into the kitchen.

Max followed. "You don't really feed him ice cream, do you?"

Jamie was already pulling a carton of butter pecan from the freezer. "Yeah. He won't go to bed for the night without his treat."

Fleas climbed from the sofa and walked into the kitchen. He sat and waited, watching Jamie's every move. She dipped ice cream into his doggie bowl, and then put some in bowls for Max and her. Fleas had eaten his by the time they carried their bowls to the kitchen table. For a moment, Jamie and Max enjoyed their dessert in silence. Max looked at her.

"I'm sorry I came down so hard on you earlier," he said. "I almost lost it when you went into Larry Johnson's apartment. I think he's dangerous."

"Or he could just be angry because he had to give up everything in the divorce. He's hard to figure, but it's obvious he doesn't have much respect for women. Still, I have a hard time believing he's a cold-blooded killer, but then I can't imagine anyone murdering another human being." Not that she hadn't witnessed killing during their trip to Tennessee, she reminded herself. She'd watched the FBI gun down two notorious mob figures, and she still had nightmares about it from time to time.

"Johnson definitely has two things against him," Max said. "Anger and booze. That can make for a deadly combination. Also, if he has financial problems he might have taken Luanne Ritter's jewelry."

"Assuming, of course, that he killed her," Jamie added quickly.

They finished their ice cream. Jamie picked up the bowls and carried them to the sink where she rinsed them out. She didn't hear Max get up, but all at once she felt his arms slide around her waist.

"I really missed you while I was away, Swifty," he said, his mouth at her ear.

Jamie tried to suppress the shiver that raced up her backbone and reached for the towel to dry her hands. "I missed you, too, Max," she said.

He turned her around so that she was facing him, and the two gazed at each other for a moment. Finally, Max kissed her.

Jamie could taste the ice cream on his tongue as he explored her mouth. She slipped her arms around his neck and drew him even closer. She had been waiting for Max to kiss her for most of the evening, and now she opened her mouth wider to receive him.

Max broke the kiss and studied her. "Remember that unfinished business back in Tennessee?"

Jamie blushed in spite of herself. Her with her skirt shoved high on her hips, Max's mouth on her, tasting. "Yes." The word was little more than a whisper.

"I'd like to finish it."

He took her hand and led her to her bedroom. He walked over to the nightstand and switched on the light. At Jamie's look, he smiled. "I want to be able to get a good look at you." He pulled her into his arms once more; this time there was a look of sheer determination on his face. Jamie welcomed his hands on her breasts and closed her eyes as her nipples contracted, despite the clothing that separated them. She gave in to the wonderful sensations his touch created.

Max reached around and unzipped her dress, kissing each shoulder as he bared it. He released the garment and it fell to her feet. Jamie kicked off her heels and was left standing there in her bra and panties, the ones she'd bought at Sinful Delights.

"Jesus, Swifty," Max said, his voice suddenly husky. "I'd like to know where you buy your lingerie."

She smiled coyly and reached for the buttons on his shirt, but her fingers trembled as she undid them. Finally, she pulled the shirt free, and Max stood there with his chest bare, looking better than anything she'd ever laid eyes on. She ran her hands over him. Her stomach fluttered. If she'd known he looked this good she would have jumped into the sack with him sooner.

Max reached around and unfastened her bra. He tossed it aside and pulled her into his arms. Skin met skin. Jamie's body responded immediately.

Max cupped her breasts in his hands and then he lowered his head and kissed the spot between them. Jamie held his head tightly against her as she felt her insides swoop upward. Max's hands suddenly appeared at her hips. He kneaded the flesh before pulling her against him where she could feel his hardness. Something hot flashed low in her belly.

Jamie whimpered his name as he buried his face against her throat. "Oh, Max."

"I know, Jamie. I know." He picked her up and carried her the short distance to the bed.

Jamie reached for his belt, fumbled with it until she was able to unfasten it. "I could use some help, Holt."

He grinned and pulled off his socks and shoes. Finally, he unzipped his pants. It took only seconds for him to dispense with them. His boxers followed. Jamie's breath caught in her throat at the sight of his lean but slightly muscular body.

Max joined her on the bed, pulled her into his arms once more, and kissed her deeply. He pulled back slightly. "Birth control?" he whispered.

154

"We're covered," she managed.

He removed her panties and sought the area between her thighs with his fingers. Jamie pressed herself against his hand.

Max teased her with his fingers, even as he continued kissing her. He began to inch his way down her body, kissing her abdomen, her tummy. He parted her thighs to receive his tongue.

The doorbell rang.

Max jerked his head up. "What the hell?"

Jamie blinked furiously, trying to awaken her dulled senses. "I wonder who that could be."

"Ignore it."

She sat up. "I can't ignore it, Max. It's almost midnight. Something must be wrong. It could be Vera."

He gave a huge sigh, climbed from the bed, and reached for his slacks. "This had better be good." He tugged them on and zipped them.

Jamie grabbed her bathrobe. She hurried into the next room, Max right behind her. Fleas was on the sofa sleeping soundly. Jamie shot him a dirty look as she made for the door. She checked the peephole. "It's Destiny."

"You're kidding. What's she doing here?"

Jamie opened the front door. Destiny was dressed in skintight faux-leather shorts and a rhinestone T-shirt that was molded to her oversized breasts.

"Don't you ever check your answering machine?" the woman asked frantically. Her eyes darted to Max then back to Jamie.

"I was out all evening," Jamie said. "I only returned home a little while ago. Do you know what time it is?"

"Of course I do," Destiny said. "I wouldn't be here if it weren't important. I've lost Ronnie."

CHAPTER
TEN

Jamie gaped at Destiny. "You're serious, aren't you?"

"Of course I am. I feel responsible for him. I was wondering if he was over here."

"Why would he be here?" Jamie asked.

"He likes the two of you. He told me. He especially likes your hound because he had one similar. Ronnie used to be an expert coon hunter," she added, shaking her head sadly. "I can't let him go off on his own because, well, because he needs my help. I'm the only one who can convince him to cross over to the other side. To the light," she added.

Jamie gave a massive eye-roll. "I don't believe we're having this conversation," she muttered.

Destiny looked past both of them. "There you are, dammit," she said to an empty space. "Ronnie, what are you doing here this time of night? I've been searching all over for you."

Jamie and Max glanced around the room. "Where is he?" Jamie asked.

"Sitting next to your dog." Destiny walked over to Fleas, once again staring at an empty space. She put her hands on her hips. "It's time to go home, Ronnie," she said. "If you don't go to the light you'll keep wandering around lost. I know you're not anxious to see your dead mother, but you've got to face her sooner or later." Destiny paused and looked at Max and Jamie. "Ronnie knows his mother is going to read him the riot act for getting drunk and falling out of that pickup truck."

Max and Jamie exchanged glances.

Finally, Destiny sighed. "OK, I'll let you hang around my place for a while longer, but you can't go running off like this because I'll worry."

Jamie was intrigued. "How come you can see Ronnie, but we can't?"

Destiny shrugged. "Everyone has some psychic ability," she said, "but they don't use it."

"What does he look like?" Jamie asked.

"He's short and bald with a beer gut." Destiny gave a grunt. "Yes, Ronnie, you do have a beer gut. Now are you coming with me or not?" She glanced at Max and Jamie. "Ronnie can be stubborn at times."

"Well, I'm sure the two of you will work things out," Max said. He walked into the bedroom for the rest of his clothes.

Jamie couldn't hide her irritation. "Destiny, you're going to have to keep up with your dead spirit. I can't have him showing up here at all hours of the night." She suddenly remembered what Max had said about dead spirits attaching themselves to other people. "Ronnie isn't, um, an evil spirit, is he?" she asked, and then realized how strange her question sounded.

"Oh, no, he's quite friendly," Destiny said, "even if he is a real pain in the ass." She paused. "Yes, Ronnie,

158

you are a pain in the ass, and I don't know why I put up with you. Now let's go home and let these people get some sleep." She crossed her arms and tapped her foot impatiently. "I'm waiting."

Max re-entered the room, still buttoning his shirt. "You haven't come up with any more information, have you?"

Destiny shook her head. "Sorry. I think I'm still blocked."

"Max said you didn't think the dentist looked suspicious."

Destiny shrugged. "He seemed harmless to me, but he did have golf clubs in his office, and I suppose one of them could have been used to kill that poor woman. Maybe something will come to me soon. In the meantime, I'll be in the office early Monday morning to pick up my mail."

"Your mail?"

"I assume I'll have responses to the new column you mentioned to your readers."

Jamie doubted it, but she didn't want to hurt Destiny's feelings. She had almost been too embarrassed to run the announcement and couldn't imagine anyone in Beaumont writing in for advice from the Divine Love Goddess Advisor, but for some insane reason she had posted it anyway.

Max stepped forward. "By the way, I was hoping you could follow one of the suspects around for a couple of days."

Destiny shrugged. "Sure."

"I don't want you to get too close, but he needs to be watched."

"How will I know what the guy looks like?"

Max described him. "Do you have a pair of binoculars?" he asked.

"They're easy enough to buy."

"His name is Larry Johnson, and he owns a local car dealership. It would be best if you parked across from his place of business. He'll probably be at the car lot all day tomorrow. He'll be easy to spot since he's the only salesman on the lot. He also hangs out in the lounge at the Holiday Inn at night. Like I said, I don't want you to get too close."

"What am I looking for?"

"I'd just like to know who he's spending his evenings with."

"OK." Destiny suddenly glanced sideways. "No, Ronnie, I don't think that's a polite question to ask."

"What does Ronnie want to know?" Jamie said.

"I'm almost too embarrassed to say, but he is asking what happened to your dog's hair."

"Coon attack," Jamie said, irritated that people were always finding flaws with her pet. "Um, it's getting late, Destiny, and I don't mean to be rude, but do you think you could take your dead spirit home now?"

Max looked amused.

"OK, I'm out of here," Destiny said. "Come on, Ronnie." She turned for the door, and then glanced over her shoulder. "We need to figure out who the murderer is right away because I have to have oral

160

surgery next week. The dentist said my wisdom teeth have to come out."

Jamie watched Destiny pull away in her Mercedes. Max came up beside her and put his hands on her shoulders. "That woman needs help," Jamie said. When Max chuckled, she went on. "And you're only encouraging her."

"I'm just trying to find a killer. Any way I can," he added.

"You don't think it's strange for a woman to show up at my door at midnight looking for a ghost?"

He grinned.

"It's not funny, Max," she said. "If you want to play ball with her and her imaginary playmate, go for it, but I'm out." He removed his hands from her shoulders, and Jamie wished she hadn't been so brusque with him.

"If you don't want her around, tell her," he said. He glanced at his wristwatch. "Look, I need to be going. I've got to make a few phone calls."

"At this hour?"

"I'm calling countries in a different time zone. Besides, we're both tired. How about I catch up with you tomorrow?"

Jamie felt her jaw drop. He was leaving? Just like that? She didn't want him to go.

Or maybe they needed a little distance. If Max stayed they would finish making love, and if that happened she was a goner. Once she made love with Max Holt she would fall hopelessly in love with him. She didn't have time to fall in love, not with a murderer on the loose.

"Maybe that's best," she said at last.

Max climbed into his car and started the engine. Muffin came on. "Boy, that was quick. I figured the two of you would go at it all night."

"Very funny."

"Uh-oh," Muffin said. "I can tell by the sound of your voice it didn't go well. Did you guys have an argument?"

"No."

"I'm confused," Muffin said. "What's the problem? Why this constant tug-of-war? It's obvious the two of you are hot for each other."

"OK, Muffin, I'll level with you. I'm beginning to worry that Jamie might want more out of this relationship than I can give her."

"So is this the part where you tell the woman in question that you can't possibly make a commitment and you try to soften the blow with flowers?"

Max didn't answer.

"Because if it is I'm telling you right now it's not going to work," Muffin went on. "You're not willing to let Jamie go. Face it, Max. You've got it bad."

Max didn't respond at first. "Do me a favor, Muffin," he said, changing the subject. "I want you to check out a Destiny Moultrie for me. I want to know everything you can find on her."

"So we're not going to talk about it, is that it?"

He didn't try to keep the irritation from his voice when he spoke. "I don't want to talk about Jamie right now if it's all the same to you."

A few minutes later, Max pulled into the parking lot of his hotel and parked. He sat there for a moment

162

before getting out of the car and making his way to his room. He gazed at the empty bed, thought of Jamie alone in hers. Shit.

Jamie awoke to the smell of Fleas's breath on her face. "Oh, God!" she cried, shoving him away. "I hope you haven't been licking yourself again."

He simply stood there, watching and waiting.

"You need to go out, is that it?" She dragged herself from the bed and headed for the back door with him on her heels. She paused to unlock the door, and he bumped into her. Dog and master exchanged looks. "You do that every time," Jamie said. "You know I'm going to have to stop and unlock the door, but you insist on running into me. Why is that?"

He thumped his tail once.

"And why am I in such a sour mood this morning?" Suddenly she remembered. She frowned as she opened the door so Fleas could go out. Max had just walked out on her the night before. Just walked out. She wished it didn't bother her so much. She wished she knew where she stood with him.

"Stop kidding yourself," she said aloud. "You know exactly where you stand." That's what hurt. It didn't matter that they were just itching to climb into bed together; the fact was Max didn't want anything permanent, and she was just going to have to accept it.

It was time she faced facts.

Fleas made straight for Jamie's one rosebush. Worse, he glanced back at her as if to say, "So what're you gonna do about it?" He hiked his leg and whizzed right on it. Jamie gave a sigh, went inside and turned on her automatic coffee maker. It gurgled to life.

Her stomach growled. She wondered if Max was going to show up with doughnuts. She wasn't counting on it; it was already seven o'clock, and he would have been there by now. He was probably sitting in his hotel room practicing his great rejection speech. Well, he could shove it as far as she was concerned. She didn't need him any more than he needed her. She had her pride.

Still, it hurt. They had been through so much together. How could a man look at her the way Max did and not feel something? How could he touch her and kiss her and remain so casual about it? Well, she wasn't made that way.

Fleas scratched at the door, and Jamie let him in, then she went into the bathroom. Fleas followed. Jamie stared at her reflection. Her hair was a mess, her mascara smudged. Her sleep shirt bore more wrinkles than Fleas's face. She glanced down at the dog.

"Would you just look at me?" she said. "I've let myself go."

Fleas cocked his head to the side as though trying to understand.

"We can't continue living on junk food," Jamie went on. "We're both at the age where we need to start taking better care of ourselves or our arteries are going to need Drano to get them unclogged. You know what that means? No more doughnuts and ice cream."

Fleas sank to the floor and put a paw over one eye. Jamie knew he didn't understand a word she said — he

164

mainly reacted to her tone of voice — but one would have thought he was capable of taking in her every word.

"Yep, this means I need to start eating more vegetables, and you need to eat that expensive dog food I buy you. I'm serious, pal," she said, trying to convince herself as much as him. "I'm going to turn over a new leaf today, and I'm going to get Max Holt out of my system if it kills me. I'm never eating one of those brownies again."

Jamie went into her bedroom and changed into a pair of sweats, an old T-shirt, and running shoes. Fleas watched her, as if he expected something big was about to happen. Jamie tried to remember when she had last done anything that resembled jogging. Jeez, she would probably have a heart attack before she cleared the driveway.

Fleas followed her outside. It was already muggy, the air thick with humidity. She could literally feel it on her face and arms. If only the weather would break. Jamie regarded Fleas. "You can't go jogging because you just got neutered," she told him. "Besides, it requires physical activity, and we both know that's not your strong suit."

As if he understood, Fleas walked over to the nearest tree and plopped down in the shade. Jamie began doing a few stretches to prepare her poor body for what she was about to put it through.

She did not see the French poodle dash across the yard, but the next thing she knew Fleas was howling in protest, and a poodle was trying to mount him. Fleas darted behind Jamie as if hoping she could protect him.

"Oh, good grief!" a woman cried. "Precious, you stop that this instant!"

Jamie glanced in the direction of the voice. The woman wore a tight polka-dot dress and spike heels, had big blond hair, and she was doing her best to walk through the high grass in Jamie's yard. "Dammit, Precious, I said stop!"

Jamie stared in disbelief as the poodle chased Fleas around a large oleander bush. Finally, Fleas skirted around the back of the house with the poodle right behind him.

"Miss, I am so embarrassed," the woman said. "Precious tries to mount everything in sight. It's like he has just gone off the deep end. It's so embarrassing."

"Your dog is a male?" Jamie asked. "So is mine."

"Yes, he's a male, but that wouldn't stop him. It's humiliating." She sighed heavily.

"I'd better check on my dog," Jamie said, worried that Fleas would pull his stitches out running from the dog. The last thing she needed was another vet bill. She hurried around the back of the house with the woman behind her. Fleas had found refuge in the old truck Jamie had parked in her back yard. The poodle was jumping up and down like a yo-yo trying to reach the tailgate.

"I think it'll be OK now," Jamie said. "Your dog doesn't seem to be able to reach the bed of the truck." She took another look at the blonde, who seemed to be in her early forties. "I don't recall seeing you before. Are you new in the neighborhood?"

"Oh, yes, I'm renting the house next door. My name is Barbara Fender."

"Jamie Swift." Jamie saw the woman's eyes suddenly widen, and she turned. Max had arrived with coffee and doughnuts.

"Who is that hunk?" Barbara whispered.

"His name is Max."

"Is he your boyfriend?"

"Well, um, it's complicated."

"All relationships are complicated," the woman said sourly. "You ask me, they're not worth it."

Jamie found herself nodding in agreement.

"Sorry I'm late," Max called out. "I had to make a lot of calls this morning." His eyes combed her in her baggy sweats. "Nice outfit."

Jamie felt like crawling beneath the truck, but she was afraid the poodle would start humping her. "I was about to go for a run."

"Why? Is your car on the blink?" Max looked at the woman beside Jamie. "Hi. I'm Max."

"Barbara."

All at once, the poodle raced toward Max and started humping his leg. "Nice to meet you, Barbara," he said, trying to shake the poodle off. "Is this your dog? I have to admit I've always had a fondness for poodles. My grandmother raised them. I just can't remember any of them liking *me* this well."

Barbara tried to get her dog under control. Finally, she grabbed him and picked him up. "Precious is going through a difficult time right now. I'm so sorry."

"No need to apologize," Max said.

"Barbara is moving in next door," Jamie explained. Max nodded, and they were all silent, each of them obviously at a loss for words. "Would you like to join us for a cup of coffee?" Jamie asked, although she knew she didn't sound sincere. She was eager for the woman to take her dog home.

As if sensing Jamie was only trying to be polite, Barbara shook her head. "I think I need to get Precious home," she said, "but thanks just the same."

Max and Jamie waited until she'd disappeared inside her house before trying to convince Fleas to get down from the bed of the truck. Finally, Max pulled out a doughnut, and the hound climbed down, took the doughnut and almost swallowed it whole before racing toward the house.

"Wow, I've never seen Fleas run like that," Jamie said.

"How come you didn't want your neighbor to have coffee with us?" Max asked.

Jamie looked at him. "What makes you think I didn't?"

"You're usually friendlier. Even to people you've just met."

"I think it had a lot to do with her kooky dog."

"You don't like her."

Jamie didn't respond because he was right. It could have been her imagination, but she hadn't appreciated the way Barbara had looked at Max. But then, he always drew stares from the opposite sex.

Oh, jeez, she had been jealous. She had all the symptoms of being in love. She could try to convince herself otherwise, but she knew better.

Problem was, Max probably knew, as well. That was the worst part.

CHAPTER
ELEVEN

Max followed Jamie inside the house with the bag of doughnuts. "About last night," he began.

"I'd rather not discuss last night," Jamie said, avoiding eye contact. "We've got a murder to solve."

"I'll grant you that, but we probably need to discuss what's going on between us."

Jamie looked at him. "And what *is* going on between us, Max?"

"It's complicated."

"Funny, that's the same word I'd use."

"I have very strong feelings for you, Jamie. The last thing I want to do is hurt you."

"Save it, Max. I think I know where this is going."

He stepped closer. "I don't think you do."

"Then tell me."

He hesitated. "I don't want to lose you. But I'm not sure what our future holds. I spent most of the night thinking about you. I need time."

Jamie knew better. Time would not change anything. "I really have a lot on my mind right now," she said, wanting to change the subject. Max did not have to spell it out for her.

"I know," he said softly. He was quiet for a moment. "So, you were going jogging, huh? You look like you're in pretty good shape to me."

She shrugged.

"I have doughnuts," he said.

Damn the man. He knew doughnuts were her weakness.

"Would you rather I leave?"

That was the last thing she wanted. "No."

Max offered Fleas another doughnut. The dog inhaled it. So much for her plan for the two of them to start eating healthy food, Jamie thought.

The doorbell rang, and Jamie turned toward the door. Max looked at her. "What is this, Grand Central Station? Don't you ever have time to yourself?"

"Vera's test-driving another car," Jamie said. "She called earlier, wants me to have a look." Jamie opened the door before Vera had time to ring the bell a second time. The woman was dressed in a purple pantsuit and hot-pink scarf. It was obvious she'd taken a lot of time with her hair and makeup.

"What do you think?" she asked Jamie, turning around so Jamie could get a better look at her outfit. "My preacher's going to have a hissy fit when he sees me coming down the aisle for communion this morning."

"You look great," Jamie said.

"I feel great. I figure age is just a state of mind, know what I mean?" She didn't wait for a response. "Quick, come check out the cool wheels I'm test-driving. I don't have much time because I'm going to the early church service, then a bunch of us girls are attending the singles breakfast. Let the guys get a load of me in this outfit. 'Course, they're too old to do anything about it if you get my drift."

Jamie glanced past Vera and found herself looking at a white Jaguar. "Oh, jeez."

"It's eight years old," Vera said, "but you'd never know it. Isn't it beautiful? The dealer said he can give me a really good deal on it."

Jamie looked at her. "Why can't you buy something sensible?"

"Because I don't want to ruin my new image," Vera said. "Besides, I can afford a car like this as long as it's not brand-new."

"I think you'd better have Max look at it," Jamie said. She turned, almost bumping into an amused Max.

"A Jag, huh?" he said to Vera.

"Yeah. Would you mind taking a look at it?"

Max followed her outside where he spent a few minutes checking it over before Vera pulled away.

"I shouldn't have lent her the red Mustang," Jamie said. "I've created a monster."

"She's just having fun," Max said. "Speaking of which, why don't you and I spend the day investigating a few of the guys, then have dinner tonight."

Jamie wrestled with the thought. It was tempting.

"Say yes, Jamie."

She wanted to go in the worst way. "What should I wear?"

"Something a little dressy," he said. "And wear that black thing underneath it."

172

Jamie's stomach fluttered. She was playing with fire, and she was likely to get burned.

Destiny arrived at Jamie's house an hour later.

"I'm sorry if I sounded rude last night," Jamie said. "I still don't believe in all this otherworldly stuff, but we do need your help."

Destiny shrugged. "Like I said, I'm used to it." She looked at Max. "I drove by Larry's car lot on the way over and saw the new Corvette you mentioned parked beside the building so he's obviously working. I also picked up a pair of binoculars."

Max handed her a photo of Johnson. "This should help."

Jamie arched a brow. "How'd you come up with such a good picture in so little time?"

"Holt Technology, Swifty."

"Why aren't you going to the police with your suspicions?" Destiny asked.

"And tell them what?" Max said. "We don't have anything on him. Yet," he added.

"He's very angry," Destiny said. "I picked up on that right away."

"You've got that right," Jamie said, then realized it was the first time she had agreed with anything Destiny said.

"Oh, by the way," Max said, "I'd like for you to try and meet with the chef today if you have time."

"What excuse is she going to use?" Jamie asked.

Destiny smiled. "I'll come up with something. I don't have trouble meeting men."

"Dumb question," Jamie said.

Max grinned. "I'm going to have Jamie pretend to have car trouble so we can get a look at the mechanic, then we'll try to set up a meeting with John Price, the accountant."

"What about the other guy? Sam Hunter?"

"Don't worry, I've been saving him for you," Max said. "Why don't you call him today and see what you can work out."

"Tell me this," Destiny said. "If he's rich and good-looking, why would he run an ad in a personals section?"

"He just moved back to town and is obviously looking for a way to meet women. He appears clean, but the fact Luanne Ritter died only a week after he moved back to Beaumont makes him a suspect. *If* the murder had anything to do with the personals section. Plus, I have his cell phone record proving he and Luanne talked. She must've written to him the minute his ad hit the paper. I suspect she contacted everyone who ran an ad."

"She must've been very lonely," Destiny said.

Jamie spoke. "They could have met for drinks or dinner, but Sam decided she wasn't his type."

"Not a very good reason to kill her," Destiny said. She suddenly looked annoyed.

"What is it?" Jamie asked.

"Oh, it's just Ronnie being a pain in the ass as usual. Like I told you, he doesn't like the fact that I might actually meet a man and find him attractive. It's like I'm supposed to be content hanging out with spooks all

174

the time. This Sam Hunter sounds like a real catch to me."

"If he's not a killer," Max reminded her.

Destiny nodded. "Yes, well, a woman has to draw the line somewhere."

"We have to work out a plan so that I'll be available at all times for each of you," Max said. "The rules remain the same. You each carry the cell phone, and you avoid being alone with these men at all costs." He looked at Jamie. "Understood?"

She nodded.

Max checked his wristwatch. "Jamie, I'm going to need the keys to your car. I'm going to pull it out of the garage and make a few adjustments under the hood so you'll have a reason to call the mechanic."

"I'm confused," Destiny said. "Why can't Jamie just call him, like I did the dentist?"

"This guy didn't list his telephone number in the ad," Max said, "so my, um, assistant had to find him through other sources."

"John Price didn't list his phone number in his ad," Jamie pointed out.

"We're going to use a different angle. You'll tell him you own the newspaper and that you were intrigued by his ad."

"Is that what you told Larry Johnson?" Destiny asked.

"No. He thought we were looking for a car."

Jamie went for her car keys while Destiny called the chef and made a date for later that day. When Jamie returned, she called the mechanic, who promised to be

175

there in an hour, mentioning there would be an extra fee for coming out on his day off.

Jamie then called John Price, explained she owned the *Gazette* and had gotten the information from his ad. At first he was cool toward her, but he finally agreed to meet for coffee later in the day. "I don't think Mr. Price appreciated me contacting him the way I did," she said after she hung up. "Perhaps I should have written him via our post office box."

"That would have taken too long," Max said. "What other impressions did you get?"

"He sounded very cautious. I have a funny feeling he's hiding something."

By the time Jamie walked into the Downtown Café for her meeting with John Price, the mechanic, a good old boy by the name of Carl Edwards, had made the necessary repairs to her car and had asked her out. She'd taken his phone number and promised to get back to him. "Edwards might be a flirt," she'd told Max once the man left, "but he didn't come off as a murderer."

Max had shrugged. "Since when do murderers wear signs?"

John Price was in his mid to late fifties, a tall man with salt-and-pepper hair, dressed in neat slacks and a golf shirt. He looked embarrassed when Jamie approached the table.

"I was afraid of this," he said, standing until she was seated.

"I beg your pardon?"

176

"I thought you sounded a little young on the telephone. I probably should have asked your age."

"Is age an issue with you?"

"It is when the woman you're meeting for coffee is the same age as your daughter."

"I doubt that," Jamie said. "I'm thirty years old, not exactly a kid."

The waitress appeared and took their order for pie and coffee. "So, you own the local newspaper," Price said.

"Yes. It has been in my family for years."

"I'm sorry if I sounded rude to you on the telephone, but I was very surprised to get your call since I hadn't listed my number in the newspaper."

"I took it off the information you sent with your ad," Jamie said. "I didn't mean to infringe on your privacy," she added, "but I was intrigued. Your ad said you were open to new experiences. What exactly does that mean?"

He chuckled. "My doctor has accused me of showing signs of a midlife crisis," he said. "First thing I did when I turned fifty was buy a brand-new Harley and start dating younger women. My second wife was fifteen years my junior. Bad move on my part; we've since parted ways." He quickly changed the subject. "Now, I'm thinking of taking flying lessons."

Jamie noticed he had an easy smile. "Sounds interesting," she said.

The waitress appeared with their order.

They talked for an hour. Finally, John picked up the check. "Jamie, I had a delightful time, but I suggest you try meeting someone your own age. With your looks, you shouldn't have any trouble."

She glanced up in surprise. "Am I being rejected?"

He laughed. "No, but I would feel silly dating a woman twenty-five years younger than me. Please don't take it personally."

They said goodbye with a handshake. Max waited just down the street at Maynard's Sandwich Shop. "Mr. Price dumped me after the first date."

Max shrugged. "That's OK, you still have me."

Jamie didn't respond.

Destiny showed up later that afternoon. "The chef is about a hundred pounds overweight. Naturally, he's looking for a long-term relationship. I think he's already found one in food. I spent the rest of the day watching Larry Johnson. He didn't leave his car lot. He was the only one working today. I'm not surprised, since it's Sunday."

The three sat around the table discussing their findings and brainstorming. Finally, Destiny left.

Max stood to leave a few minutes later. "I need to go back to my hotel and make some calls," he said. "How about I pick you up around six?"

"Sounds good," Jamie said. "Where are we going?"

"It's a surprise."

Jamie walked him to the front door. He paused and looked down at her and for a moment she thought he might kiss her. Instead, he turned and headed for his car.

She sighed and leaned against the doorjamb. Now, why, when the timing had been perfect, hadn't he

178

kissed her? She looked at Fleas. "See what I mean? I never know where I stand with that man."

Fleas responded by walking over to the refrigerator and glancing up at the freezer. "You're right," Jamie said. "When the going gets tough, the tough eat ice cream."

Muffin was waiting when Max climbed into the car. "I've taken care of everything you requested for your date tonight," she said. "Your plane will be here within the hour, and I made reservations at your favorite restaurant in New York City. Once you get off the plane, a limo will be waiting to take you there."

"Thanks," Max said. "You think Jamie will be impressed?"

"I think Jamie would be happy eating a barbecue sandwich at a local restaurant," Muffin said, "but if this is the way you want to play it, go for it."

Max was quiet. "You think I'm going overboard?"

"Hey, what do I know? She'll either think you're showing off or she'll be flattered. And since when do you worry what a woman thinks?"

"This is different."

"If I know Jamie, she'll be touched by your efforts."

"Were you able to get anything else on Sam Hunter?"

"I found nothing to indicate the man is not who he seems to be. No police record." She paused. "I'm beginning to wonder if Luanne's murder had something to do with her business. She had a lot of enemies."

"Lamar Tevis is checking into it."

"Which means we could be looking in the wrong place."

"I hope you're right, Muffin, but if you're not there's a good chance we're going to have another murder on our hands before long."

CHAPTER
TWELVE

Jamie was ready and waiting for Max by quarter of six. She wore a simple black dress with spaghetti straps, matching heels, and carried a small purse. The black see-through body suit beneath it, her purchase from Sinful Delights, was strapless and hugged her tightly. After her talk with Max she wondered why she was wearing it.

She was taking a big chance, and she knew it. She was risking a broken heart. Max Holt had made it plain he didn't know what their future held; he had not promised her happily-ever-after. But he had a hold on her heart, and there wasn't a damn thing she could do about it.

"How do I look?" she asked Fleas, who was napping in front of a kids' TV show since she did not allow him to watch anything with sex or violence. He didn't budge, didn't bat an eye. Jamie knew he was pouting because she was going out. It didn't take a genius of a dog to realize she didn't wear her best black dress every day,

And Fleas was no genius.

"OK, be that way," she said, "but I deserve a night out once in a while. It's not like I don't try to take you with me everywhere I go. Lord, you even go to work with me."

Still Fleas made no movement.

"And I was going to give you another bowl of ice cream before I left. That's two in one day for you, pal."

Fleas suddenly raised his head. He might not be a genius, but he had learned to recognize the words *ice cream* and *doughnuts*.

"I knew that would get your attention," she said.

He thumped his tail and pulled himself into a standing position. Jamie watched him make his way into the kitchen where he sat down in front of the refrigerator and waited.

The doorbell rang. Jamie had been so busy trying to get a response from her dog that she hadn't heard Max pull up. Her stomach did a series of tiny flip-flops as she opened the door. Max stood on the other side looking like something off a magazine cover in a dove-gray suit and blue shirt and tie.

Several seconds passed before either of them said anything.

Finally, Max spoke. "Are you wearing anything under that dress?"

Of all the questions he might have asked, Jamie had not expected that one. "Um, not much."

"You know, Swifty," he said, stepping inside, "we could always stay in and order takeout."

"You look pretty good yourself, Holt."

"If we don't leave soon —"

"I just need a couple of minutes," she said. "I promised Fleas he could have ice cream."

"Of course."

Max followed her into the kitchen where Jamie dipped out a healthy serving of butter pecan ice cream into Fleas's bowl. The dog never took his eyes off her. Finally, she set it down before him. "There now. He's had his dinner, and I let him out, so he should be OK until I get back." Jamie grabbed her purse, and they started for the door.

"Aren't you going to turn off the TV?" Max asked.

"No, he likes having it on while I'm gone. It helps with his separation anxiety." Max shook his head sadly as they stepped outside. He took the keys from her and locked her door while Jamie waited, then he walked her to his car. She was nervous. This seriously smacked of a date, and she and Max weren't in the habit of dating. What did it mean? Was she reading more into it than she should? Max was right. She did too much thinking. Couldn't she for once allow herself the luxury of enjoying herself without all the what-ifs? Just for once?

Max helped her into the car and closed the door. He climbed in beside her.

Lord, but he smelled good, she thought.

They were on their way in minutes. "It's quiet in here," Jamie said. "Where's Muffin?"

"She's not feeling well so I gave her the night off."

"What do you mean she's not feeling well? She's a computer."

He shook his head. "She's been researching all this pregnancy stuff for Deedee so she's suffering the same symptoms."

"Tell me you're kidding." Not that Jamie should have been surprised. Muffin had gone through menopause when it seemed as if Deedee were suffering the symptoms and Muffin had researched it. "That is the craziest thing I've ever heard," she added.

He smiled. "So is feeding your dog ice cream in front of the TV set. It's a strange world in which we live, Swifty."

Max reached over and took her hand. He raised it to his lips, and his gaze met hers. "Have I told you lately that you're beautiful?"

Jamie felt her heart in her throat. Was it her imagination or did he seem different tonight? His eyes searched her face. What was he looking for? Did he suspect the depth of her feelings? She was the first to look away. "Thank you, Max," she said at last.

It was almost as if they'd unconsciously agreed not to discuss Luanne Ritter's murder and their investigation as Max drove through town. Instead, he filled her in on what was happening at Holt Industries. Jamie was amazed at what she heard. Not only was Max on the cutting edge of technological research, he was involved in biomedical research and pharmaceuticals, among other things. He had offices all over the world. She listened as he described where some of his research could actually lead. It seemed there was nothing the man wasn't interested in exploring.

Jamie arched one brow when he took the road that led to the small airport.

"Where are we going?" she asked.

"I told you, it's a surprise."

Jamie's jaw dropped clear to her collarbone when Max pulled up near the runway where a medium-sized jet waited with the words "Holt Industries" emblazoned on the sides. Lights were flashing, and airport personnel hurried about. Two pilots stood near the steps of the plane, each dressed in khaki slacks and navy blazers.

"Good evening, Mr. Holt," one of them said as soon as Max pulled to a stop and stepped from the car.

Jamie's door was immediately opened, and the other pilot helped her out. "It's a beautiful night for flying," he told her with a smile.

Max held out his elbow as Jamie, still gaping, took it and walked with him toward the jet. "We've filed the flight plan," the older pilot said. "We're ready to go. Our ETA at LaGuardia is eight-thirty."

"LaGuardia?" Jamie asked as Max prodded her up the steps leading inside the luxury cabin. He nodded. "But that's in New York City," she said.

"I told you I wanted to take you someplace nice."

Jamie stepped inside the cabin and found herself enveloped in luxury. The sizable sitting area was done in a rich tan, but there were touches of navy blue that set it off.

She turned and looked at Max as the pilots disappeared through a curtain in the cockpit. "I've never been on a jet like this."

"It's perfectly safe if that's what you're worried about. I'll show you around if you like."

They took a tour of the front area first, the lavatory, a small galley, and a built-in cabinet that held a stereo,

185

DVD player, satellite phone, and whatever else Max might need in order to relax or conduct business during his flight. Finally, he led her to the back of the plane where a small but more than adequate bedroom was situated, complete with a bathroom that included a small tub.

"Holy mackerel," Jamie said. "It's got everything."

"I specifically designed it so I could rest during international flights." He studied the look on her face. "How about a glass of champagne?" he said. "I usually have a flight attendant on board when I travel on business, but I wanted us to be alone tonight."

Jamie smiled. She felt like Cinderella. Someone had even thought to put out a plate of hors d'oeuvres. "Except for the pilots, of course," she said.

Max nodded. "Yes, I'm afraid there was no getting around that, but they won't bother us. Please —" He motioned toward one of the sofas. "Sit down and relax, and I'll open the champagne."

Jamie did as he asked, but it was all she could do to keep from gawking. The jet should come as no surprise, she reminded herself. Any man who drove a two-million-dollar car was bound to have a nice jet.

Lord, if Vera could see her now.

She jumped when she heard the champagne cork pop. A moment later, Max carried in an ice bucket holding a bottle; in his other hand were two flute glasses. He poured them each a glass and toasted her, just as one of the pilots told them to fasten their seat belts for takeoff.

"To you, Swifty. For bringing so many good things into my life."

She didn't want to think what that meant. "From the looks of it, you already have a lot of good stuff." The plane started moving.

"A man can have all the material things he needs and still be lacking. You fill up that empty space."

Jamie couldn't have been more surprised. What did it mean? "That's the nicest thing you've ever said to me, Max." They touched glasses and took a sip of their champagne.

"Maybe I should start saying more nice things," Max said. "Seems we spend all our time chasing bad guys."

"You may have something there, Holt. Feels like we're always knee-deep in trouble."

"Yeah, but you'll have to admit we make a great team. The bad guys don't stand a chance."

She laughed. "Yeah, but we've had our share of close calls."

"I like that you're adventurous."

"I haven't had much of a choice since you came into my life."

"True. But you'll have to admit I'm not boring."

"I'd settle for boring once in a while. I'm allergic to bullets."

"I guess I like a challenge now and then."

"Now and then, Max? You would never be happy living a normal life."

"What do you consider normal?"

A house surrounded by a picket fence came to mind, but Jamie suspected the thought would scare him to death. It would smack of settling down, and she doubted Max would ever be satisfied with such an existence. "Maybe there's no such thing as normal after all," she said after a moment.

"You know what I think?" Max said. "I think you need to be challenged, too. And you know what else? I want to kiss you." He took her glass and set it on the coffee table in front of the sofa.

She didn't protest as he placed his hand beneath her chin and lifted her head slightly before gently touching his lips to hers. Jamie found herself leaning into the kiss, and she welcomed it when he took her in his arms and held her close. He kissed her temple and her eyelids and pressed his lips against the hollow of her throat before capturing her lips once more.

Jamie clung to him, loving the taste and smell and feel of the man who held her. She reached up and curled her hands around his neck. The kiss deepened, and Max slipped his tongue past her lips, exploring the inside of her mouth, tasting her thoroughly. Jamie boldly met his tongue with hers. She felt him draw a quick breath of excitement.

Max gathered her up in his arms and stood, tugging off her heels as he went. Jamie knew where they were headed, knew she wanted Max Holt as much as he wanted her.

It had been that way from the beginning. Their gazes locked as Max carried her into the bedroom. He dipped his head forward and kissed her again. Just like in the movies, she thought. Once again, lips parted, tongues mingled. Jamie could feel her insides growing

188

as soft as warm butter. For once she didn't think about what tomorrow or the next day might bring.

She was willing to take a chance.

She felt the bed sink beneath her as Max gently laid her on the mattress. He turned long enough to close the door and lock it, and then he began removing his clothes. He draped them over a chair. He never once took his eyes off her face.

He was naked and already aroused when he joined her. He raised her, up slightly, just long enough to unzip her dress, which he draped over his own clothes. "Oh, Jesus," he said, staring at the filmy black body suit. "I'm going to buy stock in the company that makes those things."

Once again, he was beside her, kissing her, running his hands over her body. Using his tongue, he teased her nipples through the fabric of the body suit.

"Oh, Swifty." He smoothed one hand over her hip, her belly, then slid one finger along the lace edge of the body suit, slowly, leisurely.

Jamie moaned and arched against him. She reached for him, but he smiled. "We're in no hurry, sweetheart. Just lie back and enjoy."

Jamie closed her eyes as he pulled the wispy fabric from her body and kissed his way down, pausing only briefly between her thighs before touching her with his tongue. She cried out softly. He flicked his tongue lightly over her before parting her with his fingers and tasting her fully. Jamie's breath caught at the back of her throat.

When she could no longer stand it, Max entered her, and it was all she could do to keep from crying out.

Max paused for a moment as if he needed time to get himself under control "Damn," was all he could say in a shaky voice.

They began to move together, slowly at first, but each thrust from Max's body brought them closer to the edge. Jamie could feel the intensity building with sweet anticipation, even as Max's brow beaded with sweat, and he gritted his teeth in an obvious attempt to restrain himself.

Jamie was the first to feel the burst of pleasure, a pleasure so intense that she called out to Max who immediately joined her in the last frenzied moments.

They clung to each other long afterward, waiting for their heartbeats to slow, waiting for the fog of passion to lift. Jamie snuggled against Max, knowing as long as she lived she would never want another man the way she did the one beside her.

"Max?"

He pulled her close. "Yeah?"

She wanted to tell him how she felt, confess her love, but fear alone prevented it. "I've never felt this way before," she said instead. There, she'd said it.

He kissed her forehead. "I knew we'd be good together, Swifty. I knew it the first time I saw you."

It was probably the closest she was going to get to what she'd wanted; an admission of love, but Jamie said nothing. Instead, she made to get up.

Max tightened his grip on her. "Where do you think you're going?"

190

"I saw a small tub in the bathroom. I thought —"

He interrupted her with a kiss. "There's plenty of time for that." He pulled her face close to his for another kiss.

Lord, she was a goner.

Jamie was touching up her makeup when Max re-entered the bedroom and told her they needed to prepare for landing. She followed him into the sitting room, fastened her seat belt, and waited until the plane touched down and came to a halt, and the captain gave them the OK to move about the cabin.

Max checked his wristwatch and ushered her off the jet into a waiting limo. Jamie had never felt so pampered. The driver immediately whisked them away.

"I've never been to New York City," she said.

"You live in one of the prettiest towns I've ever seen," he said. "Why would you want to leave it?" Max hit a button, and a window slid up, separating them from the driver. He grinned and pulled Jamie onto his lap. "It's only half an hour from here to the restaurant," he whispered. "I'm putting you in charge."

Jamie shivered when his tongue made contact with her ear. "In charge of what?" she asked.

"Not letting us get carried away back here."

"You're talking to the wrong person, pal," she whispered as she snuggled against him and raised her lips to his for a kiss.

Emilee's was an intimate French restaurant with tiny white lights attached to a dark ceiling that gave one the feeling of dining beneath the stars. After sharing an appetizer of pâté de foie gras and wafers, Max and Jamie ordered filet mignon with a béarnaise sauce that Jamie claimed was to die for. Max teased her unmercifully as Jamie ordered chocolate pecan pie for dessert, but it was obvious he enjoyed watching her while he sipped his coffee.

"You remind me of a little girl sometimes," he said, when she caught him staring. "I don't think you ever had the chance to be a little girl when you were growing up."

A slight shadow crossed Jamie's face. "It often feels like I grew up too fast, but my dad and I had some pretty good times together."

Max smiled. "Tell me,"

Jamie looked wistful. "He took me to Charleston from time to time, and we would eat at nice restaurants and visit the art gallery or the museum. I would wear my prettiest dress. My dad was the best. I don't remember a time he scolded me, except when I wanted to leave college and work full time at the newspaper. He wouldn't hear of it."

"I'm glad you have so many good memories of him," Max said.

"Vera said he spoiled me shamelessly, and I guess he did."

"Why do you suppose he never remarried?"

Jamie's eyes clouded. "I don't think he ever got over my mother leaving him. He kept her clothes for the longest time. Vera finally made him give them to the Salvation Army."

"He never dated?"

"No, And it wasn't because he didn't have the opportunity. My father was a handsome man. Would you like to see a picture?" Jamie didn't wait for a response; she was already reaching into her purse for her wallet. She flipped it open to the image of a dark-haired man and handed it to Max.

"I can see the resemblance," Max said. He returned the picture. "You must've loved him very much."

Jamie nodded. "I was devastated when he died."

"Why do you suppose Vera never married?" Max asked, changing the subject.

"Vera was in love with my father, Max," she said simply.

"I guess I've always assumed as much," he said.

"She's never admitted it to me, but I knew."

"I wonder why she never told him."

"Vera's a proud woman. She would never have made her feelings known because he spent his life grieving the loss of my mother."

"Do you miss her?" Max asked.

"How can you miss someone you never knew?" Jamie pondered the question. "There were times, of course, when I wanted a mother. I envied the girls at school whose moms helped with parties or participated in school outings. Not that Vera didn't help out," she added quickly, "but it wasn't the same."

"I'm sorry, Jamie."

"Don't be. I had all the love and attention a kid could have possibly wanted. I just hope —" She paused and blushed.

Max waited. "What do you hope?"

Jamie met his gaze. "I just hope, if and when I have children, that I'm a better mother."

He smiled. "You'll be a fantastic mother, Jamie."

"I don't know," she said. "I've already spoiled Fleas something awful, and he's a dog."

Max laughed, and the two continued conversing for more than an hour before he signaled for the bill. Once he'd paid, he looked at Jamie. "Now, tell me. Is there anything in particular you'd like to see while we're in New York?"

It didn't take long for her to answer. "Times Square."

"You got it, Swifty."

The limo was waiting when they left the restaurant. Jamie stared out the window, awed by the skyscrapers that disappeared into the night sky. "I can't believe all the people," she said, noting the crowded sidewalks. When Times Square came into view, Max had the driver open the sunroof of the limo so Jamie could peer out.

"It looks just like it does on TV," she said, feeling a surge of excitement as she gazed in delight, much like a child on Christmas morning. They spent an hour riding through the streets before Max told the limo driver to stop at Sardi's where they had coffee.

When it was time to head back to the airport, Jamie turned to Max. "Thank you," she said.

Max smiled at her enthusiasm. "It was my pleasure. I'd like to bring you back during the day so you can see Central Park. I would love to take you to other places, say, Paris and Rome and Hong Kong, just to see them through your eyes."

"Don't you enjoy them?"

"Most of my travel is business related."

"Max, this is me you're talking to. I'm sure you've had your share of lovely companions."

"Does that bother you?"

It did, but she wouldn't admit it. "It's none of my business." Still, she wondered how many women he'd taken with him on his private jet.

"There are different types of relationships, Jamie. Some are more meaningful than others."

She paused and met his gaze. Her heart thumped wildly in her chest. "Yeah?"

"Some are nothing more than two people providing, as you say, companionship. Both people are mature enough to know up front that it isn't likely to last. Then there are those worth hanging on to."

Jamie stared back at him for so long she was sure her eyes had crossed. What the devil was the man trying to say? "You know what your problem is, Max?"

"Uh-oh."

"You don't know what you want."

"Or maybe it's that I want something so badly, and I don't know where it will lead," he said ruefully. "Ever thought of that?"

Was he referring to them? she wondered. "Are you scared? That's hard to believe."

"I'm human."

Jamie saw the vulnerability in his eyes. "People take risks when they fall in love," she said softly.

"Do you love me, Jamie?"

Her heart turned over in her chest. He had just asked her the million-dollar question. "I don't know," she hedged. "I keep telling myself it would be a mistake."

"Why?"

The look in his eyes was sincere. He wanted to know. "I don't think we're looking for the same thing, Max."

"Would it matter if I told you I'm looking for a way to spend more time in Beaumont? Frankie and I are discussing the possibility of bringing much-needed industry to the area."

"How come nobody told me?"

"It's still in the planning stages."

"What would you manufacture?"

"The same material my car is made of. It's a newly identified polymer that is lightweight but has the durability of the strongest steel. Think if that same material could be used on other automobiles. It could save a lot of lives. I just need to find a way to make it more affordable to the consumer."

"And you'd lower the unemployment rate in Beaumont," she said. "Oh, Max, this is exciting news."

"It's confidential for now," he said. "I don't want it announced until we know it's a sure thing." He paused. "The main reason I'm telling you is because I want you to know I'm hoping to be around more. If that means anything," he added.

Jamie's stomach turned somersaults at the thought. "I could probably adapt," she said.

"Yeah?"

"Yeah."

196

They arrived at the airport and boarded the plane. Once they'd taken off and were able to move about the cabin, Max and Jamie found themselves back in his bedroom where they made love until the captain announced they would be landing soon. They dressed hurriedly and took their seats in the front cabin. Jamie couldn't stop grinning.

"Why are you smiling?" Max said.

"Why do you think I'm smiling? I've been flown to New York on a private jet, eaten at a fancy restaurant, seen Times Square, and I've been laid three times."

Max laughed out loud. "The things you say. That's what I like best about you."

As Max drove Jamie home shortly after three a.m., she leaned her head back in the seat and sighed happily. "Thank you, Max, for a wonderful evening."

"We should do it more often," he said.

They arrived back at Jamie's house, only to find Destiny's car sitting in the driveway. Jamie frowned. "I don't believe this," she said. "What is *she* doing here at this hour? I'm beginning to think she's following me."

"I'm beginning to think the same thing," Max said in annoyance, surprising Jamie.

Jamie suddenly felt afraid. "I hope it's not what I think it is." She rushed from the car as soon as Max parked.

"Oh, thank goodness you're finally home," Destiny said.

"What on earth are you doing here at this hour?" Jamie demanded.

"I've had several visions." She suddenly sneezed. "They were awful."

"We're listening," Max said, still sounding irritated.

"It's about the next victim," Destiny said, looking directly at Jamie. "She's going to be somebody you know."

CHAPTER
THIRTEEN

Jamie felt as though her breath had been knocked out of her. "Oh, my God!" she cried. "Who is it?"

"I can't get a fix on the person," Destiny said.

"Come inside," Jamie said, noting that the woman was trembling badly. There was fear in her eyes.

"Ronnie is with me."

"He can come in."

Jamie handed a silent Max the keys to her front door, and he started ahead of them as Jamie and Destiny waited. Once inside, Max, maintaining his silence, put on coffee.

"Now, tell me what you saw," Jamie said.

Once again, Destiny sneezed. "Like I told you, the victim is going to put up a fight, and she'll leave scratches on the murderer's arms. But I can't get an image of a face or name. But I'm positive you know her." Destiny began to wring her hands. "Do you have any friends who might answer a personals ad?"

"No one I can think of."

They moved to the kitchen as soon as Max had the coffee ready. "Max, I think we should go ahead and notify the police," Jamie said.

"Lamar can't find out the kind of information I can. Muffin is working around the clock doing background checks."

"Muffin is out of whack right now," Jamie said, "since she talked to Deedee. She thinks she's pregnant, remember?"

"She's still able to do her job."

"Your secretary is pregnant?" Destiny asked Max.

Max shifted in his seat. "She just thinks she is."

"Has she seen a doctor?" Destiny asked.

"It's a long story," he said, "but she's good at background checks. As a matter of fact, she did one on you."

Jamie turned to the woman. "Max does background checks on everyone. He even did one on me."

Destiny didn't give him a chance to respond. "So you think you know all about me, do you?" she said, anger having replaced the scared look in her eyes. "If you're so smart, tell me what you've learned."

Max didn't hesitate. "I know that before you married into money you made your living as a fortune-teller in one carnival show after another. I know you were arrested more than once for operating illegally out of your home. You've changed your name several times."

"My real name is Betty Sue Jenkins," Destiny said. "Of course I changed it. Who's going to take a psychic seriously with a name like that?"

Max looked at Jamie. "She's been married five times, and the authorities exhumed the body of one of her husbands because his children suspected poisoning."

200

Destiny hitched her chin high. "They found nothing. His kids were a bunch of spoiled brats who resented the fact I was awarded the bulk of their father's estate. And do you know *why* I was awarded it? Because I was a damn good wife to him, and I was the one who cared for him when he was sick. His children couldn't be bothered."

Jamie realized she was staring and rubbing Fleas's head frantically. The dog seemed as agitated as she was. She stood, as well. "I don't care about Destiny's past, Max. All I care about is finding a killer. You're the one who said we should use every means possible."

"I don't need you to defend me, Jamie," Destiny said. "I've lived with this sort of thing all my life. I'm going home now and get some rest." She paused to sneeze. "I'm sorry I bothered you."

She was gone. Jamie sank into her chair and looked at Max. "What's going on?"

"I'm beginning to have my doubts about her. She hasn't given us anything we could go on. I wasn't going to tell you what I found out at first, but I don't appreciate her barging in at this hour and scaring you. And think about this. Suppose she did get away with poisoning her husband. That would make her a murderer. Luanne Ritter's murder didn't occur until after Destiny Moultrie hit town, right?"

Jamie gaped at him. "You're not insinuating that Destiny killed Luanne. What would be her motive? She didn't even know Luanne Ritter."

"We don't know that. She could have done business with Luanne."

"She doesn't need money; her husbands left her well off."

"I just think it's possible that Destiny might have ulterior motives. I'm not entirely certain what they are, but her past speaks for itself."

"My instincts are pretty good, and I believe Destiny has a good heart. Her only motive for contacting me was to write a column for the newspaper, but she got dragged into this situation when she had a vision about Luanne Ritter's murder. Maybe it's all been just one big coincidence after another, but I believe she saw something tonight. You saw how upset she was. The woman was terrified."

Jamie got up and let Fleas out, then went about picking up dirty coffee cups. All at once she heard Fleas yelp. She and Max raced to the door.

The poodle next door was chasing Fleas across the back yard. "Oh, it's that damn poodle again," Jamie said, racing out the door, just as her neighbor, Barbara Fender, hurried out of her back door.

"Precious, come here this instant!" the woman cried, although the dog paid no heed. She and Jamie reached at the dogs at the same instant. Barbara pulled her dog free, and Fleas took off for the pickup truck parked close by.

"Jamie, I am so sorry," the woman said. "Precious woke up having to go to the bathroom."

Jamie noticed the woman had changed her big hair. It had been cut into a flattering style and colored, giving her a softer look. Jamie felt bad that she hadn't tried to get to know her better; the woman probably didn't know a soul in town. Then Jamie reminded herself she'd been too busy trying to catch a killer.

As though realizing Jamie was staring at her hair, Barbara touched it self-consciously. "What do you think?" she said. "I figured it was time for a change. New town, new people, new hairstyle."

"I think it looks nice," Jamie said. She smiled. "Tell you what. I'll call you first chance I get. We'll get together, and I'll tell you about my dog's emotional problems. Then you won't feel so bad."

"I'd like that," Barbara said.

Max joined them. "Come on, Fleas," he said, trying to coax the hound from the back of the pickup.

"He's not going to get down," Jamie said.

Max finally picked up Fleas and carried him into the house. Jamie and Barbara said good night, and Jamie headed for her house. She found Max inside feeding the dog cheese curls. "There you go, spoiling my dog."

"He deserves it after what he's been through. That's the ugliest poodle I've ever laid eyes on."

"Are you OK, boy?" Jamie asked her pet. But he was more interested in the cheese curls. Finally, Max poured the rest of the bag into Fleas's bowl. Max checked his wristwatch. "Wow, it's almost four a.m. I'm beat, how about you?"

"Exhausted," Jamie said.

"You need to get to bed."

"I was thinking the same thing."

He slipped his arms around her waist and kissed her lightly on the lips.

"I'm just so confused, Max. I don't know what to think anymore. If Destiny is right —" She paused and shuddered. "I don't even want to think what might happen."

"I should get going," Max said, although he looked reluctant. "You need your rest."

"Yeah, like I'm going to be able to sleep. I'm afraid, Max."

His look softened. As if to ease the tension, he suddenly smiled. "If I stay your neighbors will think you're a floozy."

She knew he was trying to lighten the mood. "Everyone already thinks I'm a floozy, not to mention the town drunk."

"Frankly, I liked seeing that side of you. I hope to see more of it." He released her.

The last thing she wanted him to do was leave. "Um, Max?"

"Yeah?"

She made a poor attempt at trying to return his smile. "If I let you stay will you still get the doughnuts after we wake up?"

When Jamie awoke it was after ten o'clock. She bolted upright on the bed, just as Max came into the room with a tray of doughnuts and coffee.

"Don't panic," he said. "I called Vera and told her you would be late coming into the office." He set the tray on the bed. "Breakfast is served."

Jamie suddenly realized she was naked. Then she recalled that, despite both of them being tired when they'd gone to bed at four a.m., they had made love again. She had needed him desperately, had needed to feel his lips on her body, feel him inside her. Only Max could chase away the fear in her heart and give her something good to cling to. Exhaustion had forced her eyes closed afterward, but at dawn she had jerked awake in the throes of a nightmare. Max had gathered her close, coaxing her to sleep once more with his steady voice at her ear.

Now with the sun up, she felt less afraid. What she did feel was self-conscious at being stark raving naked. She pulled the sheet higher over her breasts.

"No need for that," Max said. "I've already seen every square inch of you, and I like it."

Jamie blushed and reached for her cup of coffee. "How do my eyes look?" They felt gritty from lack of sleep.

"They look very blue and beautiful, as always."

She noted Max was dressed in casual clothes. "You've been up a while."

"Yeah, I drove over to my hotel and showered. I needed to change clothes."

Jamie quickly ate two doughnuts and polished off her coffee. "I've got to grab a shower," she said. She glanced around. "What happened to my sleep shirt?"

"I have no idea."

"Max?" Her voice was stern. He'd probably tossed it in the trash. "Oh, what the hell." She climbed from the bed and turned for the door leading toward the bathroom. She could feel Max's eyes on her. "Take a picture, Holt," she called back over her shoulder.

"Don't need to. I've already burned your image in my brain."

Jamie was thankful when she reached the privacy of her bathroom. She turned on the shower, waited for the water to heat up, and climbed in. She thought of Destiny's visit the night before and experienced the same sense of dread. She tried to push it from her mind. Maybe Destiny was wrong. Hadn't she admitted that her predictions weren't one hundred percent accurate? Maybe this was one of those times. Jamie prayed that was the case, but she still remembered the look of fear in the woman's eyes.

She shook her head, trying to clear it. Since when did she believe in Destiny's visions anyway? Anybody who claimed to have a dead spirit following them everywhere they went had to be a little kooky, didn't they? Didn't they?

She was too wrapped up in the case, Jamie told herself. She had other work to do. She needed to check her schedule so she could have lunch with Maxine Chambers. Or maybe she could get together with her new neighbor. Barbara was probably anxious to start making friends; and she most likely needed a break from all her unpacking.

Jamie did not hear the door open, but the shower curtain suddenly parted and Max stepped in as naked as the day he was born.

"What the —"

He smiled. "I've often wondered what it would be like to take a shower with you."

"Isn't this your second for the day?"

206

"Yeah, but who's counting? Give me your soap and washcloth."

"I can do this myself, you know."

"Come on, Swifty, give a guy a break."

Jamie did as she was told. Max lathered the washcloth and started at the nape of her neck, working his way down to the heels of her feet. The feel of his hands on her body did wonderful things to her insides, made her forget everything else.

"OK, turn around," he said.

She turned. Max busied himself washing her breasts, leaning forward to tongue each nipple once he rinsed them of soap. Jamie was suddenly enveloped in a world of sensations and tingling nerve endings. "I usually shower in half this time," she managed.

"Yeah, but think how dull it is to shower alone." He worked his way down her abdomen, her flat tummy, and finally between her thighs where he explored her with deft fingers. Jamie moaned; all logical thinking ceased, worries dissipated like smoke in a breeze. She grasped his shoulders for support as he brought her to the height of pleasure.

She was trembling by the time she climbed from the tub and toweled herself. She caught the glint of desire in Max's eyes, the slight tilt of his mouth. He knew damn well what he did to her. She glanced down at him.

"As you can see, the feeling is mutual," he said, as he dried himself. He smacked her behind lightly and chased her into the bedroom.

Jamie giggled like a schoolgirl. It felt good to laugh. "I have to go to work," she protested.

"It'll wait," he said. "Besides, I'll be there to help you."

They fell onto the bed together. Jamie suddenly felt less shy with him. She ran her fingers over his chest, and nipped one of his nipples playfully.

He shivered.

"You're asking for trouble, Swifty," he said.

"You ain't seen nuthin' yet, bubba." She toyed with his chest for a moment before lightly running her fingers down his stomach where the hair thinned slightly and then she moved lower. She stroked him. Finally, using the very tip of her tongue, she tasted him.

"Oh, God, I'm a dead man," he said.

Jamie smiled and put him in her mouth. Max gazed down at her with a look of dazed passion. The husky moan he gave prodded her onward.

Jamie swirled her tongue around him. It was exhilarating to know she could wield so much power over a man who was accustomed to calling all the shots.

Finally, he pulled away, eased her gently onto her back, and using his own tongue, brought her to the edge of orgasm. She moaned and reached for him, and he entered her. Their sighs of pleasure rose like music.

Max moved against her slowly at first, but soon they were caught up in an erotic dance, and Jamie's cries were stifled by Max's kisses.

Afterward, Max gathered her in his arms, where Jamie snuggled against him like a soft kitten. She felt safe and secure.

"A man could get used to this, Swifty," he said.

She nodded, reveling in the fact that she had Max Holt spent and naked beside her. Her hand on his chest measured each heartbeat, and she remained quiet until his breathing slowed. She could smell the heady scent of their lovemaking mixed with Max's soap and aftershave.

Jamie rose up on one elbow and gazed down at him, a self-satisfied look on her face. His own expression was lazy and contented. "A woman could get used to this, too, Holt."

"Yeah?"

"Yeah." She knew she was grinning too broadly for any sane woman; that Max would take one look at her goofy expression and guess the truth. Just as she had expected, she had fallen head over heels in love with him, and there wasn't a damn thing she could do about it.

It was almost noon by the time Max and Jamie arrived at the newspaper office, with Fleas in tow. Vera was dressed in a fire-engine-red pantsuit and tall heels that she seemed to have trouble maneuvering. She handed Jamie a large stack of mail.

"I have to leave for a while," Vera said, "because a bunch of women from my church are picketing Maxine Chamber's lingerie store this morning. I want to be there to take pictures."

"Why don't people leave the poor woman alone?" Jamie said.

"Because she's displaying unmentionables in her front window," Vera said. "And wouldn't you know it; Agnes Aimsley's grandson is the ringleader. Most folks don't like Maxine anyway 'cause she was such a snooty librarian."

Jamie gave an enormous sigh. "I don't believe this. I'm going with you, but I'll be the opposition. The woman has a right to run her business without a bunch of old church ladies interfering."

"I'm with you." When Jamie looked surprised, she went on. "After all, this is a free country. Besides, I've been thinking I might buy one of those push-up bras she has in her window. I might just give Destiny Moultrie a run for her money." She grabbed her camera. "This could be good headline material, you know."

"I need to make a few calls," Jamie said before Vera hurried out the door. "Maxine is going to need support." Deedee was first on her list. She was outraged and promised to call her friends. Jamie then called several old high school buddies, all of whom promised to meet her outside Maxine's store and rally their support. She even phoned Destiny.

"I've got to run," she told Max, who'd walked in on the tail end of one of Jamie's calls. "A bunch of old church biddies are going to picket our new lingerie store, and I'm going to try to put a stop to it."

"I thought we had a paper to get out."

"This won't take long," Jamie promised. "But I can't just sit back and do nothing while an army of angry

210

women descend on Maxine Chambers's place of business." She hurried out the door.

By the time Jamie arrived at Maxine's shop there were at least fifty women gathered out front, many of them chanting, "Close this store!" Agnes Aimsley and her grandson were right in front. A nervous Maxine peered out the window. Jamie gave her the thumbs-up, and the woman looked relieved to see her.

Jamie spotted Deedee, Beenie, and Destiny and hurried over. "How many do we have on our side?" she asked.

"We just arrived," Deedee said, "but I don't think we have more than ten or twelve. Those church ladies look pretty vicious if you ask me."

Beenie appeared anxious. "I wish I had stayed home. I'm afraid they'll kick my butt."

Jamie spied Vera on the sidelines, snapping pictures as fast as she could. "I need something to stand on," Jamie said. She hurried two doors down to Lowery's Hardware and returned with a ladder. She didn't see Max pull up across the street and get out as she climbed the ladder.

"Ladies, please hear me out," Jamie said, trying to talk above the roaring crowd of female voices. "At least give me a chance to have my say."

Brent Walker looked annoyed. "The town has spoken," he said. "We want Maxine Chambers to pack her slutwear and close shop."

Obviously feeling braver now that Jamie had arrived, Maxine Chambers stood at the front door of her shop, arms folded across her breasts, a defiant look on her face. "I have as much right to run my business as any other person," she shouted.

The crowd booed their disapproval. Jamie finally quieted them. "Maxine is right," she yelled. "As long as she pays rent she has just as much right to operate her shop as the next merchant. And without being harassed," she added.

"I can't believe you're taking her side, Jamie," Lyle Betts's wife, Lorna, said.

Jamie regarded the woman. "You don't have the right to judge Maxine," she replied. "Your husband is selling aphrodisiac-laced brownies and cakes with naked people on them."

All eyes turned to Mrs. Betts.

She squared her shoulders. "That's a lie. Lyle would never do something like that."

"Then I suggest you march right up to his bakery and demand to see his new 'Adults Only' catalog."

Brent Walker frowned. "I can't believe you're supporting this woman," he said, pointing at Maxine. "But that should come as no surprise what with your new personals ads. Men and women need to meet in church."

Jamie ignored him and turned to another woman. "And what about you, Mrs. Frazier?" she called out. "Are you going to tell me that you and Mr. Frazier don't have adult videos in your store? I know you do because I've seen them."

Mrs. Frazier looked embarrassed. "Some people enjoy watching that sort of thing. We have to keep up with our competition."

212

"And some people enjoy wearing pretty lingerie," Jamie said, "myself included."

The women gasped.

"There's a difference," Edna Wilburn said. "I love pretty nightgowns, but I wouldn't think of displaying that trash in my front store window. It's not fair that the rest of us are forced to see it every time we walk by."

Jamie hitched her chin high as she regarded the woman who was married to the owner of Wilburn's Garage. "You want to talk about what's fair, Edna?" she said. "Is it fair your husband charges a fortune for his work? Is it fair that he preys on women because he knows they have no idea what it costs for parts and labor to repair their cars?"

"Well, I never," Edna said in a huff.

"Jamie's right," Vera called out. "How do you think you got that new swimming pool?"

Edna looked shocked. "Why, Vera Bankhead, I never knew you felt that way about my George."

Agnes Aimsley stepped forward. "Maybe we can solve this like good Christians," she said in her fruity-textured voice.

Everyone glanced her way. "What do you suggest, Mrs. Aimsley?" Jamie asked.

Agnes didn't hesitate. "Why don't we all agree to stop bothering Maxine if she agrees to use a little more, um, decorum in her window display."

Brent looked at her in astonishment. "What are you saying, Gram?" He pointed to Maxine. "Why are you defending this, this —"

"Watch what you say, Brent," Jamie said. "You know what the Good Book says about judging people."

His face reddened. "I feel it's my Christian duty to clean up this town."

"Is that why you visited Luanne Ritter the night of her murder?" Jamie realized she'd gone too far the minute the words left her mouth.

The women went silent and fixed their gaze on the man. Brent shot Jamie a menacing look. "So you're the one," he said. "For your information the police have already visited me, and I've been cleared of any wrongdoing. Perhaps you should concentrate on running your newspaper, Miss Swift, and leave innocent people alone."

"Oh, why do we have to have all this bickering?" Agnes said. "Why can't we all get along?"

Jamie nodded. "Sounds like a good idea to me, Mrs. Aimsley."

The woman faced her grandson. "I like pretty nightgowns. I think Miss Chambers should be able to run her store as she sees fit. I don't know why everybody insists on making trouble for her. If people don't like what they see they should just stay away."

Finally, Maxine spoke up. "If you people will agree to leave me alone I'll take some of the more, um, offensive items out of my window."

"That sounds fair," Agnes replied.

Brent gaped at his grandmother. "Well, I for one refuse to give in to the devil's work." He looked at Maxine. "You'll pay for your actions. Mark my word." He stalked away.

Deedee stepped up. "I haven't been in your store before, Maxine, but Jamie has told me all about it. I plan to have a look before I leave here today."

"Me, too," Beenie said. "I love women's lingerie."

Jamie's high school friends promised to visit the store, as well.

All at once, a police car skidded to a stop and Lamar Tevis and one of his deputies stepped out. They were in uniform, but instead of wearing slacks, they wore shorts.

"What in the world?" Vera said to Jamie the minute she saw them. "Would you look at how Lamar and his deputy are dressed?"

"Oh, my," Beenie said, fanning himself. "Would you look at that deputy? I'd like some of that."

Even Jamie had to admit the shorts bordered on indecent. "I guess they changed to shorts because of the heat," she said.

"OK, ladies," Lamar said. "What's going on here?" He was tugging at his shorts as if he found them uncomfortable.

Jamie opened her mouth to speak, but was cut off by Lamar's deputy. "Lamar, these women are obviously picketing, and they don't have a permit. They're breaking the law. We'll have to arrest them."

This brought another gasp from the crowd. Jamie didn't know if they feared jail or were afraid the men would bust out of their shorts.

"I'm guilty," Beenie shouted, waving both hands in the air. "I insist that your deputy take me away immediately."

Lamar looked bewildered as he gazed at the crowd of women. "Are you sure about that, Joe?" he asked the deputy.

"Yes, sir."

Jamie stepped forward. "Lamar, you don't have a jail large enough to hold all these women." She tried to ignore Beenie tugging on her blouse.

"Well, that's true. But like Joe says, you're breaking the law, and I can't just stand by and do nothing."

Vera shot Lamar a dark look. "You wouldn't dare arrest us. Besides, nobody is picketing anyone. Maxine Chambers is holding a big sale, and we're standing in line to get into her store."

"I'm confused," Lamar said.

"That's obvious," Vera said, "or you wouldn't be dressed like that."

"Huh? Oh, you mean the shorts. I think the measurements were off because they're kinda snug."

Beenie moaned and bit his hand.

Jamie called out from her place on the ladder. "Ladies, Chief Tevis has the mistaken impression that we're picketing Maxine's store without a permit, which is against the law. We could all be arrested. But Vera just assured him that we're here for Maxine's grand opening sale, so what do you say? Who wants to buy a new nightgown today?"

Everyone in the crowd raised their hand.

Max looked pleased with Jamie when she crossed the street to his car. "Why are you grinning?" she asked.

216

"I'm proud of you, Swifty. You stood up for what you believed in. And from the looks of it, the lady who owns that store is going to make a hell of a lot of sales today."

Max and Jamie spent most of the day working to get the newspaper out on time and pondering what information Muffin had for them. By the time they sent the newspaper to press, both were tired. They dropped Fleas off at Jamie's house, and drove to a nearby Chinese restaurant for dinner.

Jamie noticed Max was quiet. "What's wrong?" she asked.

He shrugged. "I'm disappointed that we don't seem to be any closer to solving Luanne Ritter's murder than we were in the beginning."

Jamie nodded. "I'm worried, too, Max. Especially since Destiny said there was going to be another murder, and it would be someone I know." Max remained quiet. "I know I didn't take Destiny seriously at first, and I'm probably crazy for saying this, but what if, just what if she's right? What if the killer is still out there looking for his next victim?" When Max didn't respond, she went on. "Are you listening to me?"

"Yeah. You just don't want to know what I'm thinking."

She leaned back in her seat, noting the serious look on his face. "What is it?"

Max met her gaze. "We've never discussed this, but it's been in the back of my mind all along. If Luanne Ritter's murder had something to do with her business dealings, that's one thing. If her murder involved the personals section, that's a different story. But if he strikes again, it's a whole new ballgame, you know that, don't you?"

"What do you mean?"

"It means we're dealing with a serial killer."

Vera was oddly quiet when Max and Jamie arrived at the office the next morning with Fleas on their heels. Jamie spoke to her and grabbed the morning mail. When Vera didn't respond, Jamie looked up. The woman looked pale, the lines around her mouth drawn. "Is something wrong?" Jamie asked.

Vera glanced from Jamie to Max and finally Jamie again. "You haven't heard, have you?"

Max and Jamie exchanged looks. "Heard what?" Jamie asked.

"Maxine Chambers was found dead in the back of her store last night."

CHAPTER
FOURTEEN

Jamie dropped the mail and it scattered across the floor. She felt her stomach take a dive. All at once, her lips became numb, her knees rubbery, and she felt a blackness descending. Max noted it right away and reached for her. "Are you OK?" he asked.

"I — I need to sit."

He helped her into her office as Vera followed. "I'm sorry I just blurted it out," the older woman said, "but I haven't been myself since I heard the news."

"I think I'm going to be sick," Jamie said, sitting on the sofa.

Max immediately shoved her head between her legs. "Get some wet paper towels," he told Vera.

Fleas came to Jamie's side as though he sensed a problem. Jamie kept her head down until the nausea passed. Vera returned with the wet paper towels and handed them to her.

"What happened?" Jamie managed.

"One of Lamar's deputies saw the lights on when he drove by late last night and decided to check it out," Vera said. "The back doer was open."

"How did she —" Jamie couldn't say the word.

"Same as Luanne Ritter. A fatal blow to the head."

Jamie felt sick again; mopped her face with the wet towels.

"Take deep breaths," Max said.

She gulped in air.

"I feel so bad for her," Vera said, "Especially after everybody gave her such a hard time yesterday. I tell you, something isn't right in this town. I'm wondering if the two murders are connected in some way."

Max and Jamie exchanged looks.

Vera checked her wristwatch. "Oh, darn, I'm supposed to be at the doctor's office in fifteen minutes."

"Are you ill?" Jamie asked.

"No, it's just my yearly checkup, but if I cancel there's no telling how long I'll have to wait for my next appointment. Not that I'm in much of a mind to go," she added. She studied Jamie, as if unsure what to do.

Jamie continued to breathe deeply. "You need to go," she said between breaths. "I'll be OK."

"Are you sure?" Vera said.

"I'll stay with her," Max said.

Vera left a few minutes later. Max touched Jamie's shoulder. "How are you feeling?"

"The nausea has finally passed." She felt the sting of tears, blinked them back. "It's just such a shock."

Max retrieved the mail and placed it on the coffee table before her. "Is there anything I can do?"

"Yeah, we need to find the killer." Jamie glanced at the stack of mail and shuffled through it if for no other reason than to have something to do. There were five new ads for her personals section, but more than a dozen letters addressed to the Divine Love Goddess Advisor. She was surprised to find they'd written in so soon. She put the mail aside and looked at Max.

"Destiny was right. Not only do we have a new murder on our hands, I knew the victim personally."

"It's a small town, Jamie. You know a lot of people."

She wasn't listening. "Brent Walker," she said suddenly. "He threatened Maxine yesterday." She jumped as someone knocked on the door. Destiny peeked in.

"I heard the news on the radio and came straight over. Are you OK?"

Jamie shrugged.

"We'll find the person responsible."

"Yeah, but how many people have to die in the meantime?" Jamie's eyes glistened. "Poor Maxine. She had so many dreams for her store."

Destiny seemed at a loss for words. The three of them were quiet for a moment. Destiny glanced at the mail. "Is any of that for me?"

Jamie swiped at her eyes. "Most of it's for you."

They were interrupted by another knock on the door. Jamie wasn't surprised to find Police Chief Lamar Tevis standing there.

He glanced at Destiny, studied her a moment, then moved to Jamie. "From the look on your faces I take it you've heard."

Jamie nodded. "We all feel awful about it."

Lamar glanced at Destiny again. "Jamie, I need to speak to you and Max. In private," he added,

Jamie feared the worst was to come. "Lamar, this is Destiny Moultrie. She has been helping Max and me study the case. You can speak freely in front of her. But please, won't you sit down? Would you like coffee?"

Lamar shook his head as he sat on the sofa. "I've been up all night, had my quota of caffeine." He hesitated. "I'm afraid I have some more bad news for you. We searched Maxine's store and her house, and we found a clipping of the personals section from your newspaper on her kitchen table. We don't know if she actually called anyone, because none of the ads had been circled, but —" He paused and reached into his shirt pocket. He pulled out a sheet of paper and unfolded it.

Just what Jamie had been dreading.

"I have a court order here," he said, handing Jamie an official document, "for you to hand over any information you have on those who've placed or answered ads in your column. In the meantime, I'm going to request that you stop running the column. At least until we get to the bottom of this."

"I'll need to make copies for you," Max said, reaching into his briefcase for the file they'd started.

Jamie stood. Her knees still trembled. "I'll make them," she said, needing to do something. She hurried out to the reception area, thankful that Vera was not around to ask questions. When she returned with the copies, she handed them to Lamar.

He glanced through them. "Larry Johnson. Now there's a name I recognize. We've already had a few run-ins with him, a domestic-violence charge being one of them. Unfortunately, his wife dropped the charges."

"He has a serious alcohol and anger problem," Jamie said.

Max nodded. "When he's not working he hangs out at the lounge at the Holiday Inn."

"I see you've made notes on the rest of these guys," Lamar said. "That will be real helpful for us since me and my men have been focusing on Luanne's business dealings instead of the personals section."

"Destiny and I set up dates with these men," Jamie said. "At first blush they seemed harmless. Except for Larry Johnson."

Destiny spoke. "Don't forget he keeps a crowbar handy," she reminded Jamie.

Jamie looked at Lamar. "One in his car and one just inside his front door."

"You should probably check them for trace evidence," Max told Lamar.

"And let's not forget about Brent Walker," Jamie said. "He publicly threatened Maxine yesterday. I could be wrong, but I think the man has a few loose screws."

"He's been preaching on street corners, scaring folks half to death with talk of doom and gloom," Lamar said. "One of my deputies threatened to haul him in if he didn't stop. 'Course, Walker started yapping about freedom of speech and all that.

"We suspect he visited Luanne Ritter the night of her murder," he went on, "but we have no proof. He claims he was home reading Scripture. It's not exactly an airtight alibi; Agnes wasn't feeling well that night and went to bed early. I mean, who else would have left all that religious material in her mailbox?"

"There is one other person who could have put that religious literature in Luanne's mailbox," Max said. He told him about the Reverend Heyward. "He ran an ad. He's strange."

"Do you know if Luanne contacted him?" Lamar asked.

Max shook his head.

"Any return addresses on the envelopes of those who responded to the ads?" Lamar asked Jamie.

She shook her head. "Like I told Max, they would have wanted it confidential."

Lamar shuffled through the ads. "You've met with all these men?"

"Except for Sam Hunter," Max said.

"I've left several messages on his answering machine," Destiny said. "He must be playing hard to get."

Lamar looked at her. "If you don't mind my asking, what is your involvement in this case?"

"She's psychic," Max said.

"Oh, Lord, not one of *those*," Lamar said with a sigh.

"Actually, she has visions," Jamie told him. "She knew there would be another victim, but since we had nothing specific —"

"The scratches," Destiny interrupted. She looked at Lamar. "Maxine Chambers put up a fight before she died. She left deep scratches on the killer's arms."

Lamar looked from Jamie to Max. "Several of her fingernails were broken. I had my men bag her hands for nail scrapings. I'd like to have a look at Larry Johnson's and Brent Walker's arms. Would ya'll excuse me just a minute?" He got on his radio while Jamie and Destiny headed to the small kitchen for coffee.

"Maybe I could help you, Chief Tevis," Destiny said, once she and Jamie had returned with their coffee. "If I could take a look at the murder scene, you know, I might get a feel for something. I can't make any promises."

Lamar seemed to struggle with the idea. "The guys would laugh me right out of my job."

"But what if it works?" Max said. "What if it saves another woman's life? You won't know until you try."

Lamar finally relented. "Oh, OK, you can come with me, but don't tell the guys why you're really there. I'll think of something on the way over." They started for the door.

"I'll have to bring Ronnie."

"Who's Ronnie?" Lamar asked.

Jamie cleared her throat.

"Never mind," Destiny said.

Agnes Aimsley awoke in her easy chair with a start. She felt tired and haggard after a fitful night. She had awakened when Brent had come in after midnight, only to toss and turn for hours. She had finally given up on sleep and had risen at four a.m. She glanced at the clock, reached for her remote control, and turned on the midday news where the top story of the day brought a gasp from her lips.

Brent found her there when he came through the front door several hours later. The TV was off. Agnes hadn't moved from the chair except to answer the door once and make a cup of tea.

"What's wrong, Gram?" he said.

She didn't answer.

"Gram?"

"The police came by earlier."

He gave an exasperated sigh. "What do they want this time?"

"They didn't say. Brent, the most awful thing has happened. Mrs. Chambers was murdered last night."

"Who?"

"Maxine Chambers from the lingerie store."

"Oh, great, the police probably want to pin that on me, too."

Agnes looked at him. "What are you talking about?"

He sank onto the sofa and raked his hands through his hair. "They questioned me about that Ritter woman. I left some spiritual literature in her mailbox so they naturally assume I killed her."

"I don't understand. What was your business with Mrs. Ritter?"

Brent gaped at her. "Surely you know that she was hounding several members of the church, Gram. They had taken out loans with her and were having a hard time making payments. Ritter sent a couple of her goons out to scare them. These guys scared one of the members pretty bad. I'm surprised you haven't heard."

"I thought they were just rumors."

"Somebody had to take the woman to task," Brent said. "I felt it was my Christian duty."

"You visited her?"

Brent nodded.

"Do the police know this?"

He hesitated. "I don't want to involve you, Gram. The less you know the better."

"You've always been able to talk to me."

Brent clasped his hands together and stared down at the floor. "I had to lie to the police, Gram. I told them I never set foot inside Ritter's house. That's not true."

Agnes went deathly still. "What happened?"

"She let me in, said she'd give me five minutes to have my say. It turned into a yelling match. I was so mad." He raked his hands across his face. "I don't want to talk about it."

"You should have told the police the truth, Brent. It's not like you to lie."

"I had no choice. They're desperate to pin this thing on someone. And now they're going to come after me over that Chambers woman. I lost my temper yesterday, said some things I probably shouldn't have. My guess is somebody reported it. Probably that newspaperwoman."

Agnes suddenly looked afraid. "The police asked me if you went out last night. I told them yes, that you didn't come home until late."

Brent paled. "I was out driving around," he said. "Driving and thinking. I may as well tell you things aren't going well at school."

"Then I suggest you return immediately and straighten them out, young man," Agnes said sharply.

Their gazes locked. "Yes, of course," he said. "I can be packed and out of here in less than an hour."

Vera was not happy. "I can't believe you're going to pull the personals section to give that crazy woman more space for her Divine Love Goddess Advisor column."

"It's just temporary," Jamie said. "Did you see the stack of mail Destiny received?"

"Yes. It just goes to show you people aren't thinking straight if they're seeking information from somebody like her. They must be spending too much time in the sun. Or maybe they're eating too many of Lyle Betts's brownies."

Deedee and Beenie came through the front door. It was obvious Deedee had been crying. "We heard the news about Maxine, and we just stopped by to make sure you were OK. I know you liked her."

"Thank you," Jamie said. "It came as a real shock."

"And we wanted to invite you to lunch," Beenie said.

Deedee nodded. "That's right. We haven't had lunch together in ages. We used to do it all the time when I first moved here."

It was obvious they were trying to cheer her up. "I wish I could join you," Jamie said, "but I've been so upset over Maxine that I haven't been able to concentrate on my work, and it's going to be difficult enough meeting today's deadline. I need to stay here."

"Do you know if the police have any suspects?" Deedee asked nervously. "Do you know if Luanne

Ritter's death was connected?" she added, without waiting for an answer. "I shudder to think we have a killer walking the streets. I mean, what if he strikes again?" She had to pause to catch her breath.

"Deedee didn't take the news well," Beenie said, meeting Jamie's gaze. "She's really trying to be brave about the whole thing."

"I'm afraid the police don't know much at this time," Jamie replied, not wanting to give out too much information. But she was just as worried as Deedee about the possibility of another murder.

"Well, I for one am going to make sure my doors are locked at all times," Vera said.

Deedee took Jamie's hand in hers, squeezed it reassuringly, but it was obvious the woman was equally distressed. "Perhaps we'll have lunch soon?" Her bottom lip quivered.

Jamie offered the closest thing she had to a smile. "Of course we will. And try not to worry. It's not good for the baby."

Deedee nodded. "I promise." She and Beenie left a few minutes later.

"I need to talk to Max," Vera told Jamie, later that afternoon.

Max stepped out of Jamie's office. "Did I hear someone mention my name?"

Vera nodded. "You're just the person I'm looking for. I've decided I like Jamie's Mustang so well that I want you to find me one."

He shrugged. "That shouldn't be a problem. Any specific color?"

"Pink."

"Then pink it is. I'll get right on it."

"Just like that?"

"Just like that."

The rest of the day passed quickly for Jamie as she and Max worked together on the newspaper. By the time they sent it to press, Jamie was dog tired. Worry had etched lines on either side of her mouth, and when Mike Henderson had handed in his piece on Maxine Chambers, she'd asked Max to look at it.

Destiny came in for her mail as Max and Jamie prepared to leave the office. "I'm afraid I wasn't much help to Lamar. Ronnie was yakking in my ear the whole time so it sort of blew my concentration. He doesn't particularly like policemen since he had a few run-ins with the law when he was alive."

Jamie nodded as though it made complete sense.

"Oh, and guess what I did? I applied for a job as bartender at the Holiday Inn and they asked me if I could start tonight since they're short of help. I figured, what better way to watch Larry Johnson."

"Good idea," Max said.

"Do you know anything about making cocktails?" Jamie asked.

"No, but I suppose I can pick it up in no time. And here's the best news. Sam Hunter finally returned my call. He's going to come by for a drink tonight so we can meet."

"Just as long as you remember to stay in a public place with him," Max said. "Two women have died. We're not taking any chances."

Mike Henderson peeked in, and his eyes widened at the sight of Destiny. "Well, hello again. Have you thought any more about my offer to take you to dinner?"

Destiny stepped just outside the door with him. "I appreciate the offer," she said, "but I work nights."

"Oh, yeah? Well, that's no problem for me. I can pick you up after you get off."

Destiny smiled. "Look, Mike, I'm really flattered, but I'm sort of interested in someone."

He looked disappointed. "Oh, well, I guess that changes things," he said. "But, hey, if it doesn't work out you can always give me a call."

"How about we make it an early night?" Max told Jamie as they climbed into his car. "I'll call out for pizza. Besides, I need to be available for Destiny, even though I don't expect her to run into problems."

"Sounds good to me," Jamie said, although she didn't have much of an appetite. All she could think about was Maxine and hope the woman hadn't suffered.

Muffin came on, and Max filled her in.

"Did anyone check Larry Johnson's or Brent Walker's whereabouts last night?" Muffin asked.

"Lamar said he'd put his deputies on it," Max said.

Once home, Jamie checked to make sure her neighbor's dog was nowhere in sight, then let Fleas out of the car. After they had decided what topping they wanted on their pizza, Max placed a takeout order and started a bath for Jamie.

Jamie headed for the bathroom. She stripped off her clothes, climbed into the hot bath, and sank deep into the water.

Once again, she thought of Maxine. Maxine, who'd been so proud of her new shop, had finally taken a chance in life and gone after her dreams. Jamie had admired her for it and was sure they would have eventually become good friends.

Now Maxine was dead, and it was probably related to Jamie's new personals section. That was the toughest part.

Max returned some twenty minutes later with the pizza. Having dressed in shorts and a T-shirt, Jamie grabbed plates and silverware and set the table. She placed a slice of pizza on each plate, only to sit there and stare at her piece.

"Are you OK?" Max asked.

She looked at him. Tears pooled in her eyes. "I'll be fine."

Max pushed his chair from the table and reached for her. Jamie immediately went to him, and he pulled her onto his lap. She let her head rest against his chest.

"I feel responsible for all of this," she said.

Max pressed his lips against her hair. "Jamie, we don't know if the newspaper is involved, and even if it is, I've already told you, you can't control the actions of a cold-blooded killer." He paused. "You know, I've been thinking. Maybe we should leave Lamar to his investigative work and go away for a few days."

She gaped at him. "I can't leave while there's a killer on the loose." She didn't realize she'd raised her voice. "I can't believe you'd even suggest it. We have to find out who's behind this, Max."

"You're taking it pretty hard," he said. "I've never seen you like this."

Jamie opened her mouth to respond, but the doorbell rang. "Oh, damn, who could that be?" she said. She got up and made her way to the front door.

Beenie and Deedee stood on the other side.

"Oh, Jamie, I am so glad to see you," Deedee said, in her little-girl voice. "When you're in trouble the first person you want to see is your best friend." She walked into the living room with Beenie on her heels. He held Deedee's Maltese, Choo-Choo, Behind them stood a bevy of servants carrying luggage.

"What's wrong?" Jamie asked, noting Deedee's eyes were swollen. She'd obviously been crying again. "Did something happen?"

"It's Frankie and all his wrestling buddies," she said. "They're driving me crazy."

"Deedee needs peace and quiet in her, um, fragile condition," Beenie said. "She's not getting it at home, not with all those wrestlers around. They can be loud and obnoxious."

"So I've left Frankie," Deedee said. "I was hoping it would be OK if Beenie and I stayed with you until we found a place of our own. It is OK, isn't it?" Her staff began stacking expensive suitcases in the living room as Deedee spoke.

Jamie blinked back her astonishment. Of all times for Deedee to show up. "I, um, of course it's OK, honey. Come on in." She was only vaguely aware that Max had entered the room.

"What's wrong, Deedee?" he asked.

Beenie answered for her, "Frankie has totally lost interest in Deedee," he said. "All he does is hang out with his wrestling buddies."

Deedee burst into tears. "Beenie's right. Frankie doesn't seem to know I exist."

Fleas walked into the room and sniffed her dress. "Eeyeuuw! Is that your new dog? The one that came with the truck?" she added as she backed away.

"Yes," Jamie said, hoping Deedee wouldn't ask about the missing hair on his back. "I'm very attached to him. In fact, he sleeps with me."

"Eeyeuuw!" Deedee's jaw dropped clear to her collarbone. "What happened to his hair?"

Jamie sighed. "It's a long story, honey, but if you plan to stay you'll have to get used to him. He's really very sweet."

Deedee attempted a smile. "What's his name?"

"Fleas."

"Eeyeuuw!" Both Deedee and Beenie huddled together. Even one of the staff carrying in the luggage paused.

"You're joking, right?" Beenie said.

234

"I didn't name him that, and he doesn't really have fleas." Jamie paused. "You'll have to sleep with me," she told Deedee. Beenie can use the other bedroom."

"I thought you had three bedrooms," Deedee said.

"I converted one of them into an office a long time ago."

"I still think we should go to a nice hotel," Beenie said, staring at the dog with disdain.

Deedee almost snapped at him. "I can't go to a hotel. How would it look if the mayor's wife just up and left her husband? Especially after we've announced my pregnancy to half the town."

Max stepped forward. "Deedee, I'm sure you and Frankie can work this out. It's not often he and his wrestling buddies get together."

"Yes, but they've decided to stay a month. I can't take it. All they do is talk about the good old days and eat Vienna sausage, potted meat, and sardines right out of the can. They claim that's what they lived on before they became famous wrestlers." She shuddered. "And that's not the worst of it. Snakeman and Big John have tons of girlie magazines lying about. That's the last thing Frankie needs to be looking at since I'm going to blow up the size of a watermelon soon." She suddenly burst into fresh tears.

Beenie patted her shoulder. "There, there," he said. "You'll only ruin your makeup, and tomorrow your eyes will be twice as puffy. You're going to have to be brave for the baby's sake."

Max tried to calm her, but it was obvious he was accustomed to her dramatics. "Beenie's right," he said. "You need to calm down. For the baby's sake."

"How will I support myself?" she cried. "The only thing I've ever done is jump out of cakes at bachelor parties."

"Oh, that *is* going to be a problem," Beenie said. "You certainly won't be able to pay my salary on that." He suddenly brightened. "Oh, pooh, your husband will still take care of you. It's his child you're carrying."

"Excuse me, but where am I supposed to put these suitcases?" one of Deedee's staff asked.

Jamie pointed toward her bedroom. "How many bags do you have?"

"Only seven or eight."

Only seven or eight. Jamie realized she should be grateful there weren't more.

"Does Frankie know you've left?" Max asked.

Deedee shook her head. "He and his buddies went bowling. They'll probably go to Charlie's Sports Bar after that. No telling when they'll get in."

"He's going to call here looking for you the minute he finds out you're gone," Jamie told her.

"We won't answer the door," Deedee said.

"If he wants to see you badly enough he might break it down."

"You really think so?" Deedee looked hopeful.

"That sounds so romantic," Beenie said.

Max put his hand on Jamie's shoulder, "Listen, I hate to break up the party, but I think I'll just go back to my hotel. I have a lot of work to do. Besides, I know you're anxious to get your guests settled." Then he kissed his sister on her forehead and left.

"Well, now," Deedee said. "I suppose we should order something to eat."

"There's pizza in the kitchen that hasn't been touched," Jamie said, perturbed that Max had left her to deal with his histrionic sister. As if she didn't have enough on her mind.

"Pizza!" Deedee cried. "Eeyeuuw, that is so fattening. Do you have any lettuce?"

"You can't just eat lettuce," Beenie said. "You're pregnant. One slice of pizza isn't going to hurt you."

Jamie nodded. "Come on in, and I'll fix you a plate."

"Would you mind if I turned in early tonight?" Deedee asked. "Having all those wrestlers in my house has been exhausting, and I've been thinking about poor Maxine all day. I just want to rest."

"I second that motion," Beenie said on a sigh. "If she rests, then I can finally get some rest."

Jamie nodded. "You can turn in any time you like." She figured the sooner she got them to bed the better. At least it would give her time to think about how she could arrange a quick reconciliation between Deedee and Frankie.

Jamie was awakened at midnight by the ringing of the doorbell. It didn't take a rocket scientist to figure out who it was.

Deedee opened her eyes. "It's Frankie," she said. "Would you please tell him I'm never coming home?"

"Never is an awfully long time for a woman who is deeply in love with her husband and carrying his child," Jamie said. "As I see it we have two problems here."

"Oh, yeah?" Deedee looked at her.

"We have a woman going through hormonal changes which are perfectly normal, and we have a houseful of wrestlers who have overstayed their welcome."

"I'm too tired to go anywhere right now," Deedee said.

Jamie climbed from the bed and searched her closet for a bathrobe as Frankie began pounding on the door. The best she could come up with was a raincoat. She slipped it on and hurried into the living room. She spotted Frankie's worried expression through the peephole of her door.

"Jamie, I'm sorry to wake you," he said once she opened the door, "but I need to talk to Deedee."

He looked distraught. Jamie smiled and touched his shoulder. "Everything is OK, Frankie, so stop looking so concerned. Deedee is just very tired and needs a break from your wrestling buddies."

"She left me. She's never left me, not in twenty years of marriage."

"She's never been pregnant, either."

"It's because I haven't been giving her enough attention," he said mournfully, "but all that is about to change. My buddies are going home tomorrow, and everything will be back to normal." He took in her attire. "Is it supposed to rain?"

238

"I couldn't find my bathrobe. Listen, why don't you let Deedee sleep here tonight, and you can come over tomorrow and talk to her."

"Do you think she'll come back home?"

"Perhaps you should send roses before your visit. You know how Deedee loves roses."

It was as if a lightbulb had gone off in his head. "Yeah, that's what I'll do. And I'll start reading those baby books with her. I've been so busy with my friends I haven't had time for my own wife. Thank you, Jamie, for helping us out."

"Good night, Frankie."

Jamie closed the door and went back into her room. She shucked off her raincoat, draped it on a chair, and lay down. Deedee had already drifted off to sleep once more, her Maltese snuggled beside her. Sprawled across the foot of the bed, Fleas raised his head. He glanced at Deedee's dog, and gave a disgruntled sigh. "It's OK, boy," Jamie said. "Go back to sleep."

The dog needed no further prodding.

Jamie was pacing the floor, and Deedee sleeping soundly when the first of the roses began arriving. Beenie stumbled into the room in a satin Ralph Lauren dressing gown. He took one look at the roses and shrugged as though it were an everyday occurrence to find a living room half-filled with long-stemmed red roses.

"Coffee?" he whispered, sounding desperate.

"In the kitchen," Jamie said. "You'll find everything you need beside the automatic coffee maker."

Max arrived shortly after the second load of roses was delivered. He whistled under his breath. "Well, there goes the Rose Bowl parade this year. Have you heard from Frankie?"

Jamie told him about Frankie's visit the night before.

"Eeyeuuw!" Deedee cried from Jamie's bedroom. She appeared in the doorway a moment later in a lavish Christian Dior nightgown and robe. "Your dog is taking up half the bed." She paused at the sight of the flowers. "Are those for me?"

"Yep," Jamie said. "Compliments of Frankie. I don't know where or how he was able to find so many red roses, but it must've cost a king's ransom. Personally, I think you got his attention."

The doorbell rang. Max opened it, and Frankie stepped in looking handsome in a dark gray suit. His eyes immediately sought out his wife, and he hurried to her. "Deedee, I just dropped the guys off at the airport. Things will be back to normal now. Please come home."

"Things will never be completely normal again, Frankie," she said in her Betty Boop voice. "Don't you understand? We have a baby on the way." Her bottom lip quivered. "I'm not ready to come home. Please have the rest of my luggage delivered."

Jamie sighed inwardly. This was not going the way she'd hoped.

"Deedee, are you crazy?" Beenie said. "Frankie has put his friends on an airplane. He's willing to jump through hoops to get you back. This place is too small for three people, two dogs, *and* your luggage."

240

"I'll come back home when I'm darn good and ready," Deedee announced to Frankie, "and not a moment sooner."

A crestfallen Frankie left several minutes later, and Deedee disappeared into the bathroom for what she termed a well-deserved bubble bath.

Beenie shook his head sadly, "I'm going to have another cup of coffee," he said and made his way toward the kitchen, leaving a baffled Max and Jamie in the living room.

"Of all times for this to happen," Jamie said. "We've got a murderer to catch, and your sister and companion decide to move in. Are there any normal people in your family?"

"Yeah, a while bunch of them. But they're up in Virginia. Remind me to introduce them to you someday."

Lamar Tevis showed up at the newspaper office shortly after Jamie and Max arrived. "OK, here's what we've got so far. I have an eyewitness who claims he saw Maxine Chambers leave her shop with a man night before last. Unfortunately, it was dark so the witness couldn't give me a description of him. He recognized Maxine when she stepped beneath a street light, but the guy obviously kept to the shadows."

"Did the witness notice what kind of car the man was driving?" Max asked.

Lamar shook his head. "He didn't look since he saw nothing out of the ordinary. What we think happened is Maxine had a date with this man, and he took her back

241

to the shop afterward, probably so she could pick up her car. Maxine went back inside her shop, I believe, to pick up her deposit bag since it was her habit to make her deposits at the bank first thing each morning. Also, we found the deposit bag next to the body."

"Any sign of forced entry?" Max asked.

"Nope. She probably just ran inside to pick up the bag, not bothering to lock the door. She entered through the back. The killer had to have entered only seconds after she went in. Either her date followed her in or somebody was there waiting for her and slipped in right behind her."

"Anything taken from the bag?" Jamie asked.

"No. Which means robbery was not the motive."

"What kind of weapon was used?" Max asked.

"We found a baseball bat in a nearby Dumpster with blood and hair on it. We checked it out in the crime lab, and it's definitely the murder weapon. Unfortunately, there were no fingerprints."

"I don't know if this is going to help," Jamie said, "but Destiny Moultrie started working in the lounge at the Holiday Inn last night. Both Larry Johnson and Sam Hunter had a couple of drinks, but they left right after happy hour."

"Yeah, one of my deputies followed Johnson home. He was alone, and he didn't go back out. Could be he suspected he was being watched and decided to lay low." Lamar sighed. "I shouldn't have wasted so much time looking into Luanne Ritter's business dealings, This latest murder sheds a whole new light on things.

Two murders in a week. We don't know if and when this person is going to strike again."

Jamie felt a chill race up her spine.

CHAPTER
FIFTEEN

Vera's pink Mustang arrived later that day, looking as though it had just come off the showroom floor. The woman was ecstatic.

"I don't believe it," Jamie said to Max. "She only asked you yesterday, and you've already found one. How did you manage to find one so quickly?"

Max smiled as he watched Vera circle the car in delight. It was obvious he was enjoying her excitement. "Muffin and I had already made a lot of contacts when I was picking out the red one for you. It was just a matter of getting it here overnight." Max had already sent the driver to the airport in a taxi; the man would be flown home courtesy of Holt Industries.

Vera couldn't stop grinning. "It's perfect," she told Max, "and it fits the new me to a T. Wait till my friends see me driving it." She paused and suddenly looked worried. "Can I afford it?"

Max suddenly looked ill at ease. "I was hoping you would accept it as a gift. For all you've done for Jamie."

It was the first time in Jamie's life that she could remember Vera being speechless. Finally, the woman hitched her chin high. "I can't do that. It would feel as

244

though I were accepting charity, and I've always worked for what I wanted."

"It's a gift plain and simple," Max said. "If you don't want it then I'll have to go to the expense of sending it back. Now, why don't you take a spin in it and see how it runs."

Vera thought long and hard. "I don't know what to say," she said, looking genuinely touched.

"Just say thank you," Jamie told her.

"Thank you doesn't seem to come close," Vera replied, eyes suddenly tearing, "but thanks just the same." She hugged Max. "I can't wait to get behind the wheel."

Jamie was glad they had something to smile about after the past week. Luanne and Maxine's murders had left a dark cloud hanging over everyone's head. But Vera, more than anyone, deserved to be happy.

Jamie raised her eyes and met Max's gaze. His look seemed to reach right out and touch her. She offered him a silent thank-you, and was rewarded with a tender look.

That's what love is, she thought.

They were still standing in the parking lot of the newspaper office when Lamar Tevis pulled up. Vera showed him her new car, and although he tried to look excited about it, Jamie could tell his thoughts were elsewhere. She hoped it wasn't more bad news as she ushered him inside her office a few minutes later.

"You were right about Larry Johnson," he said. "I visited his ex-wife, and she told me he could be rather heavy-handed with his fist at times. The only reason she didn't file for a divorce on the grounds of physical cruelty was because Larry agreed to all the terms of the divorce, which means he walked away with the clothes on his back. Guess he didn't want folks to know he was a wife beater."

"I knew he was scum from the beginning," Jamie said.

"Yeah, he's real tough where the ladies are concerned," Lamar said, "but he didn't act so tough when we questioned him. He and Maxine Chambers had drinks together the night of her murder."

"So that's who the witness saw lurking in the shadows," Jamie said. "Maybe there was a reason Larry didn't want to be seen."

"Of course, Larry claims he never went inside her place of business," Lamar went on. "Said he met her at the door and drove her to the Holiday Inn. They had a couple of drinks and left. Said they didn't hit it off. Not a very good reason to kill someone if he's the one," Lamar added.

"Does he have an alibi for later that night?" Max asked.

Lamar shook his head. "Nope. But he offered to let us have a look at his apartment and car, so my deputies are combing them now."

Vera glanced at herself in the rearview mirror and tried to smooth the frown lines on her forehead. She was clearly irritated as she followed the highway that led to

Moseley, the next town, and the restaurant where she was to meet her date.

She sighed aloud. "This is ridiculous driving almost twenty-five miles for dinner," she told her reflection. "Whoever heard of such?"

Still a bit peeved, Vera turned off the highway a half hour later and located the restaurant. She checked her lipstick and stepped from the car. The air hung thick with humidity, but she didn't seem to notice as she smiled at her new Mustang. She stepped inside the cool restaurant a moment later and made her way toward the lounge where her date had suggested they meet. It was not yet six o'clock. John Price had agreed to meet for an early dinner so Vera wouldn't have to drive home in the dark.

The lounge was empty except for a couple at one end of the bar, and a man with broad shoulders and salt-and-pepper hair. He was neatly dressed in a navy blazer and white slacks. He stood and hurried over.

He smiled warmly. "You must be Vera. I'm glad you could make it."

She offered her hand. "I just want you to know I don't usually do this sort of thing, and I've most certainly never been in a bar, but your ad sounded so interesting I felt I should respond."

"I promise you won't regret it," he said.

"So what I'm thinking, once we find the killer — and we will find him, Jamie — we need to get away," Max told her once they left the newspaper office shortly after seven. It had been a long day, trying to deal with a

247

murderer on the loose and meet deadlines, as well. They'd been late finishing up, but the production manager, who normally would have complained about it, had taken one look at Jamie's face and kept quiet.

Now, Jamie was exhausted.

"We could fly up to my place in Virginia," Max said. "You need the rest and a little pampering. It'll take your mind off things."

Jamie didn't respond to his suggestion; she had more pressing matters on her mind. "Do you think Deedee had a change of heart and went back to Frankie today?" she asked.

"Oh, man, I'd forgotten about her," Max said. "Who knows?" Five minutes later, they had their answer when they found a catering truck in the driveway. The grass had been cut, the flower beds weeded and filled with pansies.

"Wow, would you look at that?" Jamie said, glancing at her house to make sure they were at the right one. "Are you responsible for this?"

He shook his head. "No, but it's pretty impressive. Looks like my big sister has been busy. Probably trying to keep her mind off her troubles." He parked and they went inside.

"Surprise!" Deedee said.

Jamie glanced around. "Deedee, what have you done?" Jamie asked, going from room to room. Most of the furniture had been replaced, and new window treatments put up.

"I called my decorator as soon as you left for the office this morning, and I told her you needed all new stuff. You'll have to admit yours was old and worn. I described your house, and she immediately sent a truckload of furniture in from Charleston. She's been here all day, just finished putting up the new curtains before you arrived. She left not five minutes ago. Isn't it to die for?" Deedee said.

Jamie shook her head, trying to take it all in. How Deedee had managed to get it all accomplished in one day was beyond her. Of course, she'd probably had a dozen people working as hard as they could. "I don't know what to say."

Beenie spoke. "I told Deedee you wouldn't appreciate her barging in and changing everything." He had his hand on one hip. "I just want you to know I had nothing to do with it. Oh, I did insist that Deedee not get rid of a couple of pieces that looked like antiques."

"This must've cost you a fortune," Jamie told her friend. She and Max went into the kitchen where they found two men filling cabinets and her refrigerator with various food items.

Deedee waved off the remark as she followed them. "I'm rich so I can afford it. You were out of groceries. Don't you ever buy food?"

"Fleas and I eat out a lot."

"Well, from now on you can eat healthy food. My chef is coming over soon to cook. We're having salmon with cream sauce, new potatoes, and Caesar salad. I've decided to go off my diet for the baby's sake."

Jamie looked at Max. "May I have a word with you?"

"Sure."

"Don't let us stop you," Deedee said. "We've got plenty left to do." She went back to supervising the men.

Max and Jamie stepped outside. "Has your sister lost her mind?"

"Probably," he said, "but you'll have to admit it was a nice gesture, and everything looks great."

"But I liked my place the way it was. I mean, I don't want to sound ungrateful, but it's going to take some getting used to. I'll be afraid to sit on the sofa."

"Do you like what the decorator chose?" he asked.

"It's beautiful."

"Then let Deedee do this for you," he said. "I'm sure it means a lot to her. When you've been given a lot in life it feels good to give something back."

"Is that why you gave Vera the Mustang?"

"I wanted her to have the Mustang and not worry about paying for it," he said. "But I was truthful when I told her the main reason. She's been like a mother to you. I can't help but appreciate that kindness."

"I guess I owe Deedee a genuine thank-you," Jamie said. "But that still doesn't solve the immediate problem. My place isn't large enough to accommodate three people and two dogs."

"So tell her."

"I can't tell her."

"Then I'll tell her."

"No, you can't tell her, either," Jamie said quickly. "It'll hurt her feelings. Plus, I'd feel like a real jerk after all she's done."

"OK, Jamie, what do you want me to do?"

"I want you to think of a way to get her and Frankie back together right away. I can understand that Deedee is going through all these hormonal changes, but why hasn't Frankie been a little more insistent about her coming home?"

"His pride has probably been hurt, plus he could be embarrassed. I'll drive over and see if there's something I can do. Frankly, I'm getting tired of worrying about everyone else. It leaves us little time to worry about what's really important here, namely us. And I want more time alone with you."

"I'm beginning to think that'll never happen."

"We have to make it happen."

"Things should settle down once all this is behind us," she said.

"I'm going to drive over and talk to Frankie now," he told her, a resigned look on his face.

Max headed for his car and Jamie turned toward her house. Beenie met her at the door. "Oh, darn, I wanted to ask Max if he'd stop by the store for me."

"Do you need something?" Jamie asked.

"Yes. Deedee made me pack in such a hurry that I didn't get a chance to bring all my toiletry items, and I really need to exfoliate."

"Can't you borrow what you need from Deedee?"

"I'm allergic to the products she uses." He tapped his lips with his index finger. "Oops, I almost forgot. Lamar Tevis called only minutes before you arrived. Wants you to call him right back. I hope he solves those two murders soon because I'm afraid to go out at night and Deedee is beside herself with worry."

Deedee came up behind him. "Beenie, why would you even bring up those poor women at a time like this? You know how upsetting it's been for me. I'll never get to sleep tonight thinking about it."

Jamie reached into her purse for her cell phone. She didn't want to make the call where she could be overheard, but the phone wasn't in her pocketbook, and she couldn't remember using it that day. Must've left it in her car, she thought.

"I have to run out to the garage," she told them. "I'll be right back."

Jamie hurried through the laundry room that led to her garage. Since Max had arrived she'd spent most of her time riding with him and using his cell phone, which probably meant hers was dead. She opened the door to her car and found the phone lying on her console. She reached for it.

All at once, she felt the hairs on the back of her neck prickle. She jumped and turned and found herself staring into Larry Johnson's face. A rush of adrenaline hit her.

"Hello, Jamie," he said.

She blinked several times. "What are you doing here?"

"I want to know what you told the cops. They've been on my ass ever since our date."

Jamie could smell the alcohol on his breath. "I don't know what you're talking about," she said, knowing it was best to lie.

"They questioned me about those two women who were murdered, and then they proceeded to search my

252

car and apartment. They took both crowbars." He stepped closer. "Don't you think that's a coincidence?"

"What I think is that you have no right hiding in my garage," she said, knowing he'd had to pick the lock on the door that led from the garage to the back yard. "You're trespassing."

"You're not only a tease, you're a bitch. Just like my ex-wife." He flexed both hands. "Somebody needs to teach you a lesson."

Jamie stiffened. "Are you threatening me? Because if you are, I'm going to scream this house down over our heads. My guests will come running. Now, get out of here and stay off my property or I'll have you arrested." Jamie punched the automatic garage door opener, and the door swung open. "Now," she ordered.

Larry's look turned menacing. "I'm not done with you yet, lady. You cause me any more trouble, and I promise you'll regret it." Jamie waited until he'd cleared the door before closing it. She suddenly realized she was trembling. She reached for the phone and called Lamar.

"I just wanted to let you know we didn't find anything on Larry Johnson," he said.

Jamie's voice quavered as she spoke. "He just paid me a visit." She told Lamar what had happened.

"Do you want me to pick him up?" Tevis asked.

"No, I think it would be better if your men just kept a close eye on him."

"Try not to go anywhere alone if you can help it," he said. "I think Johnson's dangerous, but I can't pin anything on him. I promise we'll keep trying."

253

"That was a wonderful dinner, John," Vera said to the man sitting across the table from her. The hostess had seated them in the dining room where all the tables were draped in crisp white tablecloths and napkins were folded fanlike at each place setting. "Thank you for inviting me."

"You only took a few bites of your prime rib."

"I guess I'm a little nervous," Vera confessed, her gaze falling on the small glass-enclosed candle between them.

John reached across the table and touched her hand. "I feel very fortunate to have met you."

Vera shifted in her seat. "John, may I ask you a question?"

"Of course."

"In your ad, you said you wanted to meet a woman for a discreet relationship. Why are you so concerned about discretion?"

He didn't answer right away. "I'm a very private person, Vera, and the last thing I want people to know is that I ran an advertisement in the newspaper to meet a woman. I know it's silly, but that's how I feel."

"Yes, well, my minister would certainly frown on that sort of thing."

"I've dated a couple of women in town, and I could tell up front that nothing would come of it, but I must say, you and I seem to have a lot in common." He grinned. "Anybody who drives a pink Mustang is definitely my kind of woman."

Vera smiled. "It's a new acquisition."

254

"Plus, if I might say so, you're very attractive."

Vera patted her hair. "Why, thank you, John."

The waiter brought their check. John Price pulled out a credit card and handed it to him, and the man hurried away. "I hope we can get together again soon," John said.

"I'd like that, too."

"Is tomorrow night too soon?"

Vera laughed. "Well, gee, I guess tomorrow is OK." She paused in thought. "You know, I wouldn't normally do this, and I don't wish to sound forward, but how would you like to come to my house for pot roast tomorrow evening? Everybody always raves about my pot roast."

"Wow, a home-cooked meal. It sounds great to me since I eat out so much. I'm afraid I'm not much of a cook."

Vera pulled a small notebook from her purse on which she wrote out her address and telephone number. "I'll expect you around seven."

John walked Vera to her car and waited until she climbed in. "I'll see you tomorrow night," he said.

She started her engine and pulled away. She was humming a tune under her breath as she turned onto the highway leading home. She did not notice that she was being followed.

"I can't believe Deedee just up and left me," Frankie told Max. "We've never had a serious argument in our life."

"Your wife is pregnant," Max said. "She's going to be moody once in a while. She needs you right now more than she's ever needed you before."

"What can I do when she refuses to come home?" Frankie asked.

"Jewelry might help."

Frankie seemed to ponder it. "I'll take care of it first thing in the morning. I need to run by the bank as soon as it opens. I've got something in my safe-deposit box that just might do the trick."

Max, Jamie, Deedee, and Beenie shared a gourmet dinner in Jamie's small kitchen that evening. Once the chef and his assistant finished up, Max suggested he and Jamie take a walk. It wasn't until they had cleared Jamie's yard that Max spoke. "You've been awfully quiet this evening," he said. "I can tell something is wrong."

Jamie told Max about Larry Johnson's visit. She sensed his anger before he even responded.

"I'd like to get my hands on Johnson and show him what it's like to fight a man," he said, "but I have a feeling I wouldn't stop until it was too late."

"Too late for what?" Jamie asked.

"Never mind." He stopped walking. "Look, Jamie, I want you to come back to the hotel with me tonight."

"And leave Beenie and Deedee?"

"Larry Johnson isn't interested in hurting them. I'll ask Tevis to keep an eye on the place. Besides, Frankie is coming over in the morning, and I think he'll be able to convince Deedee to come home this time."

256

Jamie smiled. "Meaning diamonds will exchange hands."

"Something like that," Max said, but he didn't look amused. "Either way, I'm not leaving you alone tonight. You'll have to stay with me or I'm camping out on your sofa."

"I'll go to your place," she told him, "as long as you don't mind having Fleas along. I don't think he likes sharing our place with Choo-Choo."

"But I'd feel guilty running you out of your own house," Deedee said when Jamie broached the subject of staying with Max at his hotel. "It's bad enough that we just showed up on your doorstep without warning."

"Not to mention completely re-decorating her house without her permission," Beenie said.

"Which was very sweet of you," Jamie told her. Even though it would take her time to adjust to her new surroundings, Jamie knew her friend had had good intentions. "You're my best friend," Jamie told her. "Of course I would expect you to come here."

Deedee suddenly looked sad. "Frankie hasn't even called me."

Jamie could see that her friend was truly in pain, but she was sure Deedee's pride would not let her call him. "I think Frankie's feelings are just hurt," she said. "I wouldn't be surprised if he showed up on my doorstep tomorrow. In the meantime you need to rest."

Deedee nodded. "I think it's great that you and Max will have a chance to spend some private time together. Will you be taking Fleas?" she asked hopefully.

"Yes. I'll make sure you and Choo-Choo have the bedroom all to yourselves tonight."

Jamie packed a small bag and climbed into Max's car a few minutes later. Fleas sat in the back seat. "They're not going to allow us to have a dog in the room," Jamie said when she saw that Max had booked a room in one of the nicer hotels.

"See, that's where being rich comes in handy," Max said. They went inside the hotel with Fleas on his leash, and although they were awarded several stares from the staff, nobody said anything.

"How much did you have to pay to get permission to bring my dog in?" Jamie asked Max.

Max looked at her. "Don't worry about it."

"Not everything comes with a price tag," she said as they waited at the elevator.

"You're right," he said. "You can't pay for what's really important. I did what I had to do because I wanted you with me tonight. I was afraid for you."

Max's cell phone rang as soon as they stepped inside his room. From the conversation, Jamie could tell it was Destiny calling. Max hung up a few minutes later. "Destiny said Larry hasn't been in tonight. I'm calling Lamar to make sure they've got someone on his tail." Max placed the call. Once he was finished, he hung up and faced Jamie. "Brent Walker left town today. Agnes Aimsley told Lamar he had to return to school."

"I don't know whether to be worried or relieved," Jamie said.

"Lamar has already informed the police in Atlanta. Walker will be questioned." He paused. "You look exhausted." He pulled her into his arms and kissed her softly on the lips. Finally, he raised his head and smiled. "I like you, Swifty," he said. "What do you think of that?"

CHAPTER
SIXTEEN

Jamie stared back at him. She didn't know what to make of it. *Like* was not the word she hoped for. "It's the sex," she said, trying to sound flippant so he would not read the disappointment in her eyes.

"The sex is fantastic, but that's not why I like you so much. I like your spunk, and the fact you've never been a quitter. I like that you stand up for what you believe in, like when you rallied to keep Maxine's store open."

"I suppose you know the feeling is mutual," she said, determined to keep it light.

"Like I said, you're going to be seeing a whole lot more of me in the future. No more three-week intervals." He kissed her again. "So what do you think? Think you'd like to see more of me?"

She nodded. It was a start.

Frankie arrived at Jamie's house before eight a.m. the following morning. "Deedee, I can't live without you," he said to his wife, who was still in her nightgown. They both looked tired from lack of sleep. "I promise to get more involved with the preparations for the baby, but I need for you to come home. It's where you belong."

Deedee gazed lovingly into his eyes. "I feel the same way. I've been miserable without you."

He reached into his pocket and pulled out a small velvet box. "I brought you a gift."

"Oh, Frankie, you didn't have to do that. I would have come home anyway." Deedee opened the box. "Oh, my, it's the ring I saw in Tiffany's."

"I've had it for some time," he said. "I was saving it for a Christmas gift, but this seems the perfect time. After all, we're celebrating a baby on the way."

Deedee looked genuinely touched. "I have a lot of luggage with me."

"I brought some of the staff," Frankie said. "They're waiting outside."

"You're mighty sure of yourself," she teased.

"Oh, I was planning to convince you to come home no matter what," he told her. "Even if I had to pick you up and carry you out."

"Oh, Frankie, that's so romantic."

He pulled her into his arms for a kiss.

Beenie came into the room, still wearing his silk pajamas. "Oh, thank God you've made up. I'm ready to go home. I can't sleep on cotton sheets. They irritate my skin."

Max and Jamie had awakened early and made love, only to spend the next hour cuddling and talking. As Jamie showered, Max ordered room service, and they took their time enjoying breakfast together. It was almost nine by the time they climbed into Max's car and started for the office. Muffin came on right away.

"I've done some more digging on John Price, and I think I may have hit on something."

"I'm listening," Max said.

"Price was questioned by the Atlanta PD six months ago about a murder that took place in his neighborhood. The woman lived two doors down from him. The reason it didn't show up when I checked to see if he had a police record is because he was one of about ten who lived in the area that were questioned. I would never have found it had I not thought to look for murders in Atlanta over the last couple of years. And get this. Same MO. Somebody bashed in her head."

Max looked at Jamie. "Very interesting."

"Not only that, I found the service provider he uses for his cell phone. The reason it took so long is because the company is brand-new. It's called In Touch Communications. They weren't in the telephone book; the Better Business Bureau doesn't even have them listed yet."

"Oh, crap," Jamie said. "I completely forgot about them. They ran an ad with me a couple of weeks ago offering free phones for those who signed up. Muffin's right, they just opened for business. As a matter of fact, they've got salesmen going door to door."

"They obviously convinced Price to try their service because that's who he's using," Muffin said. "But I've been saving the best for last. Price was in touch with Luanne Ritter only three days after his personal ad hit the newspaper. She must've written to him immediately, probably the same day his ad came out."

"Bingo," Max said. "What about Maxine Chambers?"

"No record of a call placed to her number, but he could have called from another phone. I haven't found her name listed with any service provider in the area. As hard as it is to believe in this day and time, she must not have had a cell phone."

"Anything else?"

"I followed up on the dentist, the chef, and the mechanic. The dentist and chef checked out fine, but the mechanic, Carl Edwards, had had a run-in with the police. Seems he and another guy got into a fist-fight outside a bar a couple of years ago. Nothing serious; just a couple of good old boys who had too much to drink and one of them accused the other of cheating in a pool game."

"How come it didn't show up on his record?" Max asked.

"I suspect the cops just talked to them and sent them on their way because neither of them was officially charged. I found the information by checking on calls made to the dispatcher in the last three years. They list complaints in the computer, even if there are no arrests made."

"Good work, Muffin," Max said. "From here on out I want you to make Price your top priority. Find out why he left Atlanta so soon after the murder in his neighborhood."

"Will do."

"By the way, did you happen to get anything else on Sam Hunter?"

"Nothing looks suspicious. No police record, not even a parking ticket. He kept the same job for ten years. His cell phone records indicate that he was somewhat of a ladies' man, but all his ex-girlfriends are alive and well and working in New York City. Max?"

"Yeah?"

"After we figure out who committed these murders I'm taking some time off. I don't feel so good."

"Muffin, you are *not* pregnant," Max said. "You're just having the symptoms because Deedee fed you the information."

"Then why are my hormones acting up?"

Max sighed. "You don't have hormones, you're a computer."

"Yeah, and you programmed me to have emotions. I do too have hormones. Just ask my friend at MIT. He's accused me more than once of having PMS. Just this morning, as a matter of fact."

"I thought the two of you broke up."

"You know how it is, on again, off again. I can't get him to make a commitment. I think I intimidate him, but what can I say? Besides, he's just a laptop, and he's not being fed information from experts around the clock like I am. He needs an upgrade; somebody needs to install more memory in him."

"Let's just try to concentrate on the case, OK?"

Muffin sounded testy when she spoke. "I've never once let my personal feelings get in the way of my work, but I do need a life." With that she was gone.

Max looked thoughtful. "I'll inform Lamar about Price, but I think it would be a good idea to drive by his house tonight and see if there's any activity."

"Only if you promise not to break in again," Jamie said. "I don't think my nerves can take it."

"Deal," Max said.

"Well, Destiny will be relieved that Sam looks clean," Jamie said, changing the subject. "I think she has a crush on him."

"Don't get her hopes up," Max said. "Until we find the murderer, everybody is a suspect."

Max and Jamie worked throughout the day, breaking only for lunch, which consisted of sandwiches at Maynard's.

"Is it me or does Vera seem to be in a really good mood today?" Jamie asked as they left the sandwich shop and walked back to the office.

Max grinned. "Maybe she's getting laid."

"Max!"

"Well, you asked."

They left the office at six p.m., only to find that the night had not cooled,

"This has been the hottest summer I can remember," Jamie said. "No wonder people are acting kooky in this town, Vera included. There's definitely a change in her." Jamie was almost certain the woman was wearing padded bras.

They arrived at Jamie's house and found a note from Deedee saying she had made up with Frankie and gone home. "Well, that's one less thing to worry about," Jamie said.

"Frankie must've taken my suggestion and bought something nice for her," Max said with a grin.

"I don't think Deedee is as materialistic as you think, Max," Jamie said. "She genuinely loves Frankie. Twenty years is a long time to stay married these days."

"Not if two people work at it," Max said. "Do you think you'd want to be with somebody that long or longer?"

Jamie couldn't have been more surprised with his response. Had Max Holt just made a favorable comment about marriage and commitment? She felt like pinching herself to make sure she wasn't dreaming, and then realized he was waiting for her answer. "I wouldn't get married unless I was prepared to do just that," she said.

There was plenty of food in Jamie's cabinets and refrigerator, thanks to Deedee. Once they'd eaten, Jamie took a shower and changed into shorts while Max made calls to Holt Industries. They waited until dark before getting into Max's car. "We're going by John Price's house," he told Muffin.

"Speaking of Price, I discovered a few more things you might find interesting," Muffin said. "His divorce a year ago was less than amicable."

"Most divorces aren't real friendly," Max said, although his had been, thanks to his generosity.

"Yeah, but listen to this. Price swore out a warrant shortly after the separation, claimed his ex was stalking him. The police checked into it but no charges were filed for lack of proof."

Max looked thoughtful. "How soon can you get me a complete file on her?"

"I'm about to send it through the printer now. She has an apartment in Atlanta, but her employment history is spotty. She obviously quit work after she married Price because I can't find anything after that."

Max was thoughtful. "If Price thought she was stalking him that might explain the guard dogs, and the expensive security system."

"I wonder if he's afraid she'll find him," Jamie said. After a moment, she changed the subject. "We should probably check in with Destiny." Max made the call. He was frowning when he hung up. "Larry Johnson is there with a woman."

Jamie felt a chill race up her spine. "I hope she's armed."

"Sam Hunter is sitting at the bar. Destiny says they've really hit it off."

"I wonder what Ronnie is making of Destiny's crush on Sam," Jamie said, if for no other reason than to lighten the mood. She could see that Max had a lot on his mind. "Maybe Ronnie will finally take the hint and be on his way. Toward the light," she added with a smile.

They drove by John Price's house twenty minutes later and found it dark. Max frowned.

"What's wrong?" Jamie asked.

"Something doesn't seem right here. I get the feeling we should be someplace else."

★ ★ ★

John Price arrived at Vera's house at precisely seven o'clock carrying a bouquet of flowers.

"Oh, John, how thoughtful," she said, as she put them into a vase with water. Vera had put the pot roast in a Crock-Pot that morning before leaving for work, then cut up new potatoes, carrots, and onions and placed them in the pot on high so they'd be ready in time. Although her house was kept neat, she'd dusted and vacuumed before freshening her makeup. It was obvious she'd wanted to make a good impression.

"May I offer you a glass of sweet tea?" she asked John.

"I would love something cold after coming in from that heat," he told her, wiping his brow. "I took a shower before I left the house, but I was perspiring before I got to my car."

"This has been the hottest summer we've had in years," Vera said, "and the humidity doesn't help. I dread seeing my power bill because I've used my air conditioner so much this season. Now, why don't you take a seat on the sofa, and I'll get us both something cold to drink. Dinner should be ready soon."

"I'm in no hurry," John said. "I'd much rather get to know you better."

"I'm afraid my life would sound boring to you," Vera said, returning with two tall glasses of iced tea with lemon. She took the chair opposite him. "I've lived in Beaumont all my life. Never traveled more than a couple of hundred miles away, and that was with my church friends. I'm sort of a homebody."

"I used to do a lot of traveling with my job," John said. "My ex-wife didn't like my being gone so I tried to cut back as much as I could."

"She obviously missed you while you were gone."

John shifted uncomfortably in his chair. "She was somewhat, um, possessive. She liked being able to put her finger on me at all times." He took a sip of tea. "I'm sorry; it's rude of me to discuss her with you."

"Oh, no, I don't mind, How long were you married?"

"A year."

Vera looked surprised. "That's all?"

"The marriage was doomed from the beginning, but I fancied myself in love. She was quite a bit younger than me. Plus, it was a second marriage. I hadn't been divorced all that long before I met her. I was married to my first wife for twenty-seven years. I regret that we drifted apart." He sighed. "Anyway, I married Celia less than three months after I met her. I guess I was just lonely after the divorce and wasn't thinking straight."

"Do you have children?"

"Oh, yes, a beautiful daughter by my first wife. She studied business at college and graduated with honors, and then decided she wanted to go into nursing. She graduates in the fall." He glanced around. "Your place is very cozy. You have a real eye for decorating."

"Thank you. I study the latest magazines for ideas. Luckily, I sew," she added proudly. "I was able to make the slipcovers for the sofa and I made all the draperies as well. But you're probably not interested in hearing all that."

He smiled. "On the contrary," he said. "You sew, you cook, you decorate, and you're a devoted employee. I'm beginning to think there's nothing you can't do."

Vera blushed. "Oh, I have my faults," she said. "I'm a very impatient woman. I want things done right away because I don't believe in wasting time. People at the office will tell you I can be quite demanding at times."

Price nodded. "You're obviously a hard worker." He paused. "Vera, I'd like to continue to keep our friendship discreet for a while longer."

She gave him a funny look. "Well, of course, if that's the way you want it."

"Maybe we could continue to meet privately for a while," he said.

"I suppose so." But Vera was frowning as she got up to check the vegetables. "Dinner is ready," she called out. "I hope you're hungry."

Business was slow in the lounge at the Holiday Inn, which didn't seem to bother Destiny at all since Sam Hunter was the only one at the bar.

Sam watched Destiny closely, as though trying to size her up. His eyes followed the way her short skirt lifted each time she reached high for the bottle of Johnnie Walker Red which two men at a nearby table were drinking, to the way her oversized breasts bounced as she washed glasses. Finally, Destiny sashayed toward Sam, took one of his hands in hers, and turned it over so that she was looking at his palm. "I didn't tell you I was a palmist, did I?" she asked.

He smiled, showing off his good looks. His thick brown hair had not begun to gray at the temples like that of a lot of men his age. "You failed to mention it," he said.

"I'll be happy to give you a reading," she said, "No charge, of course."

He chuckled. "Of course."

"This is your lifeline," she said, tracing one of the lines that ran across his open palm. "It shows that you're going to live a long life."

"That's good to know."

"And this line —" She paused and gave him a coy smile. "It says you're going to meet a beautiful woman. You will quickly become smitten with her."

Sam smiled and captured her hands in his. "I think I already have. What time do you get off?"

Destiny didn't respond. If Sam noticed her staring across the room at the couple leaving, he didn't say anything. "Would you excuse me," she said. "I need to make a quick phone call."

Max's cell phone rang, and he picked it up. Destiny spoke from the other end. "Damn," he said. "How long ago?" He listened. "OK, thanks."

"What is it?" Jamie asked.

"Larry Johnson just left the Holiday Inn with the woman. I hope Lamar is doing his job." He paused. "Maybe we should drive over."

"And do what?" Jamie asked. "We can't exactly knock on his door."

Max looked thoughtful. "If he took her to his place I think she's relatively safe. Johnson isn't dumb enough to try anything at his apartment. My concern is he'll take her home. That might put her in danger. We might be wasting our time, of course," he added. "I think Johnson suspects he's being watched. If that's the case he's not going to take any chances."

"Unless he gets drunk enough and lets down his guard," Jamie said. "Then anything is possible."

"Vera, that was the best pot roast I've ever had," John said. "I can't believe you never married, what with your looks and cooking skills."

Vera waved off the remark. "Flattery will get you everywhere. Wait until you see what I've made for dessert."

"Dessert? I'm already busting out of my pants from that meal."

Vera got up and cleared their dishes away before cutting them each a slice of Key lime pie and filling two cups with coffee. She carried them to the table on a silver tray.

"You shouldn't have gone to so much trouble," John said.

"It wasn't any trouble. I love to cook."

John waited until she sat down before he spoke. "Tell me something," he said. "How come you never married?"

Vera shrugged. "I was in love once, but he wasn't able to make a commitment."

"I find that hard to believe."

272

Vera looked sad for a moment. "I wasted a lot of years hoping he'd change." Finally, she shrugged. "But I had a job with the newspaper that I loved, and I was always busy with church activities so it wasn't like I sat aroumd moping about it."

John shifted in his chair. He suddenly looked nervous. "You didn't mention our date to anyone at the *Gazette*, did you?"

"Of course not."

He looked relieved as he took a sip of his coffee. He watched her closely from over the rim of his cup. He didn't make a move for his pie.

"Aren't you going to eat your dessert?" Vera asked.

"Could you make it to go?"

"Oh, are you leaving so soon?"

"I'm afraid my day has caught up with me," he said. "I was at the office before six, and what I need right now is a good night's sleep. I hope you don't mind."

"Well, of course not. Actually, I was thinking of turning in early myself."

John left a few minutes later after promising to call the next day. Vera locked up after him, and began cleaning the kitchen. The phone rang, and she answered.

There was no response.

"Is anyone there?" she said after a moment.

Finally, a click.

"Well, now, that was odd," she said to herself as she hung up.

Ten minutes later she had another silent phone call.

She was in the process of preparing for bed when the telephone rang for the third time. She picked it up. Once again, no answer. "Listen, I can hear you breathing, what do you want?"

Nothing.

"I'm sick and tired of you calling this house. Don't call me again, do you hear?" She slammed the phone down. "Probably a bunch of kids playing pranks," she said.

"I have more news for you," Muffin said as Max and Jamie headed for Larry Johnson's apartment. "It concerns John Price. Do either of you know a Barbara Fender?"

"That's my new neighbor's name," Jamie said. "Why do you ask, Muffin?"

"Bad news," Muffin said. "Barbara Fender aka Celia Brown Price is John Price's ex-wife."

Max and Jamie exchanged looks. "Are you sure?" he asked.

"Am I ever wrong?" Muffin asked.

Jamie stared at Max in disbelief. "She followed John from Atlanta."

"I don't like what I'm thinking," Max said.

"Tell me anyway."

"John Price filed charges that his ex was stalking him, but there was no proof so they were dropped. And later, he was questioned about a woman murdered two houses down from him. I'm willing to bet he was involved with her." He sighed. "It never occurred to me that the killer could be a woman. What I don't understand is why she's doing it. Unless she's insanely jealous," he added.

Jamie felt the familiar sense of dread. "Or maybe she's trying to set him up for a murder rap. She must really hate him. This is scary, Max."

"We need to talk to Price right away."

"Problem is, he isn't home, and he could unknowingly be putting someone else at risk," Jamie said. She had begun to fidget with her hands. "Assuming he isn't the killer."

"First we need to find out if Barbara Fender is home." Max whipped his car around and headed back to Jamie's house, making the drive in record time. Barbara Fender's car was not in the carport.

"This isn't good," Jamie said.

"If she was really stalking Price, odds are she's somewhere watching him. Do you have his phone number handy?"

"Yes, it's in his file."

"Why don't you call and see if he's home yet."

Barbara Fender drove slowly past Vera Bankhead's simple ranch-style house. Darkness had descended; lights burned bright in the windows. Barbara parked her car down the street, cut her headlights, and turned off the engine.

And waited.

Vera grabbed a quick shower, changed into her nightgown, and climbed into bed. "Oh, that feels good," she said, yawning wide as she slipped between the sheets. She didn't read her daily Scripture as was her custom; instead, she turned off her lamp and closed her eyes. She was asleep in minutes.

Jamie dialed John Price's number. He picked up on the third ring. "Mr. Price, this is Jamie Swift from the *Gazette*," she said quickly. "I'm terribly sorry to bother you, but it's important."

"How may I help you, Miss Swift?" he asked.

"My partner and I need to speak with you. Is it OK if we come over?"

"Actually, I was just getting ready for bed. Can this wait until tomorrow?"

"It's rather urgent or I wouldn't be calling. We only need a minute of your time."

Silence. "In that case, please come over."

Vera opened her eyes and stared into the darkness as the clanging of something metal sounded from the back of her house. "It's that stray dog in my garbage can again," she muttered. "I'll have a mess to clean up in the morning." She dozed off again.

CHAPTER
SEVENTEEN

Jamie and Max arrived at John Price's house in half the time it would normally have taken. As they climbed from Max's car, they heard the dogs barking. John called out from the doorway.

"Don't worry about the dogs," he said. "I've got them penned."

Max and Jamie hurried up the front walk. John stepped back to permit them inside. "Mr. Price, I'd like you to meet my partner, Max Holt," Jamie said.

Price arched one brow. "Not the Max Holt I've read about in all the financial magazines."

"That's me," Max said.

Price looked impressed as he motioned them toward the living room. "Please come in and sit down. And call me John." Max and Jamie sat beside each other on his sofa. Price took the chair on the other side of the coffee table. "You said this was urgent. How can I help you?"

"We're here to discuss the ad you ran in the newspaper," Jamie said, "among other things."

Price glanced at Max, then back at Jamie. He looked embarrassed. "I was hoping that would be kept confidential."

"It would have been," Jamie said, "but a couple of women have been murdered, and we think it may be related to the personals section. I'm surprised the police haven't already questioned you. I was served with a court order to release the files."

Price looked annoyed at the news. "I read about the murders," he said after a moment.

"We know you were in contact with Luanne Ritter," Max said. "What about Maxine Chambers?"

Price hesitated. "I received replies from both ladies right after my ad came out. I took each of them to dinner, but that was the extent of it." He glanced from Max to Jamie. "I had nothing to do with their murders."

"You were questioned about the murder of a woman in Atlanta," Jamie said. "I believe she was a neighbor."

He looked surprised. "You've been checking on me. I wasn't the only one questioned in that incident."

"Were you involved with her?"

"We had coffee once or twice. We were both going through a divorce at the time; we sort of used each other as a sounding board. It was nothing more than friendship."

"The murder was never solved," Max said.

"I regret that. She was a nice woman."

"John, didn't you think it odd that both women you dated were murdered?" Jamie asked.

Once again, he hesitated. "Of course I did, but since I had nothing to do with it I felt no need to go to the police. I'm new in town, and I've recently started my own business. The last thing I need is to get entangled in a murder investigation."

"Why did you leave Atlanta?" Max asked.

"I had my reasons."

"Did they concern your ex-wife?" Jamie asked.

Once again, he looked annoyed. "Why all these questions?"

"It could be a matter of life or death," Max said.

Price's eyes widened. "My ex-wife was hounding me. She didn't want the divorce, and she did everything possible to make my life a living hell once I left her. My apartment was ransacked twice, and the tires slashed on my car. She even started calling my boss. I swore out a peace bond against her, but it didn't help. I couldn't prove she was behind any of it. So I decided to move away and start over."

"Does anyone know you're here?"

"Only my daughter and first wife. I still send money for our daughter's education."

"Where do you mail the checks?" Max asked.

"To my first wife's mailbox, of course. She lives in Marietta, Georgia, just north of the Atlanta area."

"Did your second wife know her address?"

"It was listed in our address book. She would have seen the address where I mailed the checks."

"That might be one way Barbara found him," Jamie told Max. "She could have gone through his first wife's mailbox."

"Who's Barbara?" Price asked, obviously confused.

"That's the name your ex-wife is using," Max said. "She's going by the name Barbara Fender."

Price instantly paled. "Oh, God."

"What is it?" Max asked.

"That's the name of the neighbor in Atlanta who was murdered."

Price stood and shoved his hands in his pockets. "Her real name is Celia." He paused and regarded them. "Look, I knew Celia had problems, but I don't think she's capable of murder."

"We don't have proof of anything," Max said, "but there are a lot of coincidences."

"She's moved in next door to me," Jamie said.

John was quiet, as though trying to take it all in. "I don't know what to think. Celia was jealous of everyone I had anything to do with, my daughter, and my friends. She followed me when I left the house. I was always looking over my shoulder because I didn't know what to expect. I asked her to get help, but she refused. When I filed for divorce she threatened to get even."

"Does she hate you enough to try and pin a murder rap on you?" Max asked.

John met his gaze. "She could be cruel. I didn't know about her problems before we married, but it didn't take long before she began showing her true colors, so to speak. I regretted the marriage almost from the beginning, but I thought I could help her."

"You went out earlier this evening," Max said, changing the subject.

"I had a dinner engagement."

"With a woman?"

"Yes. She answered my ad."

"Do you mind telling us who the woman was?"

"I would like to keep that confidential. For her sake," he added.

"John, she may be in danger," Jamie said.

He suddenly covered his face with his hands, and his voice trembled when he finally spoke. "I thought it was finally over. I thought I could start living a normal life again. If Celia was responsible for the death of those women then it's because I asked them out."

"John, we have to know who you were with tonight," Max insisted.

He looked at Jamie. "She works for you," he said. "Vera Bankhead."

Jamie felt the blood rush to her ears.

The sound of breaking glass woke Vera a second time. She bolted upright and reached for her telephone to dial 911. The line was dead. Quietly, she climbed from her bed.

"My purse," she whispered to herself. "Where did I leave it?" She started down the hall, feeling her way. The house was bathed in shadows.

There was a click at the kitchen door, the sound of the lock being turned. A hand fumbled, found the chain, slid it free.

Vera reached the living room, her hands searching the sofa blindly for her purse.

The kitchen door creaked.

Vera found her purse and reached inside for her gun. She raised it, aimed it toward the dark kitchen. "I don't know who you are or what you want, but I'm holding a thirty-eight Smith and Wesson, and I know how to use it."

Suddenly, a bright light hit her face. Vera was blinded. She raised her free hand to cover her eyes, as a baseball bat came down hard on her arm. Vera cried out and dropped the gun. It hit the carpet with a dull thud. "Why are you doing this?" she cried, trying to see the face behind the light.

"It's a pity you won't live to find out," the woman said with gritted teeth. The bat came down a second time. Vera cried out again and sank to the floor.

Jamie was the first to spot Barbara's car parked a couple of houses down from Vera's. "There it is!" she cried. "Hurry, Max!"

Max whipped his car into the driveway. "Muffin, hit the siren, and call 911."

Barbara Fender raised the bat high, a determined look on her face as she aimed for Vera's head. She jerked around as a siren split the night, and then turned once more for Vera. She shone her flashlight on the floor as Vera reached beneath the sofa for her gun.

Jamie felt the adrenaline gush through her body as she raced toward Vera's back door with Max on her heels. "Vera!" she called out loudly.

Inside, Barbara ignored both the siren and the voice and raised the bat once more. Vera rolled away, and the bat slammed against the sofa. She raised her gun and fired twice.

The woman staggered once and fell.

Jamie reached the dark kitchen and searched frantically for a light switch. She turned it on and gasped at the sight of Vera pulling herself up and Barbara Fender, with big blond hair, sprawled on the floor. A wig, Jamie thought.

"I think I hit her in the stomach," Vera said, dropping her gun as the woman writhed in pain.

Jamie saw that Barbara had been hit; her dress was already blood soaked. "Help is on the way," she said, although she found little reason to pity her. She reached down and checked her arms. Sure enough, she found several deep scratches.

Jamie paced the waiting area in the emergency room as she waited to see Vera. Celia Price had been rushed by ambulance and was undergoing emergency surgery; Vera had ridden in another ambulance. Lamar Tevis had arrived on the scene only minutes after the injured women had been whisked away. He sat in the waiting room with Max, Jamie, and John Price, as he waited for a chance to question Vera, who had suffered a broken arm.

"I honestly had no idea Celia would resort to murder," Price told Lamar, "but it all adds up. I feel terrible about this." He'd already told Lamar about the murder in Atlanta, and his suspicions that his ex might have been responsible.

Jamie noted the man's face was a chalky white. He was obviously in shock. "It's not your fault," she said. "You can't control the actions of others." She said it as much for herself as for him.

Lamar nodded. "I'll notify the authorities in Atlanta to reopen the case." He frowned. "Why do you suppose she did it?"

Price shook his head. "Revenge, maybe. I think part of me suspected she would find me one day." He looked at Max. "That's the reason for the dogs. Still, nothing could have prepared me for this."

A nurse stepped out. "Is there a Mr. Price here?"

"I'm John Price," he said, standing.

"Miss Bankhead is asking for you."

John followed the nurse through the metal doors leading into the ER. He stepped inside a small room where Vera wore a cast on one arm.

"Max told me everything as we were waiting for the ambulance," she said.

"Vera, I'm so sorry," he said. "I don't know how I will live with this."

"You're not responsible, John. You had no way of knowing."

"I should have put two and two together. I should have known Celia would stop at nothing to get back at me for leaving her. Those poor women." He raked his hands through his hair. The look on his face was bleak. "She could have killed you."

"But she didn't, and it's behind us now. Your ex-wife, if she survives the surgery, will never have the chance to kill again."

John stepped closer to Vera's bed and took one of her hands in his. "I'm almost afraid to ask, but where does this leave us?"

Vera hesitated. "I don't know, John. I need time."

He nodded. "I guess we both do. At least until we get through this."

"We can still be friends."

A look of vulnerability crossed his face. "Thank you. I'm going to need a friend."

Destiny and Sam rushed through the doors to the ER. "What's wrong?" Destiny demanded.

"What on earth are you doing here?" Jamie asked.

"I had this feeling that something was terribly wrong. Even Ronnie agreed. I called the police. All they would tell me was that there had been a shooting. So I asked Sam to give me a ride over. Who's hurt?"

Jamie filled her in.

Sam regarded Destiny with a look of awe. "You were right. You *are* psychic."

"I tried to tell you," she said.

"Hello, Sam," Jamie said. "It's been a long time." They shook hands, and she introduced him to Max.

"What do you think of Destiny's friend, Ronnie?" Max asked Sam, as though to lighten the mood.

Sam offered him a blank look. "Who's Ronnie?"

Destiny shot Max a look, reached for Sam's hand and patted it. "We'll talk about it later, honey." She turned to Jamie. "This is probably a bad time to bring it up, but I answered most of the mail."

"More has come in since the last batch," Jamie said. "The responses have been overwhelming."

"I knew that. I'll pick them up and give you the other letters tomorrow. After it stops raining," she added. "I like to sleep late when it rains."

"That makes two of us," Sam said. They shared a private look.

"Rain?" Jamie said. "The weatherman isn't forecasting rain. In fact, the temperatures are going to be even worse than they have been."

"The weatherman is wrong," Destiny said with a shrug. "It's going to rain and finally cool things off. And not a moment too soon, if you ask me."

Destiny and Sam stayed and chatted a while until John Price joined them and told Jamie that Vera was asking for her. Jamie joined the woman a moment later.

"How are you?"

"How the heck do you think I am? I have a broken arm. But don't worry, I'll still be able to work."

"Maybe you should take a vacation," Jamie said. "You've certainly earned it after what you've been through."

"Oh, fiddlesticks, a broken arm isn't going to stop me. Besides, who will run the newspaper if I'm not there?"

"True."

"I called you back here because I want first dibs on this story."

Jamie arched one brow. "I should have known."

"I'll give you editorial control, but I think it's high time you let me write some of the articles. I am the assistant editor, after all, and I'm tired of watching Mike get all the glory."

"OK, Vera, whatever it takes to make you happy."

"So, what do you think of John?"

"He's a very nice man, but he's having a hard time dealing with all this. So am I."

Vera took her hand and squeezed it. "I know, honey. But we've gotten through tough times before, and we'll get through this." She brightened. "So, you think I should let John sleep over tonight?"

"Vera!"

"Just kidding. But if I start dating him, I'm going to need a few pointers."

Jamie was glad Vera could be so upbeat after what she'd been through. "It's always a good idea to follow your instincts. Don't do anything until you know you're ready."

Vera sat up in the bed. "I've got to get out of this place. If I stay here any longer I'm going to catch something. Would you please find my doctor and tell him I said to get his fanny in here. He's the young one who looks like Andy Garcia. If I were forty years younger I'd jump his bones."

"Vera?"

"Yes, dear?"

"Lay off the brownies."

Jamie awoke the next morning to the sound of rain. "Holy cow!" she said to Max. "Destiny was right."

Max smiled beside her. "You know what this means."

"Um, we're going to need an umbrella?"

"Nope. It means you're going to be late for work." He reached for her.

"I can't be late for work. Vera's got a broken arm."

"That's not going to stop her, and that's why I'm not worried about taking you back to Virginia with me for a few days. We'll take the small six-passenger plane so Muffin can have some time off."

Jamie did a bit of eye-rolling. "Max, do you know how that sounds? I've never been involved with a man who owned a fleet of airplanes and a two-million-dollar car. I'm going to have to get used to your being so rich."

"It has certain advantages."

Jamie suspected it wasn't a bad idea. She needed to get away. Somehow, she had to put the terrible stuff behind her and go on, and she found solace in Max's arms. She smiled. "So you're taking me to Virginia, huh?"

"I want you to meet my family, Jamie."

"Jeez, Max, that sounds serious."

He gazed back at her. "I guess it does. Maybe it's time I let down my guard and went with my feelings."

Jamie waited for him to say more. "What does that mean exactly?" she asked when he didn't elaborate.

"You're asking me to go out on a limb here." His look grew serious. "Jamie, do you love me?"

She was surprised he hadn't figured it out for himself. "Men are so dumb."

"Is that a yes?"

Jamie glanced away; afraid he would see it in her eyes.

"I haven't used that word in a long time, Jamie," he said, "and I ended up being wrong."

"So take a chance, Holt."

"I asked you first."

"Come on, Max, give it up."

"It certainly feels like love. The fact that I don't want to be without you, and I can't stop thinking about you when you're not with me is a good indication that something serious is going on between us." He grinned. "Your turn."

"You didn't say the words, Max."

His look turned tender. "I love you, Swifty."

Jamie felt her heart turn over in her chest. "See, that wasn't so hard. I love you, too, Max. I have for some time."

He looked relieved. "This smacks of commitment, you know. I usually run as fast as I can when a woman mentions that word."

"And now?"

"I'm tired of running. I love you," he repeated. He suddenly grinned. "It gets easier every time I say it."

Jamie studied him. He was sincere; she could see the love in his eyes. "You know what else I love?"

"What?"

"Rainy days."

"It's still early. I know how we could fill the time." He kissed her deeply. Before long they were aching for each other. Max began to unbutton her gown.

"Uh-oh," Jamie said. "Something tells me I'm going to be really late for work. I'll miss out on the fresh doughnuts."

He laughed. "Those doughnuts are going to be very stale by the time you show up."

EPILOGUE

ONE WEEK LATER

Dear Divine Love Goddess Advisor:

I'm a single gay male, and I have a crush on a policeman. Every time I see him in his shorts I get hot all over — he's got a behind to die for. I've watched him closely, and I suspect he's gay as well, but he doesn't seem to know I exist. I've tried jaywalking, not putting change into parking meters, and parking more than eighteen inches from the curb. He writes me tickets but he's all business. What I want to know is whether or not I should confess my feelings to him and risk rejection or take a chance.

Signed,
Flaming Hot in Beaumont

Dear Flaming:

The Divine Love Goddess strongly suspects this man feels the same about you, but he is trying to come to terms with his sexuality. My advice to you

291

is to confront him, and see where it leads before you go broke paying fines. Who knows, maybe he'll handcuff you, take you home, and show you his nightstick. You might just end up on his Most Wanted list.

See you at the policemen's ball!

Signed,

The Divine Love Goddess Advisor

Dear Divine Love Goddess Advisor:

I have been married for a long time to a wonderful man. I recently found out I was pregnant. I am concerned my husband won't be attracted to me once I begin to gain weight because I have always taken very good care of myself, maintaining a perfect size-six figure. How can I be certain he will love me when I'm big as a house?

Signed,

Growing Day by Day

Dear Growing:

The Divine Love Goddess knows that your concerns are unwarranted. Your husband loves you very much and looks forward to sharing this special time with you. Many men find pregnant women very sexy, and I suspect your husband will, as well.

I suggest you not worry so much about your figure and concentrate on the miracle growing

inside of you, because your husband is going to love you even when your feet swell to twice their size, you blimp out, and start waddling like a duck.
Signed,
The Divine Love Goddess Advisor

Dear Divine Love Goddess Advisor:
I am a gay policeman who recently became attracted to another man. I think the feeling is mutual because he follows me everywhere. I think he might be trying to get my attention because he's racking up fines for parking violations. Should I come clean with this man and give him the frisking of his life?
Signed,
Uncertain

Dear Uncertain:
I am positive this man has strong feelings for you. (Read "Flaming Hot in Beaumont.") Don't wait until he becomes so desperate he has to call 911 to get your attention.
Signed,
The Divine Love Goddess Advisor

Dear Divine Love Goddess Advisor:
I am in love with a wonderful man who recently confessed his love for me. I feel insecure at times

because he's gorgeous and filthy rich and has dated his share of celebrities. Can you tell me what the future holds for us?
Signed,
Head over Heels

Dear Head over Heels:
One word: Fireworks.
Signed,
The Divine Love Goddess Advisor

Also available in ISIS Large Print:

Full Speed

Janet Evanovich & Charlotte Hughes

Jamie and Max have intense chemistry — even though they drive each other crazy. Max thinks Jamie is a magnet for trouble and Jamie thinks Max is the most annoyingly sexy, mysterious man she's ever met. She knows she should stay away from him, but there's something irresistible about the millionaire playboy.

Jamie, as small-town newspaper owner, is after the scoop of a lifetime. Max Holt is right in the middle of that story. What follows is the tale of a corrupt minister, a gang of mobsters on the loose, a hound dog called Fleas, a wise-cracking computer genius, and lots of love in the fast lane.

With loveable, dysfunctional characters, villains you love to hate and plenty of fast action, Full Speed is filled with suspense and hilarity from these best-selling authors.

ISBN 0-7531-7025-6 (hb)
ISBN 0-7531-7026-4 (pb)

Full Tilt

Janet Evanovich & Charlotte Hughes

Jamie Swift has one priority in quiet Beaumont, South Carolina: running the local newspaper. Romance runs second. But with the arrival of her silent partner, the notoriously mysterious and sexy Maximillian Holt, Jamie's life gets shaken up.

A former wrestler, Frankie Fontana, is now taking his shots in the political ring. Beaumont could use a mayor with scruples, but what it gets is a crime — and what Jamie gets is a story that's taking her for a ride on the wild side, complete with two assassins, a washed-up stripper and an insane poacher. Between a spray of bullets and a fast getaway, nothing could be more romantic — or dangerous. Max and Jamie are betting their lives on a long shot.

ISBN 0-7531-7023-X (hb)
ISBN 0-7531-7024-8 (pb)

ISIS publish a wide range of books in large print, from fiction to biography. Any suggestions for books you would like to see in large print or audio are always welcome. Please send to the Editorial Department at:

ISIS Publishing Limited
7 Centremead
Osney Mead
Oxford OX2 0ES

A full list of titles is available free of charge from:

Ulverscroft Large Print Books Limited

(UK)
The Green
Bradgate Road, Anstey
Leicester LE7 7FU
Tel: (0116) 236 4325

(Australia)
P.O. Box 314
St Leonards
NSW 1590
Tel: (02) 9436 2622

(USA)
P.O. Box 1230
West Seneca
N.Y. 14224-1230
Tel: (716) 674 4270

(Canada)
P.O. Box 80038
Burlington
Ontario L7L 6B1
Tel: (905) 637 8734

(New Zealand)
P.O. Box 456
Feilding
Tel: (06) 323 6828

Details of ISIS complete and unabridged audio books are also available from these offices. Alternatively, contact your local library for details of their collection of ISIS large print and unabridged audio books.